SENHORA
Profile of a Woman

The Texas Pan American Series

SENHORA

Profile of a Woman

by José de Alencar

translated by
Catarina Feldmann Edinger

 University of Texas Press
Austin

FIC

First edition, 1994

Requests for permission to reproduce material from this work should be sent to
Permissions, University of Texas Press, Box 7819, Austin, TX 78713-7819.

The paper used in this publication meets the minimum requirements of American
National Standard for Information Sciences—Permanence of Paper for Printed Library
Materials, ANSI Z39.48-1984.

LIBRARY OF CONGRESS CATALOGING-IN-PUBLICATION DATA

Alencar, José Martiniano de, 1829–1877
[Senhora. English]
Senhora : profile of a woman / by José de Alencar ;
translated by Catarina Feldmann Edinger.
p.   cm. — (The Texas Pan American series)
ISBN 0-292-70449-6 (alk. paper). —
ISBN 0-292-70450-x (pbk. : alk. paper)
I. Title. II. Series.
PQ9697.A53S413 1994
869.3—dc20
93-791

CONTENTS

ACKNOWLEDGMENTS

My deepest gratitude goes to my husband, Robert Edinger, and to my parents, Rosa and George Feldmann, for their continuous support during the years I worked on this project. Whenever I needed books or any other information from São Paulo, my father would promptly respond to my request, contacting old colleagues, going to libraries and *sebos* (old book dealers)—and always succeeding. It would never have been possible to do all the research without his help from thousands of miles away. And I can't thank my husband enough for the countless hours he spent helping with revisions and making excellent suggestions. Above all, I appreciate the patience and understanding he and my son Richard demonstrated during these years, giving up our time together, homemade suppers, and peaceful weekends.

Without the contribution of Clifford Landers, who edited the manuscript carefully and creatively, making innumerable suggestions for improvement, this English version of *Senhora* would never have acquired fluidity. Between his dictionaries and mine we solved the meaning of many nineteenth-century colloquialisms that made absolutely no sense at first sight. I am very grateful for his dedication to the project.

A special thank you to Daphne Patai who enthusiastically vouched for the translation of Alencar's novel and made some invaluable recommendations concerning tone and formality of nineteenth-century dialogue.

For the time they took from their own work to read parts of this translation and discuss alternatives with me, I must thank my colleagues Stephen Hahn and James Barszcz. Their interest in the project reinforced my belief that it was worth the effort. I am also grateful to Stephen for assisting me in obtaining different editions of *Senhora*.

I must also thank Dona Maria Itália Causin, Technical Director of the Library at the Instituto de Estudos Brasileiros of the University of São Paulo, for her assistance in providing me with an 1875 edition of *Senhora* and other invaluable material.

And to all those unnamed here who at one point or another assisted me, my heartfelt thanks. —C.F.E.

INTRODUCTION

Author of twenty novels, six plays, and numerous newspaper articles and speeches, José de Alencar is considered the father of Brazilian literature. He was born in the northern state of Ceará in 1829 and died of tuberculosis in Rio de Janeiro in 1877. A graduate of the law school of São Paulo, he became a journalist and later a senator, rising to Minister of Justice under Emperor Dom Pedro II. His writings signal the beginning of a literature that is unmistakably Brazilian in genre, in themes, and in language. They reflect the different intellectual, political, social, and cultural currents found in Brazil during the reign of Dom Pedro II, a period known as the Second Empire (1840–1889).

During the Romantic period (roughly corresponding to the mid-nineteenth century), Brazilian literature, in search of its national identity, focused on local color and on the new nation's geography and social make-up, exalting its representative population, be it the Indian, the gaúcho, the slave, or the middle-class man and woman, along with their values. José de Alencar's works span all of these aspects. His novels deal with most of the historical moments of Brazil, evincing the variety of its cultural heritage and bringing to the fore its most relevant issues.

However, this wide-angle picture of nineteenth-century Brazil is not Alencar's only contribution to Brazilian literature. He invested greatly in the creation of a vernacular, borrowing from a variety of models. But mainly he was always attuned to the popular Brazilian diction with its differences from the language imported from Portugal (the position of pronouns, for example). He was fascinated by and tried to adapt the agglutinations of Tupi, an Indian language, and was interested in the etymology of words as sources for his metaphors. He was praised and criticized for his innovations, attacked for trying to create a new language different from Portugal's. But having always been conscious of his craft and well versed in matters of language and style, he was able to refute these accusations, and in so doing brought these issues to the national intellectual consciousness, proving to his opponents that the development of a national vernacular was indeed unavoidable.

As he explains in *Como e Porque Sou Romancista*, from an early age he envied the admiration bestowed upon novelists, and aspired to emulate them. First he was taken by the tearful, emotional response of his mother and relatives whenever he read to them; later, he appreciated the homage his law school colleagues paid to Joaquim Manuel de Macedo who had just published the first significant Brazilian romantic novel, *A Moreninha*. He set out to find his models, to prepare himself to attempt a "poem of real life," as he envisioned the novel at the time. The writers who influenced him most were Chateaubriand, Balzac, Sir Walter Scott and Cooper—but, as he cautions, the Cooper of the sea novels, not of the Leatherstocking Tales; he denies having written his Indianist novels based on Cooper.[1]

Alencar's vast production may be classified in various ways. The writer himself revealed a scheme to his work, albeit after having written extensively. He explained that his novels dealt with three historical phases: the native—that of legends (prior to the European invasion); the historical—the interaction of two cultures, including the question of miscegenation; and the national—"the childhood of our literature" (emphasizing what was characteristic of the new nation and its struggles against foreign influences). In more general terms, we may divide his works into Indianist (*Iracema, O Guarani*), historical (*A Guerra dos Mascates, As Minas de Prata*), regional (*O Gaúcho, O Sertanejo*), and urban (*Senhora, Lucíola*). Antônio Cândido refers to "three Alencars": one who appeals to a male audience, describing heroism and gallantry, creating some of the myths of the new culture, like the Indian Peri; one who addresses a young female audience, presenting sentimental stories, always centered around a woman and leading to a happy ending; and an adult one (which includes *Senhora* and *Lucíola*) concerned with darker psychological, moral, and sociological issues, with a depth that distinguishes these novels from the sentimental, weaker ones, such as *Diva* or *A Pata da Gazela*.[2] Alencar's best known books are *O Guarani* (1857), *Iracema* (1865), *Lucíola* (1862), and *Senhora* (1875).

From its social revolutionary beginnings, Romanticism derived a dissatisfaction with both the old order of things, primarily the dominance of the aristocracy, and with the present one, the still inept and provincial bourgeoisie. Not always highly cultured, the bourgeoisie had become materialistic either as a means of survival or in a search for power. Unable to solve these conflicts, the romantic *I* tends toward evasion, valuing and glorifying things that remain at a distance, either in space or in time, infusing them with the imaginary. Hence the appeal of the chivalrous Middle Ages and of picturesque, faraway regions. Alencar wavered between the elegance and gracefulness of aristocratic customs, the sweet simplicity and solid values of the middle class, the heroic endurance of the Indian, the gaúcho, the *sertanejo* (northern backwoodsman), and the drama inherent in some less desirable forms of behavior like violence, seduction, and prostitution. He was a romantic influenced by Balzac's realism; his was a Brazilian consciousness following French revolutionary models. Hence the prevailing dichotomy in his works between realistic social criticism and romantic ideology, and the consequent inconsistencies and unevenness. As a journalist, he presents an admirably objective portrait of the times, offering in well-tuned diction details of life in the wilderness as well as of Rio's bourgeoisie during the second half of the century. But the reader senses, intermingled with these objective descriptions, the romantic imagination responsible for the delightful, but occasionally rather unseemly plots—the emphasis on the power of love, the nobility of the soul, the significant position of women in society. In *Senhora*, for instance, he criticizes the custom of the marriage of convenience and the institution of the dowry. However, in spite of the materialistic, sadistic, or self-interested mesh of motivations, in the end it is money earned through responsible work coupled with romantic love that redeems the characters.

Historically, it should be noted, the middle of the nineteenth century marks the decline of the custom of endowing daughters. Women were left freer to choose a marriage for love; in fact, by that time, the judge officiating at a wedding had to certify the bride's free will and consent. The elimination of the custom put an end to dowry hunters, as well. Moreover, the lack of a dowry meant that, even though men still incorporated their wives' property and inheritance through marriage, they came into the family as partners and/or had to support their families through hard work.[3]

It was the centrality of a feminine protagonist that drew me to Alencar when I first compared mid-nineteenth-century Brazilian and American novels. Cooper, Hawthorne, and Melville seldom give their fictional women any relevance or historical significance; theirs is mainly a world of men, in which women appear as intruders, often to disturb their enjoyment of life and nature. Hawthorne, of course, is the exception, having created several strong-minded female characters. Hester Prynne, in *The Scarlet Letter*, is an example of a self-determining individual, who resists the oppression of the Puritan, patriarchal social order. But her power remains rather subdued, and she survives by being silent and performing typically feminine tasks: sewing and caring for the sick. In the end her strength yields wisdom, but also loneliness. Joyce Warren points out in *The American Narcissus* that "All of the studies of the American character are analyzing men in America, for it is the man who has been encouraged to achieve, who has sought the expansion and development of the self." She thus laments the nonexistence of female role models for women readers: "Women are associated with the pressures of society and seen as entrappers, unattractive adversaries of the 'American' experience. For the woman reader to identify with the men in the novel is to identify against herself."[4] Not so in Brazil. Mindful of the sight of his mother and aunts crying as he read novels to them, Alencar surely had a feminine audience in mind as he wrote his own novels. Besides, women, mainly those of the higher classes, enjoyed a powerful social position in Brazil in those days. Antônio Cândido reminds us that behind the sentimental complications of the romantic novels published in the mid-nineteenth century "There is an infrastructure determined by the position of women, in this shy society of salesmen, public officers, and farmers. Women were one of the most important transmitters of property, a means of acquiring fortune or qualification."[5] As does the fictional Seixas, the critic Afrânio Coutinho explains that marriage was a means toward social classification: "A factor in social categorization, [women] represent and transmit family assets and confer to the intelligent, but poor, man the opportunity to fulfill his aspirations."[6]

Many of Alencar's novels have female protagonists. In *Iracema*, as in *Senhora* and *Lucíola*, man and woman engage in meaningful dialogue, facing each other at an equal level. Highly significant in comparing Brazilian and American mid-nineteenth-century fiction is the Indianist novel *Iracema*. The protagonist, for whom the book is entitled, is a beautiful honey-lipped Indian woman, portrayed as self-sufficient, intelligent, and knowledgeable of the forest's ways and secrets, much like Cooper's Uncas or Chingachgook. However, her life suffers a decline as a consequence of having fallen in love and eloped with a Portuguese settler. Unlike the tendency in American literature, here it is the man who entraps the woman.

Senhora features a female protagonist who took control of her life and steered it according to her own wishes, first evading, then overcoming male supremacy whenever it stood in her way. *Senhora* in the title means not only a lady, a married woman, but also mistress, the feminine of *senhor*, master; Aurélia is the owner, the proprietress, the power-holding figure. She embodies the image of individualism preached by some American writers: intelligent, self-assured, and self-reliant, in charge of her life. And she maintains this position against a patriarchal social context, represented by her guardian who time and again tries to veer her decisions to his own advantage, and by suitors after her beauty and, later, after her wealth.

All this, however, would not suffice to make Aurélia the intriguing character that she is. Her depth lies in the antagonistic forces that drive her, her internal dichotomy. Her behavior in society does not coincide with her nature. Her aggressiveness, her ironic tone, and her air of superiority, deriding all who seek her for her social status, are only a façade. To herself, she is sweet, melancholy, torn by the events in her life. When the character assumes her businesslike, haughty self, the author describes it as ". . . an upheaval taking place. The woman's vital core abandoned its natural focus, the heart, to concentrate itself in the brain, where a man's speculative faculties reside." On these occasions, Aurélia resembled a statue, "cold, paused, inflexible." This mineralization of the heroine, as some critics have expressed it, betokens a conflict "between the so-called masculine qualities, required to survive in the money-dominated world outside, and the more typically feminine, domestic attributes of love, warmth, and purity of thought. This polarity often presents itself, not only to the author, but to the character herself."[7] The insoluble polarity lends inner dimension to the heroine.

Aurélia harbors yet another kind of dualism. Antônio Cândido refers to "disharmony" as the dynamic factor in Alencar's plots. Usually this disharmony is a conflict between good and evil. However, as he sees it, sometimes it appears in a more "refined" form—"a certain preoccupation with a deviation from physiological or psychic balance." In *Senhora*, "due to the unusual and compelling situation it determines, a strange sado-masochistic repression emerges from beneath the greatness of Aurélia's soul and her gentility, which lends sinew and relief to a plot which, without it, might not go beyond *Diva* or *Sonhos d'Ouro*."[8] But this rather unusual trait in Aurélia's personality only enhances her power of resolution, her freedom of thought and action and her radical desire to follow the path of happiness. Roberto Schwarz suggests that "Aurélia belongs to the ironclad and absolute family of avengers, alchemists, loan sharks, and the ambitious, etc., of *The Human Comedy*; like them she heads a quest—one of those that had captivated the century's imagination—without which life for them appeared to be empty."[9] She may be compared with Zenobia of *The Blithedale Romance*, with whom she shares beauty, intelligence, and a prominent social position; both authors cause an irreconcilable dichotomy between reason and feelings to transform these characters into marbleized, statue-like forms. But there is a cultural difference in the way the novels end: Alencar granted his heroine a happy ending whereas Hawthorne murdered his.[10]

It should be underscored, however, that even though the striking protagonist of Senhora had always despised the "matrimonial market" and shown a disdainful attitude, her scornful, sadistic treatment of her suitors and the circumstance that allowed her to humiliate Seixas came only as a result of her inheritance. The picture of her poorer days is bleak and is comparable to the descriptions of the way Seixas's mother and sisters spent their days. Ironically, or surprisingly, the placid attitude of these other women toward their fate contrasts with the bitter criticism behind Aurélia's behavior. These secondary characters and the subplots lack the ideological impulse that provides the power behind the main story line, creating a certain thematic imbalance in the novel. As Roberto Schwarz points out in "Criando o Romance Brasileiro," the descriptions of the landowner's farm or the shameful position of Aurélia's mother do not embody any vehement social attack or justification; they appear as mere aspects of life, typical Brazilian life, that escaped the impact of the revolutionary ideology that brought forth the realistic movement in fiction. In an amazing turn, Schwarz's article concludes by suggesting that the mineralization of the protagonist implies paganism and refusal of sensual satisfaction; "In short," he writes, "the object of economic criticism has 'sexual prestige.'" Quoting from Senhora—"Such is the world; the satanic fire of that woman's beauty was her greatest seduction. In the embittered ardor of her rebellious soul, one could fathom abysses of passion that foretold tempests of sensuality promised by the love of the virginal bacchante"—he draws his conclusion: "Explicit subject matter: money represses natural feelings; latent subject matter: money, scorn, and refusal make up an eroticized context which opens more exciting perspectives than conventional life. In other words, money is detrimental because it separates sensuality from the existing familial context, and it is interesting for the same reason. Hence the convergence, in Alencar, between wealth, feminine independence, sensual intensity, and the sphere of prostitution."[11]

Money of course stands at the center of Alencar's preoccupations. Yet his concern with the ugliness that stems from materialism troubles the writer only in certain instances. His romantic eye for the colorful and the picturesque renders him blind to the inconsistencies that result from the unevenness of his treatment of the theme. He does criticize the "mercantile mentality of the end of the Empire," as Alfredo Bosi indicates, "but only when the crude villainy of self-interest surfaces, not when it is clouded by the fumes of aristocratic refinements: the glory of the salons, the luxury of the alcoves, the pomp of the costumes."[12] Alencar showers the reader with touches of elegance—magnificent gowns, men's suits, and pieces of furniture are described in detail, with mention of specific kinds of wood, inlays, metal adornments. Seixas's confession (that he was brought up in a society that promoted marriage as a means of gaining wealth) appears to be a sign of his awareness of wrongdoing; but his taste is condoned when the narrator explains that Seixas was "rather of an aristocratic nature" and only admired beauty, "the supreme feminine grace, the humanization of love . . . in a woman crowned by the halo of elegance." Even Seixas's foot is described, certainly without criticism, as having "the firm arch of an aristocrat."

The emphasis on the visual, on appearance, often serves as a means to suggest inner truths. The meticulous rendering of objects has an artistic, literary function, often signaling states of mind and internal conflicts. Seixas and Aurélia's evening walks, when they stroke flowers and feed birds and fish, are choreographed to reflect their emotional movements as well. Similarly, the reference to Seixas's change in type of clothing from dandy to a more subdued elegance, and Aurélia's simple attire in contrast to Adelaide's adorned luxury on their evening together at the theater denote mental states. The "staging" of the wedding night and the final scene in the same apartment, with Aurélia wearing the same green robe, reveals Alencar's concern with form, with setting, and with detail. On the whole, these minutiae add up to a vivid picture of Rio's life in the mid-1800s. As one critic remarked, if you want to know how the rich lived, read the description of Aurélia's mansion; for a simpler, poorer kind of dwelling, look for the details about Seixas's house.[13]

My purpose in translating *Senhora* was to familiarize American readers with this powerful novel that features a heroine very different from those found in American works of the same period, and thus to develop an appreciation for the literary production of other nations of the Americas.

THE TRANSLATION

Had I known the problems that Alencar's text poses to a contemporary translator, I think I would not have started this project. On the other hand, discovering the hidden treasures of Alencar's novel in details of both plot and style was thrilling. "Discovering" indeed it was, because the meticulous reading required for the translation yielded elements I had previously overlooked. Like every Brazilian student, I had read *Senhora* at least three times in the past; how could I then not have realized the extent of the paganism and sensuality of the vocabulary? How many sentences did I read, or skim, not perceiving the serious misprints? How could I have overlooked so many nineteenth-century idioms whose meanings totally escaped me? The translation forced me to face them. Here are two examples. "*Eu é que não estou pelos autos*," says Lemos, wondering if Seixas would demand more money. I finally found the expression in Antonio de Moraes Silva's 1878 dictionary, meaning "I won't consent." Clifford Landers discovered "*há viver e morrer*" in *Tesouro da Fraseologia Brasileira* by Antenor Nascentes; it means "to secure in writing."

The translation was based primarily on *Senhora*, eighth edition, Editora Ática, 1977. However, in view of the number of misprints or phrases that seemed flawed, I also consulted the Artes e Letras edition of 1964 and the text included in the *Complete Works*, Editora José Aguilar, 1959. Most of the time, the correct version became quite evident based on syntax or common sense. José Olympio prefaces his edition of Alencar's *Complete Works* by acknowledging the existence of "countless editions, many of them truly criminal, such is the number of errors that infest them and the amazing adulteration of texts, omissions, accretions, substitutions . . . ." To be certain that I was choosing the phrases closest to Alencar's original text, I verified some of my doubts against the 1875 Garnier edition in the Library of the Instituto de Estudos Brasileiros of the University of São Paulo—variations such as *abordar/abortar, segunda/seguinte folha de papel, palavras inspiradas pelo moço/palavras inspiradas do moço, casca/casta de bípedes*. To my surprise, Alencar himself faced editorial problems. The Garnier edition includes a long errata which points out misprints such as: "salinha térrea de Sta. Tereza, não Lapa"; "Alfredo, não Lúcio," "embalar o coração, não abalar."

Alencar was concerned with form and mastered a variety of tones—humorous, realistic, poetic. His diction can be very formal or very colloquial, even slangish. Aurélia's rather formal and eloquent speech is a far cry from Lemos's, as is the narrator's language in referring to one or the other. References to Lemos come always steeped in humor and contemporary idioms which posed several problems. He was *"rolho e bojudo como um vaso chines"*; his body *"rechonchudo tinha certa vivacidade buliçosa e saltitante que lhe dava petulância de rapaz . . ."* The descriptions are flippant, funny, and extremely visual. In the process of transposing the writer's wonderful choice of words, tone, euphony, and rhythm into the target language, the translator becomes fully aware of Alencar's felicitous expressions. There are also the more typically romantic, mystic, clouded, evanescent metaphors, precise (in their imprecision) and beautiful in the images they evoke. The vocabulary is of a very high register, and the equivalent often difficult to find, especially when one considered the sound quality of these passages. I often read Hawthorne or Cooper before translating to familiarize my ear to diction, images, and tone. The juxtaposition of the texts always yielded results: similar constructions or similar metaphors, and, I hope, fluidity of language.

Another issue was what to do with the currency of the time. *Mil-réis* could be left as such. But then came *contos*; since in English I could use *thousand* without having to repeat *mil mil-réis*, I opted to avoid another untranslated term and, at the same time, clarify the amount. The names of meals had to be reconsidered as well, for they differ from today's breakfast at seven or eight, lunch at noon, and supper at seven. I translated *almoço* as *breakfast*, having in mind *petit-déjeuner*. It took place around ten in the morning and included steak and seafood. The word *lunch* was eliminated as a possibility because it is used elsewhere in a reference to the English term *lunch*, Lusitanized as *lanche*, meaning a snack early in the afternoon. It was important to keep the difference. *Jantar* remained as dinner, even though it was eaten at five in the evening; *ceia*, served much later, was translated as *supper*.

Alencar has left us a wonderful picture of life during the latter half of the nineteenth century: from food to wardrobes, from means of transportation to different kinds of amusements, from what people saw in the theater, to the books they read, the games they played and the songs they sang, from the ways of life of different social classes to various political or cultural attitudes. The novel includes an amazing number of references to poets and novelists, to novels read at the time, to operas, to customs that have been lost. Occasionally the need arose for cultural or linguistic adaptation. In most instances, however, the names are world famous or the context clarifies the meaning so I decided to leave them as used by Alencar, devoid of extraneous explanations or notes. My main concerns were to maintain the novel's flavor and richness, and to do it justice.

NOTES

1. José de Alencar, *Como e Porque Sou Romancista* (Salvador: Livraria Progresso Editora, 1955), 58. For a comparison of Cooper and Alencar see Renata M. Wasserman, "Re-Inventing the New World: Cooper and Alencar," *Comparative Literature*, Spring 1984: 130–145.

2. Antônio Cândido, *Formação da Literatura Brasileira*, 2d ed., 2 vols. (São Paulo: Livraria Martins Editora, 1964) 2: 218–222.

3. For a study of the dowry in Brazil, see Muriel Nazzari, *Disappearance of the Dowry: Women, Families and Social Change in São Paulo, Brazil, 1600–1900* (Stanford: Stanford University Press, 1991).

4. Joyce Warren, *The American Narcissus: Individualism and Women in Nineteenth-Century American Fiction* (New Brunswick: Rutgers University Press, 1984), 6 and 2. See also Nina Baym, "Portrayal of Women in American Literature, 1790–1870," in *What Manner of Woman: Essays on English and American Life and Literature*, edited by Marlene Springer (New York: New York University Press, 1977), 228.

5. Cândido 2: 140. The translations of critical texts are mine.

6. Afrânio Coutinho and Eduardo de Faria Coutinho, eds., *A Literatura no Brasil*, 3d. ed., 6 vols. (Rio de Janeiro and Niterói: José Olympio Editora and Universidade Federal Fluminense, 1986) 3: 261.

7. Catarina Edinger, "Machismo and Androgyny in Mid-Nineteenth-Century Brazilian and American Novels," *Comparative Literature Studies* 27.2 (1990): 135.

8. Cândido 2: 227–228.

9. Roberto Schwarz, "Criando o Romance Brasileiro," *Argumento* 1.4 (February 1974): 31.

10. For a comparison of Alencar's and Hawthorne's works see Catarina Edinger, "Hawthorne and Alencar Romancing the Marble," *Brasil/Brazil* 4.3 (1990): 69–84.

11. Schwarz 46.

12. Alfredo Bosi, *História Concisa da Literatura Brasileira* (São Paulo: Ed. Cultrix, 1975), 154.

13. M. Cavalcanti Proença, "José de Alencar na Literatura Brasileira." Introduction, *José de Alencar: Obra Completa* (Rio de Janeiro: Aguilar, 1959), 1: 73.

SENHORA
Profile of a Woman

TO THE READER

This book, like the two that preceded it, is not authored by the writer to whom they are usually attributed.

The story is true and the narrative comes from the person who, directly and in circumstances of which I am unaware, received the confidence of the principal actors in this curious drama.

Strictly speaking, the supposed author is merely an editor. Of course, in taking it upon himself to correct the form and give it new literary polish, he in some way appropriates not the work but the book.

In any case, in these pages the reader will often find an exuberance of language and a boldness of imagination that would never spring from the sober and reflective pen of a writer devoid of illusions and enthusiasms.

I was tempted to erase some of those more overdone pictures or at least to dim the bright and sparkling tones.

But should I sacrifice to graybeards these artistic whims of style which might constitute, to the refined advocates of esthetics, the book's most delicate hue?

And is the prominence of those scenes merely the painter's fantasy and decoration of form, or does it, above all, serve as contrast to a character's fine degree of perfection?

There is in fact a heroism of virtue in the pride of this woman who resists every seduction, the impulses of her own passion as well as the rapture of the senses.

—José de Alencar

FIRST PART

The Price

Some years ago, a new star appeared in the skies of Rio.

From the moment she rose, no one challenged her scepter; she was proclaimed queen of the ballrooms.

She became the goddess of the balls, the muse of poets, and the idol of eligible suitors.

She was rich and beautiful.

Two opulences that enhance each other like flowers in an alabaster vase; two splendors that reflect each other, like a ray of sun on the facet of a diamond.

Who can forget Aurélia Camargo, who crossed the heavens of the court like a shining meteor, suddenly to vanish amidst the wonder that produced her fire?

She was eighteen when she first appeared in society. No one knew her; and all searched immediately, avidly, for information about the great novelty of the day.

They said many things I shall not repeat here, for in due course we shall learn the truth, stripped of the petty comments in which telltales are wont to dress it.

Aurélia was an orphan; she lived in the company of an elderly relative, a widow, Dona Firmina Mascarenhas, her constant companion in society.

But this relative was merely a mother of convenience to comply with the scruples of Brazilian society, which at that time had yet to accept a certain emancipation of women.

Maintaining toward the widow a respectful deference due her age, the young lady never wavered for a moment from the firm purpose of running her household and acting in the manner she pleased.

Aurélia was also said to have a guardian; but this unknown entity, to judge by the character of his ward, must have exerted as little influence over her will as did the elderly relative.

It was generally believed that the girl's future depended exclusively on her own inclinations and whims; and therefore all types of veneration were laid directly at the feet of the idol.

Besieged by a mob of suitors who vied for her like a spoil of victory, Aurélia, wondrously shrewd for her age, assessed the dangers that threatened her and the difficult situation in which she found herself.

Hence, perhaps, the rather disdainful attitude and a certain air of coquettishness that ruffled her beauty, otherwise so proper and sculpted for the sweet and serene expansion of her soul.

Had the beautiful face not constantly betrayed, even in moments of contemplation and distraction, this tint of sarcasm, no one would see it as Aurélia's true visage, but as the mask of some deep disillusionment.

It is hard to believe that nature would limn such pure and clear features only to mar their harmony with a pungent, sardonic smile. God would not soften such large, wide eyes with charming tenderness if He had intended them to fire sparks of contempt.

Why that statuesque, perfect silhouette, if instead of breathing deep with the gentle flows of love, it only raged with scorn?

In the living room, surrounded by admirers, amid splendid reflections of beauty, Aurélia, far from becoming intoxicated by the adoration evoked by her beauty and by the homage paid her, on the contrary, showed only indignation toward this vulgar, contemptible horde.

It was not a triumph she considered worthy of her, these people's abject humiliation before her riches. It was a challenge she thrust upon the world, proud to crush it beneath her heel like a poisonous reptile.

Such is the world; the satanic fire of that woman's beauty was her greatest seduction. In the embittered ardor of her rebellious soul, one could fathom abysses of passion that foretold tempests of sensuality promised by the love of the virginal bacchante.

If the sinister glimmer were to vanish suddenly, leaving that beautiful statue in the soft penumbra of sweetness and innocence, the pure and chaste angel borne within her as in all young women, might pass unnoticed amidst the whirlwind.

Aurélia's most impetuous rebellions were directed precisely against the riches that enthroned her and without which, for all her gifts, she surely would never enjoy, disdainful as a queen, the vassalage rendered her.

It was for this reason that she considered gold a vile metal that debased men; and in her heart, she felt deeply humiliated thinking that to all these people who surrounded her, she, herself, merited none of the flattery that they dedicated to each of her thousands in capital.

Never from the pen of some unknown Chatterton came more excruciating diatribes against money than those that often vibrated on the perfumed lips of this young enchantress in the bosom of opulence.

One line is all we need to sketch her from this perspective.

Convinced that all those who professed love for her, without exception, sought only her wealth, Aurélia reacted to this affront by responding to these individuals in kind.

Thus she would indicate the relative merit of her suitors by attributing to each a certain monetary value. She quoted her worshipers in the language of finance, referring to the price each might reasonably be expected to bring on the matrimonial market.

One evening, at the casino, Lísia Soares, who was very close to her and would have liked to see her married, made a comment about Alfredo Moreira, an elegant young man who had just arrived from Europe.

"A very distinguished gentleman," replied Aurélia, smiling. "He is worth about a hundred thousand as a fiancé, but I can afford a more expensive husband, Lísia; this one is not good enough for me."

Everyone laughed at these remarks of Aurélia's and considered them jests of a witty young girl. The majority of ladies, however, especially those with young daughters, were unrelenting in their criticism of this brazen conduct as improper for a well-bred young lady.

Aurélia's suitors knew of the value placed upon them in the girl's ledgers, for she made no secret of it. Rather than being upset at her honesty, however, they enjoyed the game—which often resulted in an increase in their stock in the nuptial business.

This happened whenever one of these young men was fortunate enough to do something that pleased the girl and fulfilled her fantasies. In such case, she raised his price, just as she similarly lowered that of those who displeased her or fell into disfavor with her.

Greed must have inured these men, or passion blinded them, for them not to see the cold scorn with which Aurélia deceived them in these silly games they took as girlish vanity, but which were, in fact, the impulses of a hidden, perhaps morbid, anger.

The truth is that they all persisted; at times caught up in temporary despair, but soon restored by an obstinate hope, none chose to abandon the field; least of all, Alfredo Moreira, who appeared to head the list.

I shall not follow Aurélia in her transient passage through the salons of the court, where she saw, coupled to her triumphant chariot, everything our society boasts of the most elevated and brilliant.

All I propose is to tell of the intimate and strange drama that decided the fate of this unique woman.

∞ II ∞

It must be about nine o'clock.

The hot March sun strikes the blinds that cover the balcony of a drawing room in Laranjeiras.

The light filtered through the green draperies outlines in its glow Aurélia's graceful bust against the velvety scarlet wallpaper of the study.

Reclining on the settee with her eyes wandering about the twilit room, the girl seems deeply immersed in thought. Her reverie dissolves from her features, as from her demeanor, the caustic sparks that usually emanate from her like the sulfurous flame of a bolt of lightning.

But the serenity that envelops her, if in some way attenuating her beauty, renders her irresistible by bathing her in an indescribable flow of sweetness and tenderness.

Her eyes no longer exhibit those tawny sparks, which burn like the cloud-covered sun, that they issue in the salons. On her lips, instead of a stinging smile, there springs forth a soul reflecting on innermost raptures.

Casting a shadow over her beauteous visage, there lingers a melancholy tone that, although not seen for some time now, could nevertheless be deemed more suitable for those delicate features. There are women whom the perfume of sadness elevates to perfection. The most violent passions are inspired by these angels in exile.

Aurélia is totally concentrated within herself; no one, seeing this sweet young girl, so calm and peaceful in appearance, would believe that at this very moment she is deliberating and deciding upon the problem of her existence, and preparing to sacrifice irredeemably her entire future.

Somebody, entering the study, tore the beautiful, pensive girl from her lengthy meditation. It was Dona Firmina Mascarenhas, the lady who served as Aurélia's chaperone.

The widow approached the settee and kissed the girl on the cheek, rousing her from the profound absorption in which she found herself.

Taken by surprise, Aurélia glanced about the room and consulted a miniature watch she carried around her waist on a matte gold chain.

Meanwhile, Dona Firmina, accommodating her fifty-year-old girth in one of the large armchairs next to the settee, was ready to wait for breakfast.

"Are you tired from yesterday?" asked the widow with the affected tenderness demanded by her role.

"Not really, but I feel faint; it is probably the heat," replied the young lady seeking an excuse for her meditative attitude.

"These balls that finish so late cannot do anybody's health any good; that is why there are so many thin and pale young girls in Rio de Janeiro. Why, yesterday, when they served supper it was almost time for the bells of Santa Teresa to sound matins. And the first quadrille began at the sounding of Aragão's curfew! There was a great deal of confusion; the service was not bad, but everything was jumbled—"

Dona Firmina went on and on describing her impressions of the previous evening's ball, without taking her eyes from Aurélia's face, on which she fixed her gaze to discern the effect of her words, ready to withdraw any comment at the slightest sign of disagreement.

The young woman let her speak, desirous of unburdening herself of her cares, and lulling in the sound of this voice she heard without understanding. She knew the widow was speaking of the dance, but did not follow what she was saying.

Suddenly, however, she interrupted her:

"What did you think of the Amaral girl, Dona Firmina?"

The older woman assumed the expression of attempting to remember.

"Amaral? That girl all in blue?"

"With silver sprigs in her hair and in the folds of her skirt, simple and in very good taste."

"I recall her. A very charming girl!" confirmed the widow.

"And well-bred. They say she plays the piano to perfection and that she has a very pleasant voice."

"But she does not usually appear in society. It is the first time we have met her. I do not remember seeing her before."

"It *was* the first time!"

As she pronounced these words, the girl seemed to feel her soul refract once again, drawn imperiously by the secret thought that absorbed her.

But she reacted against this preoccupation and said to the widow in a lively and urgent tone:

"Tell me something, Dona Firmina!"

"What is it, Aurélia?"

"But you must be honest. Do you promise me?"

"Honest? More than I am, madam? Why, that is my greatest shortcoming!"

The girl hesitated.

"Go ahead, madam."

"Whom do you find prettier, the Amaral girl or me?" Aurélia finally blurted out, turning slightly pale.

"Well, well!" laughed the widow. "Are you joking? How can the Amaral girl compare with you?"

"Be honest!"

"Others, much more beautiful than she, do not hold a candle to you."

The widow mentioned the names, which I no longer recall, of four or five girls then at the height of acclaim.

"She is so elegant!" said Aurélia as if completing an intimate thought.

"It is a matter of taste."

"In any case, is she more well-bred than I?"

"Than you, Aurélia? It is difficult to find in all of Rio de Janeiro another young lady with your upbringing. Even there in Paris, which they talk about so much, I doubt there is one."

"Thank you! Is this your honest opinion, Dona Firmina?"

"Yes, madam; my honesty lies in my telling the truth, not in hiding it. Besides, this is what everybody sees and repeats. That you play the piano like Arnaud, sing like a prima donna, and talk to politicians and diplomats, and bewitch them. And why should it be otherwise? When you so wish, Aurélia, you speak in a way that sounds like a novel."

"I can see that you are not at all flattering. You do not recognize my *gifts*," interrupted the girl stressing the last word with a slight ironic smile. "Don't you know, Dona Firmina, that I have a *golden style*, the most sublime of all styles, whose enrapturing eloquence none can resist? The ones who speak like a novel, in common prose, are those pale and romantic girls who are always dissolving into sighs; I speak like a poem: I am poetry that shines and dazzles!"

"I understand what you mean; money makes the ugly into beautiful; it provides everything, even health. But look here, your greatest admirers are precisely those who cannot aspire to your wealth; some are married, others already old . . . "

"When somebody smoked near you for the first time, didn't you feel sort of dizzy? Well, gold has an invisible smoke that intoxicates more than that from a Havana cigar, and even from that disgusting paper cigarette that young men today are so taken with. All those people who surround a rich old man—ministers, senators, and noblemen—certainly have no intention of marrying the man's coffers, but they are drawn by the attraction of money."

"At this very moment, Aurélia, you are saying that I am right, and displaying your education. Who would say that a girl of your age knows more than many of the men who attended the academies? And that's good; otherwise, with the wealth your grandfather bequeathed you, alone in the world, you would surely be duped."

"Would it were so!" replied the young lady, retreating into her meditations.

Dona Firmina still uttered some words, continuing the conversation, but noticed that the girl was not paying attention; rather, she seemed to avoid any impression from without to concentrate even more deeply on her thoughts.

Then, with the tact of those souls molded for moral domesticity, Dona Firmina rose, and taking some steps around the room, feigned interest in the alabaster statues and porcelain vases sitting on the red marble consoles.

Her back toward the settee, she appeared to take no notice of Aurélia's reverie for, upon her return from the distraction, the girl would surely take umbrage at anyone divining through her gestures the secret of her thoughts.

Scarcely five minutes had elapsed when Dona Firmina heard a crystalline, fluttering sound that she knew well from having heard it so often. She turned around and saw Aurélia, whose pink lips still vibrated with the chords of that harsh smile.

The gentle girl had emerged from her pensive languor, resembling a wax statue that, suddenly transforming itself into jasper, stood proud and disdainful, emitting livid, tawny reflections like those of polished marble.

She walked toward the windows and with a nervous, petulant gesture abruptly raised both blinds, which seemed excessively heavy for her thin and gentle hands.

The flood of light rushing through the open windows filled the room; the young lady advanced onto the terrace to bathe herself in the cascades of sunlight that swept over her forehead crowned by a tiara of brown hair and rippled down her magnificent shoulders like a golden tunic.

She steeped herself in light. One who saw her at that moment, so radiant, might believe that beneath the pleats of the fine linen robe undulated voluptuously the nymph of the flames, the lascivious salamander into which the enchanted fairy had suddenly transformed herself.

After drenching herself in sunshine, like the milky white poppy that blushes at the kisses of its royal lover, the young woman went to the piano and threw it open with an abrupt movement. From the maelstrom of the raucous chromatic storm that roiled the keys came Norma's magnificent imprecation, when raging with jealousy, she lashes out at Polion's betrayal.

Tempering the boldness of that dizzying arrangement in order to accompany it, the girl began to sing; however, at the first notes, feeling confined by her position, she abandoned the piano, and standing in the middle of the living room, trailing the skirt of her robe as if it were the train of a Gaulish canopy, she reproduced in voice and gesture that epic of a broken heart, one she had so often seen performed by Lagrange.

Never, even by that finest singer, had the ferocity of the woman betrayed, the rage of the wounded lioness, been expressed in a more resounding voice, in a more sublime gesture. The notes that flew from her lips, vigorous and harmonious, left behind a tremor that recalled the serpent's hiss, especially when her delicate, well-turned arm lunged out suddenly, stiffly, in a gesture of supreme contempt.

Dona Firmina, although quite accustomed to Aurélia's eccentric nature, was surprised at what she saw, and suspected that something extraordinary must have occurred in her life to first make her so pensive and then produce this outburst of emotion.

Nonetheless, as voluble as when she rose from the settee, she ran to Dona Firmina, and locked her hand about the lady's wrist as if she were Polion, giving a comical twist to the scene which ended in laughter.

∞ III ∞

It was time for breakfast. The two ladies sat at the table. Aurélia distinguished herself by her composure, a consequence of her temperament and upbringing. This does not mean that she belonged with that group of fluttering girls who live on the pollen of flowers, and for whom eating is prosaic and inelegant.

Quite the opposite. She understood that nutrition provides beauty its vitality, without which colors fade from cheeks and smiles from lips, like the pale and ephemeral blossoms of a sickly rose bush.

So she was unashamed of eating; and without vanity she believed that the enamel of her teeth was not less charming when they made low sounds like a pearl necklace; nor was the hue of her lips less tasty when they sucked into a fruit, or opened slightly to receive nourishment.

On this occasion, however, the young lady made an exception to her habitual sobriety; she, who did not care for spices, and only touched a few drops of spirits now and then, wished to try all the sauces and spices to be found in the house and finished with a glass of sherry.

Dona Firmina, while not neglecting her breakfast, continued to observe the girl, ever more convinced that something important must have happened to alter the girl's usual serenity.

This event, in the widow's view, could only be the one that affects eighteen-year-old girls so deeply, especially if they depend on no one for their freedom.

Dona Firmina was therefore sure that the disdainful Aurélia had finally felt some inclination; the widow was eager to meet the fortunate man who had had the power to captivate the proud queen of the salons, as worshiped as she was cold and indifferent.

She sifted in her mind the memories of last night's dance to make sure that no unknown young man had appeared with whom Aurélia might suddenly have fallen in love. It must therefore be one of the old suitors whom she scorned, who, for some inexplicable reason, had at last succeeded in winning her heart.

She could contain herself no longer; at the risk of displeasing the girl, she dropped a hint so as to start a conversation, and, depending on the response, lead up to the point.

"I do not know what to make of you today, Aurélia! You seem so happy, and even more beautiful than usual, if that is possible!"

"Really!"

"I am not exaggerating. Listen! Young girls, when they dress to go to a ball where they expect to meet someone special become more beautiful than they actually are. But you, today, are more beautiful than at the balls. I have never seen you this way. You must be keeping some secret."

"Do you want to know about it?" asked Aurélia, smiling.

"I am not a curious person," answered the widow, feeling the bitterness of that sharp smile.

"I have decided to become a nun."

"A good idea."

"But my convent will be this very world we live in, because no other would offer me more penitence or mortifications."

Immediately belying the seriousness of these words with mocking laughter, Aurélia left Dona Firmina in the dining room, astonished that a girl so immensely rich and beautiful, desired by all, could harbor such thoughts, even in jest.

Aurélia, who had gone to her dressing room, sat at a desk made of *araribá* wood with golden bronze reliefs and wrote a short letter.

The girl executed each detail of this simple operation with deliberation, folding the paper, placing it in the envelope, melting the wax, and pressing the seal, with greatest attention and care.

Either the letter was intended for one who deserved everything from her, or by this painstaking manner she was trying to disguise the vacillation that took her by surprise as she was about to carry out an idea previously decided upon.

After addressing the envelope, the young woman removed from a secret compartment in her desk a small sandalwood box with ivory inlays.

There, among letters and wilted flowers, lay a yellowed card which she placed in her velvet purse and then hid in the pocket of her robe.

At the sound of the bell, a servant appeared. Aurélia handed him the letter with a rapid gesture and a brief word, as if fearful of second thoughts.

"To Mr. Lemos! Quickly."

Aurélia felt then the tranquility that follows struggles of the heart. She had finally solved the intractable problem of her life; and instead of drifting with chance and allowing herself to be swept by the world's turmoil, she had found the strength in her soul to shape events and control the future.

Hence the peace that fell over her as she left the dressing room, which once more imparted to her beauty a sweet expression of melancholy and resignation.

Dona Firmina, as usual, was waiting for Aurélia to determine how they would spend the morning, for the widow had no occupation other than to please the girl, keep her company, and satisfy all her desires and whims.

For this, she received, besides her meals, a generous monthly allowance that she put away for difficult times such as those she had faced soon after she had lost her husband.

"You are not going out today, Aurélia?"

"Perhaps. But do not feel obliged to stay with me."

"Will you stay by yourself?"

"I have things to do. Serious business!" responded the girl, smiling.

"Is it already some small penitence?"

"Not yet; it is the vocation, the calling of the novice."

The girl was still laughing when they announced Mr. Lemos, who was immediately shown into the living room.

"I received your letter en route. I was going to Botafogo; José ran into me at the Largo do Machado. I am at your service, Aurélia."

Mr. Lemos was an elderly man, short, not overly fat, but plump and bulbous like a Chinese vase. Despite his chubby build, he was lively and sprightly, and this lent him a certain youthful brashness offering a perfect match for his small, mischievous eyes.

To be introduced to him was to recognize him immediately as one of these merry fellows well supplied with hearty laughter to celebrate themselves.

When Lemos, as her uncle, was appointed by the Court of Orphans as Aurélia's guardian, there occurred an incident that determined from the outset the nature of the relationship between guardian and ward.

The old man expected to take the girl to live with his family.

Aurélia opposed the idea formally, and declared that it was her intention to live in her own house, in the company of Dona Firmina Mascarenhas.

"But listen, my girl, you are still a minor."

"I'm eighteen years old."

"Only at twenty-one can you live by yourself and control your life."

"Is that how you feel? I'll ask the judge to give me another, more obliging kind of tutor."

"What did you say?"

"And I will present him with such arguments that he will surely heed my wishes."

In view of this assertive tone, Lemos pondered, and found it more prudent to avoid antagonizing the girl. The idea of her asking the judge to take away the guardianship displeased him. Rich and beautiful women, he concluded, never want for influential protectors.

Soon after the greetings, Dona Firmina left in order to let the young lady be at ease. In truth, the widow would have liked to be present at these conferences that Lemos held now and then with his ward to discuss the accounts of the guardianship; but Aurélia was extremely reserved about this and disliked anyone's concern with what she called her business.

"If you please, Uncle!" said the girl, opening a side door.

This door led to an elegantly furnished study, in the center of which was an oval bench, of *érable* like the rest of the furniture, covered with a blue cloth with red fringes. On the table, on a silver tray, lay the inkwell and other writing implements.

Just as Aurélia, after seeing Lemos in, was about the enter the office, Bernardina, an old woman whom the girl protected with alms, appeared at the door of the sitting room. The creature stopped shyly, waiting for permission to come in.

Aurélia approached her inquisitively.

"I wanted to come yesterday," whispered Bernardina, "but I could not; I had an attack of rheumatism. I meant to tell you that he has arrived."

"I already knew."

"Oh! Who told you? It was yesterday, about noon."

"Come in!"

Aurélia cut the dialogue short, pointing to the hallway that led to the inside of the house and, entering the study, closed the door behind her.

This detail did not escape Lemos, who judged the importance of the conference by its solemnity.

"What story will she tell me today?" the jolly old man wondered.

Aurélia sat at the *érable* desk, inviting her guardian to take the armchair opposite her.

ಇ IV ಊ

Anyone who observed Aurélia at that moment could not but notice the new appearance her beautiful face had assumed, which also infused her entire being.

It was a cold, studied, inflexible expression, that marbleized her beauty, lending her something akin to the iciness of a statue. But the sparkle of her large brown eyes shone with radiant intelligence. An upheaval was taking place within her. The woman's vital core abandoned its natural focus, the heart, to concentrate itself in the brain, where a man's speculative faculties reside.

On these occasions her spirit acquired such lucidity that Lemos felt a chill run down his spine, in spite of the solid flesh nature provided the chubby old man with which to line the trunk of his nervous system.

It was astonishing to strangers, and frightening to a guardian, to see the cleverness with which this eighteen-year-old girl approached the most complicated questions, the perfect knowledge she evinced of her finances, and the ease with which she completed, often in her head, the most difficult and intricate mathematical operation.

On the other hand, Aurélia showed no trace of the ridiculous pedantry of certain girls who, having garnered some vague ideas from superficial reading, set out babbling about everything.

Quite the opposite. She was reserved about her experience, and made use of it only when her own interest demanded it. Aside from such occasions, no one ever heard her discuss business or give her opinion about things alien to her realm of unmarried young lady.

Lemos felt uneasy; he had lost the high spirits that lent him a pleasant bubbly air. In the unusual momentousness of this conference, experienced and shrewd as he was, he could see serious consequences.

So he was all ears, heedful of the girl's words.

"I took the liberty to disturb you, Uncle, to discuss a very important subject."

"Oh! Very important?" repeated the old man shaking his head.

"My marriage!" replied Aurélia, with great coldness and composure.

The old man sprang from his chair like an elastic balloon. To disguise his agitation, he rubbed his hands quickly one against the other, a gesture that for him indicated great excitement.

"Don't you think I am old enough to start thinking about it?" asked the girl.

"Certainly! Eighteen years old . . . "

"Nineteen."

"Nineteen! I thought your birthday was not—Many girls get married at this age, and even younger; however, that is when you have a father or mother to choose a worthy husband and push certain scoundrels aside. As an orphan, with no experience, you would be well advised not to marry until you come of age and know something of the world."

"I know it only too well," replied the young girl, in the same serious tone.

"So, have you made up your mind?"

"So much so that I asked for this conference—"

"I know. You want me to point out someone—to find you a fiancé with the necessary qualifications—Hmm!—It's difficult—some character who would be courting a young lady like you, Aurélia? All right. We shall undertake the search!"

"No need to, Uncle. I have already found him!"

Lemos had another shock that made him jump in his chair once again.

"What? Do you have your eye on someone?"

"Excuse me, Uncle, I do not grasp your figurative language. I am telling you that I have chosen the man I am to marry."

"I understand. But you see! As guardian, I have to give my approval."

"Certainly, but as my guardian, sir, you are not going to be so cruel as to deny your approval. If you do, which I do not expect to happen, the Court of Orphans will overrule it."

"The court? What kind of stories have they been putting into your head, Aurélia?"

"Mr. Lemos," said the girl slowly, meeting the old man's perplexed look with a cold stare, "I am nineteen. I can request an age waiver showing that I am capable of governing my own person and my belongings; with reason on my side, I will obtain from the Court of Orphans, in spite of your opposition, a license to marry whomever I wish. If these legal arguments do not satisfy you, I will offer you a personal one."

"Let's see!" replied the old man.

"It's my willpower. You have no idea what it is worth, but I swear that to carry this out I would not hesitate to sacrifice my grandfather's inheritance."

"Typical of the age! Only at nineteen does one come up with such ideas; and even this is becoming increasingly rare."

"You forget that of those nineteen years, I lived eighteen in extreme poverty and one in the lap of luxury into which I was suddenly led. I have learned the two great lessons of this world: that of poverty and that of wealth. In the past I knew money as a tyrant; today I know it as a submissive captive. Therefore I must be older than you who have never been as poor as I was or as rich as I am."

Lemos regarded with astonishment this girl who spoke of such profound worldly lessons and a philosophy hitherto unknown to him.

"It would not be worth having so much money," continued Aurélia, "if it did not afford me the marriage I desire, even though it might require spending a few miserable thousand."

"That's where I see the problem," retorted Lemos, who had been looking for an opportunity to gainsay her. "You are aware, Aurélia, that as your guardian I cannot spend a cent without the judge's authorization."

"You do not want to understand me, my dear guardian," replied the girl, with a hint of impatience. "I know that, just as I also know of a lot of things that no one ever dreams of. For example, I know my stock dividends, interest rates, stock exchange prices. I know that I can calculate compound premiums as accurately and precisely as an exchange table."

Lemos felt dizzy.

"And finally, I know I have a list of everything my grandfather owned, in his own handwriting and given to me by him personally."

At this, the ruddy old man turned pale, a frightening symptom for such a full and massive pile of flesh as the one that stuffed his imported trousers and black morning coat.

"That means that, if I had a guardian who opposed and displeased me, when I became of age I would not discharge him before examining the accounts he had administrated. For that purpose, fortunately, I am not in want of a lawyer or bookkeeper."

"Yes, madam; you are within your rights," replied the old man contritely.

"However, since I am fortunate enough to have a friendly guardian who always accedes to my wishes, like you, Uncle—"

"Oh, how true!"

"In that case, instead of exhausting my patience and bothering with records and accounts, I consider everything in order. Moreover, I know that the guardianship is unremunerated, but it should not be when the orphans have more than enough to compensate for the troubles they cause."

"No, none of that, Aurélia. I have accepted the charge as a sacred obligation to the memory of your mother, my good and sorely missed sister."

Lemos wiped away a tear he managed to squeeze from the corner of his eye, unless he invented it, which is more likely. And the girl, in honor of her mother's memory evoked by the old man, stood up for a moment, on the pretext of looking out the window.

When she returned to her place, Lemos had fully recovered from the shocks he had just undergone and appeared natural, vigorous, sprightly, and cheerful.

"Do we understand each other?" asked the girl, as judicious as she had been throughout the conversation.

"You are a sorceress, Aurélia; you do with me as you please."

"Think about this, Uncle. I am going to entrust you with my secret, a secret I have told no one else in the world, and one that God alone knows. If after hearing it you do not wish to help me or do not know how to, I shall never forgive you."

"You need have no fear of trusting me with your secret, Aurélia; I will prove worthy of your trust."

"I believe, Mr. Lemos, and to remove any scruples that might assail you, I swear by the memory of my mother, that if there is any happiness for me in this world, it is that which you can give me."

"I am at your disposal."

Aurélia paused for a moment.

"Do you know Amaral?"

"Which one?" asked the old man, somewhat embarrassed.

"Manuel Tavares do Amaral, a customs employee," said the young woman consulting her small notebook. "Please take this down. He is not rich, but has some holdings; he arranged his daughter Adelaide's marriage to a gentleman who was absent from Rio de Janeiro, and to whom he offered a dowry of thirty thousand."

As she uttered these words, one could sense a fleeting tremor in the girl's voice, usually so clear, but it quickly assumed a harsh tone.

Lemos, already flushed, turned purple; and to disguise his embarrassment he shook his head, ill at ease, loosening his collar with his finger as if it were choking him.

Aurélia's cold gaze lingered a moment on the old man's face; then, turning her eyes slowly so as to focus on the opened page of her notebook, she allowed her uncle some time to recover; it took him only a short time. He was skilled in the ways of the world.

"Thirty thousand—" he remarked. "Not a bad start!"

Aurélia went on:

"We must break this marriage arrangement as soon as possible. Adelaide must marry Dr. Torquato Ribeiro, whom she loves. He is poor, and for this reason her father rejected him; but if you assured Amaral that this young man has about fifty thousand of his own, do you think he would refuse him?"

"Suppose I did so. From where would this money come?"

"I shall provide it with the greatest pleasure."

"But why, my dear, should we interfere in other people's business?"

"You are sufficiently intelligent to understand what I would in vain try to hide from you. I would rather trust in your loyalty without reservations."

The girl made an effort.

"This young man who is engaged to Adelaide Amaral is the man I have chosen for my husband. As you can see, since he cannot belong to both, I must fight for him."

"You may count on me!" replied the old man, rubbing his hands, as if he could foresee the benefits that this passion held for an astute guardian.

"This young man—"

"His name?" he asked, dipping his pen. Aurélia signaled him to wait.

"He arrived yesterday; it follows that he should now be taking care of preparations for this marriage which was arranged almost a year ago. You should look him up as soon as possible—"

"This very day."

"And make the offer. These arrangements are quite common in Rio de Janeiro."

"It is being done every day."

"You know better than I how such arranged betrothals are executed."

"Well . . . !"

"I warn you that my name must never be mentioned in any of this."

"Ah! You wish to maintain anonymity."

"Until we meet. However, you may disclose enough for them not to fear that it might be an older woman or an invalid."

"I understand!" reassured the old man, laughing. "A romantic marriage."

"No, sir. No exaggerations. You are authorized to say only that the bride is neither old nor ugly."

"Do you want to prepare for the surprise?"

"Possibly. The terms of the offer—"

"Excuse me! Since you want to remain unknown, should I also stay out of sight?"

Aurélia thought for a moment.

"I do not want this to go beyond you. In case he recognizes you as my uncle and guardian, couldn't you convince him that I have nothing at all to do with this? That it is something being done by the family or relatives?"

"A good thought! I shall work it out; do not worry."

"The terms of the proposal should be as follows; pay close attention. The family of this mysterious young woman wishes to see her marry with a prenuptial agreement that keeps husband's and wife's assets separate, offering to the groom the sum of one hundred thousand as dowry. If one hundred is not enough, and *he* demands more, it shall be two hundred."

"I am sure it will be sufficient. No fear of that!"

"In any case I want you to understand my thinking very well. Naturally I want to obtain what I desire as cheaply as possible; but it is essential that I obtain it; therefore, up to half of what I own, price is no object. It is my happiness I am buying."

The girl uttered these last words in an undefinable tone.

"Won't it be expensive?"

"Oh!" exclaimed Aurélia. "I would give my entire fortune for it. Others have it for free, sent directly from heaven. But I cannot complain, for, in denying me this gift, God took mercy on me and sent me, when I least expected it, such a large inheritance that I can fulfill the dream of my life. Don't they say that money brings every happiness?"

"The greatest happiness money provides is having it; the rest is secondary," said Lemos, an expert on the subject.

Aurélia, who for a moment had allowed herself to be carried away by her emotions, resumed the cold and judicious tone in which thus far she had discussed her future.

"I still have to point out one thing, Uncle. Words are subject not only to being forgotten but also to being misunderstood. Would it be possible to put this matter in writing?"

"You mean have the fellow sign a contract? Certainly; but if he wriggles loose, nothing can force him to marry."

"It does not matter. I would rather submit myself to this person's honor than to the courts. With a commitment to which he pledges his word, I will be satisfied."

"It can be arranged."

"That is what I expect from your friendship, Uncle."

Lemos overlooked the irony which stressed the word *friendship* and held perpendicular before him the sheet of paper on which he had taken his notes, turning it to the light.

"Let us see! Tavares do Amaral, customs employee . . . his daughter, Dona Adelaide, thirty thousand . . . Dr. Torquato Ribeiro . . . guarantee fifty . . . The other . . . from one to two hundred. All I need is the name."

Aurélia took a card from her purse and presented it to her guardian. As he was about to read the name aloud, she cut him off with the short and authoritative word which occasionally curled her lips.

"Write it down!"

The little old man copied the information on the card and returned it.

"Anything else?"

"Nothing, except to repeat once again that I have entrusted to your hands the only happiness that God has reserved for me in this world."

The girl uttered these words with a profound conviction that penetrated the old man's good-natured skepticism.

"You will be very happy; I guarantee it."

"Give me this happiness, which I covet so much; I will give you whatever is left over."

"You can count on me, Aurélia."

The old man shook Aurélia's hand, and left. The girl's last promise had touched his heart.

When he arrived home, Lemos still was not entirely recovered from the shock he had experienced.

∽ V ∾

There used to be on Hospício Street, near the field, a house that disappeared with the latest rebuilding.

In front, it had three windows with parapets—two belonged to the living room, the third to an adjoining study.

The exterior of the house, like its interior, bespoke of the poverty of the dwelling.

The living room furniture consisted of a sofa, six chairs, and two console tables of *jacarandá* wood, with no visible signs of its former polish. The wallpaper had gone from white to yellow, and here and there one could notice skilled patching.

The study offered much the same appearance. The paper, originally blue, had acquired the color of dried leaves.

In the room there was a cedar dresser that also served as a dressing table, a mahogany closet, a desk, and finally a settee, made of iron, like the handbasin, and covered with a green mosquito net.

All of these, even if they possessed the same appearance of age as the furniture in the living room, were, like the latter, carefully cleaned and dusted, breathing the most scrupulous neatness. No spiderwebs were to be seen on the walls, nor a hint of dust on the knickknacks. The floor revealed here and there scratches in the wood, but not a stain on the scoured planks.

This part of the house had another unique trait: the striking contrast between the hidebound poverty of the two rooms and certain objects in them, used by the resident.

Thus, on the back of one of the old *jacarandá* chairs, one could see at this moment a swallow-tailed black coat, which by the superior quality of the fabric and above all by the elegance of style and neatness of finish, could be recognized as boasting the "chic" of the House of Raunier, already the tailoring establishment in vogue those days.

Beside the coat lay the rest of a formal outfit, all the product of the same fashionable scissors, a very fine folding hat from the best manufacturer in Paris, straw-colored Jouvin gloves, and a pair of boots of the type Campas made only for his favorite customers.

A box of Havanas, of the most coveted brand then on the market, had been placed on one of the consoles. They were exclusive luxuries enjoyed by perhaps only the ten most refined smokers in the empire.

On the old dark wicker sofa, there was a blue satin cushion embroidered in chenille and gold. Not even the most sumptuous rooms of Rio de Janeiro were arrayed with tapestry work more delicate or more exquisite than this, embroidered by aristocratic hands.

Passing on to the bedroom, on the shabby desk covered with a faded cloth and cluttered with stacks of books, mostly novels, were disused gold-toned bronze ink wells, cigar holders of various tastes, oddly shaped ashtrays and other fanciful objects.

The dresser top looked like a veritable perfumist's counter. On it lay every type of comb and brush and other toiletries of a fashionable young man, as well as the finest English and French scents with labels indicating that they had come from the establishments of Bernardo and Louis.

In one corner of the room, an assortment of umbrellas and canes could be seen, some of them quite expensive. Some were gifts, like other artistic curiosities in bronze and jasper thrown carelessly under the table, and whose value certainly exceeded the total cost of the furnishings in the house.

Any observer would recognize in this discrepancy material proof of the complete divergence between the outward life and the domestic life of the person who occupied this part of the house.

The building and its fixtures, either stationary or of personal use, revealed a scarcity of means, if not extreme poverty; but the clothes and the objects by which he represented himself proclaimed a certain social level boasted only by the wealthiest and most reputable gentlemen of the court.

This characteristic of the room was repeated in its inhabitant, Seixas, sprawled at this moment on the living room sofa, reading one of the daily newspapers opened over his raised knees, which thus served as a convenient stand.

He is a young man, not yet thirty. His face is as noble as it is seductive; handsome features, fine skin whose whiteness accents the soft brown beard. Large, bright eyes that occasionally coalesce in a rapture of tenderness, but natural and foreign to affectation, which must render them irresistible when kindled by love. His mouth, topped by an elegant mustache, shows its graceful shape without losing the serious and austere expression that befits the organ of the manly word.

His casual posture does not totally conceal the elegance of his shape, visible even as his body draws into itself. He is slender, without being thin, and quite tall.

His foot, now resting in a slipper, is not small, but is narrow and has the firm arch of an aristocrat's.

Wearing a velveteen robe that clashes with the delicate slippers of embroidered camlet, he is obviously still in that morning disarray of one who has just risen from bed. His hair, as yet uncombed, assumes its elegant waviness even when left to its own devices.

Having washed his face and donned his robe, he had come to the living room to pick up the day's newspapers at the door that led to the staircase; for he was one of those people who feel as if they are fasting or empty-headed if, upon arising, they do not stretch their spirits on these towels of paper with which civilization dries the public's face each morning.

He had then lain face down on the sofa to read more comfortably, and mechanically ran his eyes over the headlines in search of some scandal that might spur his curiosity, numbed by the fatigue of a prolonged sleepless night.

Somebody appeared at the stairway door, peeking in and saying, "Are you up, Brother?"

"Come in, Mariquinhas," answered the young man from the sofa.

The girl approached the sofa and leaned towards her brother who, without changing his position, encircled her waist with his left arm, drawing her down so that he could place a kiss on each cheek.

"Would you like your coffee?" asked Mariquinhas.

"Bring it, girl."

Moments later the girl returned with a cup of coffee. While her brother, now sitting upright, sipped the aromatic drink of the sybaritic poets, she went to the bedroom to get a cigar, of superior brand, and lighted a match.

All these details she carried out with perfect awareness of her brother's habits, surmising from his pleasure how delightful it must be to smoke a cigar early in the morning after a cup of coffee.

The indolent brother accepted these services as would a sultan from his favorite dancer; he was so accustomed to them that he did not even thank her, convinced that for the girl it was a privilege that he deigned to let her serve him.

When her brother had lighted his cigar, she sat by him on the edge of the sofa.

"Did you have a good time, Brother?"

"It was all right."

"It finished very late. It was about three when you came in."

"And it was not worth it; I wasted the evening, when I could have been recovering from the bad nights I spent aboard ship."

"That is true; it was unwise to go to a ball the same day you arrived."

The young man followed with his eyes the spiral of a white cloud of smoke from his Havana until it completely dissipated in the air.

"Do you know who was there? And was the queen of the ball? Aurélia!"

"Aurélia—" repeated the girl, searching her memory for the name.

"Don't you remember? Look!"

And, crossing his left foot over his right knee, the brother showed her, with a wave of his delicate white hand, the camlet slippers.

"Ah! I know," the girl cried out. "The one who lived in Lapa?"

"Precisely."

"You really used to like her, Brother."

"She was the great love of my life, Mariquinhas!"

"But you left her for the Amaral girl," observed the sister, smiling.

Seixas shook his head slowly and melancholically; after a pause, during which his sister gazed at him with compassion and regret for having awakened old feelings, he continued, lively and in good spirits.

"Yesterday, at the casino, she was magnificent, Mariquinhas! You can hardly imagine! You women share this with the flowers, that some are daughters of the shade and open up in the evening, while others are daughters of light and need the sun. Like these, Aurélia was born for riches. I always thought so! When I admired her beauty in that small ground-floor living room in Santa Teresa, she seemed to live there in exile. She lacked the tiara, the throne, the galas, the submissive masses; but the queen was there in all her splendor. God had destined her for wealth."

"Is she rich, then?"

"She has suddenly come into an inheritance—from a grandfather, I think. Nobody could really explain it to me; however, the fact is that today she has, according to what I was told, about a million."

"She also loved you very much, Brother!" remarked the young girl, with an intent that did not go unnoticed by Seixas.

He took his sister's hand.

"Aurélia is lost to me. As many as admired her yesterday at the casino may pursue her, although they risk being rebuffed. I alone do not have that right."

"Why, Brother? Because of the Amaral girl, whom they say you will marry?"

"That has not yet been decided, Mariquinhas, as you well know. It is for a different reason."

"What, then?"

"One day—one day I will tell you."

A third voice joined the dialogue with these words:

"You can tell her now, Brother; I am leaving. I do not want to eavesdrop on your secrets."

The person who spoke was another young girl who had entered the living room shortly before this and had heard the last remarks of the conversation.

"Come here, Nicota, and I will whisper my secret in your ear!" replied Seixas, laughing at his sister's annoyance.

"I do not deserve it. It should be for Mariquinhas!" answered Nicota, from afar.

"What is this now, Nicota! Because I was talking to Fernandinho? Is that a crime?"

"That's not it," replied her sister, her eyes brimming with tears. "You deceived me by saying you were going to iron your dress and then coming to peek in to see if our brother had already woken up so you could bring him his coffee."

"I was really going to iron, but then I heard Brother open the door—And you, why did you stay?"

"I was just finishing that lady's sewing, which as you well know has to be ready today. I had asked mother to call me as soon as Fernandinho woke up; and since she did not hear him whistling as usual, she thought he was still sleeping from the exhaustion of the trip and the ball."

Seixas followed with a mocking, but tender and proud smile the confrontation of the two sisters.

"But how am I to blame, Nicota, for what Dona Mariquinhas did? Will you tell me?"

"I am not blaming you, Brother. Is anybody at fault for loving one person more than another?"

"You are jealous!" exclaimed Seixas.

The young man arose and went to the middle of the room to Nicota, who remained resentfully aloof, leaning against the farthermost chair.

"There is no need to be annoyed at me; I will not allow these fits of pique. The more you frown, the more kisses I will give you to wipe away these ugly wrinkles."

"That is what she wanted!" observed Mariquinhas by now a bit jealous.

"Let us find out, Miss Ungrateful," said Seixas, bringing Nicota over to the sofa and seating her beside him. "What have I done to make you think that I like Mariquinhas more than you? Have I not cut my heart into two absolutely equal slices, of which each of you has her own?"

"But you would rather talk to Mariquinhas, so much so that you spent the whole morning telling secrets."

"Is that the reason for the complaint? Well, Dona Mariquinhas, please leave. I want to spend some more time talking to Nicota, and to her alone. Are you happy now? Does that satisfy you?"

Nicota smiled, still somewhat piqued, like a ray of sunlight through a cloud.

"What about the coffee?"

"Oh! Do we also have to deal with the coffee? Well, little one, go get another cup, and I will gratefully receive it from your hands. And you can also bring me a cigar, and I will smoke half of it, instead of this stub. Anything else?"

Seixas's good humor and tenderness not only vanquished Nicota's complaints, but also reestablished the cordiality between the two girls who loved each other with great affection, shaken only by the jealousy over this darling brother.

∞ **VI** ∞

Son of a public servant and an orphan at eighteen, Seixas had to abandon his studies at São Paulo College because his mother found it impossible to continue his allowance.

He was already in his third year, and if nature, which had endowed him with excellent qualities, had given him energy and willpower, he could have overcome a few minor difficulties and obtained a degree, especially since a classmate and friend, Torquato Ribeiro, had offered him lodging until his father's will was probated and the widow settled the estate.

But Seixas was one of those spirits that prefer the beaten path and deviate from their routine only when impelled by a great passion. So, a degree in law held no great attraction for his magnificent intelligence, more inclined toward literature and journalism.

He acceded, therefore, to the entreaties of his father's friends, who managed to secure for him a position as apprentice in a government office. Thus he began that social vegetation in which so many talented men consume the best years of their lives, performing thankless tasks, and continually tormented by disappointments.

While continuing the career as public servant, forced upon him by necessity, Seixas searched for a more prominent field to satisfy his superior spirit, and found it in the press.

Having been hired by one of the court's daily newspapers, first as mere translator, and then as reporter, he became with time one of the more elegant writers of Rio's journalism. We will not say *celebrated*, as is fashionable nowadays, because in this land of ours, applause and fame followed the steps of blissful mediocrity.

Seixas's father had left his meager patrimony encumbered by a mortgage, in addition to several minor debts. After a difficult and protracted settlement in which the widow found herself enmeshed, the sum of twelve thousand plus four slaves was all the family could call their own.

After the division of assets, Seixas's mother, Dona Camila, at the advice of friends, put the money into a savings account, from which she withdrew the interest at six-month intervals to cover her domestic expenses, with the help of income from renting out two slaves and what she and her daughters earned from sewing.

Fernando wanted to contribute from his salary to the monthly expenses, but both his mother and his sisters refused. On the contrary, they regretted not being able to save a small amount to add to the little they made, which barely covered the young man's wardrobe and other expenses.

Ordinarily, this sole male child, in the absence of the natural head of the household, should have served as his family's mainstay. Not so in the eyes of these three creatures, who lived only for this loved one. Their destiny consisted of making him happy; though they neither thought about nor could express it, they did it.

That such a handsome and gifted young man as their Fernandinho should dress according to the latest fashions and with the greatest elegance; that instead of staying at home bored, he should seek out amusements and the company of friends; in short, that he should always cut the best figure in society was for those ladies not only fair and natural, but essential.

While Fernandinho ostentatiously attended the theater, they spent their evenings in the dining room, around the lantern that illuminated their nocturnal task. More often than not, by themselves; on occasion, in the company of a rare guest who visited them in their modest and humble dwelling.

The topic of conversation was invariably the absent one. They never tired of singing his praises. Each spoke of her dream of how certain wishes and hopes would come true, for, by this time, Fernandinho had gotten into the habit of making them confidantes of his smallest secrets.

Whether the one he liked so much would be at the ball; whether she would give him the favorite quadrille, the fourth, reserved for the chosen one, not only because it was infallible, but also because it took place when the party was at its height; whether Fernandinho would finally succeed in letting her know of his passion, and how the girl would react to his declaration—such were the grave concerns of these three creatures who, deprived of all entertainment, worked by lamplight to earn part of their necessities.

On other evenings, they wondered how the wife of some bigwig to whom he was supposed to be introduced would receive the young man. Seixas counted on winning her favor, with an eye to attaining through her the minister's protection toward a promotion. His mother and sisters, to whom he had confided the plan, worried about the results and prayed that he would succeed, unaware, in their naiveté, of the nature of this feminine influence supposed to sway the minister.

Thus Seixas imperceptibly became accustomed to his double life, which daily grew more and more separate. A family man within his home, sharing with his mother and sisters their inherited poverty, in society, where he appeared by himself, he projected the image of a wealthy young man.

From the showy life he flaunted in society, Seixas brought to the intimacy of his home not only material proofs but also confidences and seductions. He was still too young to consider the danger of awakening in the virgin hearts of his sisters desires that might torment them. Later, when reason should have warned him, the gentle habit of confidences had already lulled it to sleep. Fortunately Dona Camila had given her daughters the same strict upbringing that she had received—old-fashioned Brazilian upbringing, quite rare in our days which, if it did not mold romantic young ladies, prepared women for the sublime forbearance that protects the family and makes of a humble home a sanctuary.

Mariquinhas, older than Fernando, saw the years of her youth slip by, in serene resignation. If anyone mentioned that the fall, considered the wedding season, was passing by with no hope of a marriage, it was not she, but Dona Camila, her mother, who felt her heart ache whenever she noticed her daughter's youth fading.

Occasionally Fernando also shared her sorrow but, for him, the bustle of the world soon erased it.

Nicota, the younger and more beautiful, still blossomed in the prime of life, but she was approaching her twenties and, with the sheltered life her family led, it was not very easy to find suitors for the hand of a poor and unprotected girl. Therefore, the good mother's concerns and sadness increased whenever she thought that this daughter too would be condemned to the unfortunate fate of the social deformity called celibacy.

Upon Fernando's coming-of-age, Dona Camila conferred upon him the authority she enjoyed at home and the administration of the modest patrimony left upon her husband's death, which, although officially divided, remained intact and in joint property.

The interest from the savings account and from the rented slaves came to something like $1,500 annually or $125 a month. However, since the family expenses came to $150, the three ladies provided the rest with their sewing and ironing, with the help of two black woman servants.

When he took over running the house, Seixas modified this rule. He declared that he would contribute the $25 that was lacking, leaving whatever the ladies earned from their work for their own private expenses, with which he promised to help them as soon as he could.

At that time, he had been appointed second in command, with hopes of being promoted to first, and his income, together with what he earned with his constant contributions to the newspaper, added over three thousand. Later it rose to seven as the result of a commission given to him by the minister, who had taken a liking to him.

Thus, his annual income amounted to $8,500. Deducting $1,800, which he gave his family in installments of $150 a month, he was left with $6,700 for his expenses, an amount at that time not spent on themselves by many wealthy bachelors who cut a fine figure in society.

One evening, Seixas suffered a romantic disappointment as he entered the ballroom and withdrew, slighted. With nowhere to while away his time and annoyed at the social scene, he returned home. The misadventure prodded his muse, melancholy by nature. He recalled his Byron, and the imitations he had done of some of the English bard's most acerbic upbraidings.

It was quite uncommon for Fernando to spend the evening at home. To avoid explanations, he decided to enter unnoticed, and he climbed the stairs very quietly. He opened the living room door with the key he carried on a ring along with the one to the outside door, so as not to disturb the family when he arrived at a late hour, and made his way to his bedroom.

Dona Camila and her daughters were having tea. A family from the neighborhood was visiting. The girls talked loudly and amid the chatter Fernando overheard them mention an opera that was being presented at the opera house.

The friends had attended the latest performance and related it in detail to his sisters, enhancing the entertainment with praise.

"You have not seen it yet? You should not miss it. It is worthwhile. Ask your brother."

Taken aback by the direct question, the two sisters instantly lost some of their interest in the description of the show.

They both became silent. But the others, with a touch of malice, insisted and Mariquinhas, the more outspoken of the two, answered:

"Fernandinho has already invited us several times, but one thing or another always gets in the way."

"That's true!" observed Nicota.

For the first time Seixas saw clearly the contrast which, incidentally, lay before his eyes every day, every minute, and of which he himself was one of the terms.

While the hours were insufficient for the pleasures with which he sated himself, those three ladies spun long evenings with no amusement other than their daily chores or the echoes of the world that reached them through some rare visitor.

Merely on himself he spent more that three times what the entire family needed to subsist. That very evening, just to attend a ball he had left almost as soon as he arrived, he had squandered an amount more than sufficient to afford his sisters the pleasure of an evening at the opera.

These ideas took hold of his spirit. Instead of striking the match, already in his hand, to light both the lamp that would illuminate his poetic vigil and the cigar that would opiate his muse, he threw himself on the bed, buried his head in the pillow, and slept the sleep of the just.

On opening night of the opera, Fernando took his family to the theater. For the three ladies it was a party. Despite her unaffectedness and humility, Dona Camila felt, as she made her way through the crowd on her son's arm, the sweet fragrance of pride, but a pride imbued with fright, more the awareness of one's own humbleness, rather than self-importance. Her daughters shared this feeling and believed that all the other young ladies envied them their brother.

When Fernando, after settling his family in their box, left to move about, he met someone he knew:

"Say, Seixas, where did you dig up that trio of peasant-like women? I bet you do not have good intentions. One of them is not bad! How dreadful!"

Fernando cut this dialogue short, with the excuse of greeting an acquaintance who had just come by.

When he left home, hurriedly and in the dim light of the lamp, he had not noticed how his mother and sisters were dressed. In the box, however, in the bright gaslight, the odd attire of the three ladies, completely out of touch with fashion and social customs, did not escape his eyes, strict in matters of elegance.

The rest of the evening, which seemed endless to him, he avoided the box, and when he stopped by there, he never went to the front.

For some days, Seixas remained sullen and preoccupied with the incident. He even went so far as to feign an illness in order to stay at home and avoid amusements. It is true that this rejection of society was also a reaction to the umbrage that occurred the evening of the ball. Finally, this crisis led to a rationalization that appeased our journalist.

Since he diligently attended social functions and had become a rather distinguished figure, establishing relationships and cultivating friendships with influential persons who received him warmly, it was natural that he, Seixas, led a brilliant career. He might, at any moment, arrange an advantageous marriage, as many others had done who enjoyed less favorable situations than he. Nor was it difficult to foresee that the royal road of ambition, called politics, might suddenly open up for him.

Once rich and famous, he would build a house commensurate with his position.

Then his family would participate not only in the material pleasures of this opulent way of life, but also in the glitter and prestige of his name. Interaction with society would impart to them the seal of distinction they would need to show themselves at their best. He would arrange good marriages for his two sisters and thus bring happiness to all these dear creatures entrusted to his care.

If, on the contrary, Seixas burdened himself very early, at the beginning of his career, with the weight of his family, entangling himself in an obscure life from which he could never free them, not even at the sacrifice of all of his income, what could he expect but to vegetate in the shadow of mediocrity and fruitlessly expend his youth?

Seixas therefore hardened his conviction that luxury meant not only the infallible struggle of a noble ambition, but also the only pledge for the happiness of his family. Thus his misgivings vanished.

Seixas had just arrived from Pernambuco, where he had spent eight months; he had landed the day before, in time for the casino.

The ostensible motive for this trip had been some commission, that of presidential secretary, I believe. It was said, however, in political circles, that our writer had been laying the foundations for a future candidacy. Without denying the facts, some envious souls added that he had been driven to the North by the fire in the beautiful dark eyes of a tawny young girl from Pernambuco, the talk of the last parliamentary session.

All these circumstances indeed influenced Seixas's decision, but the primary cause that led him, a proud native of Rio, to absent himself from the court for eight months, we shall learn in due time.

∞ VII ∞

Fernando was playing with his sisters, when someone clapped at the foot of the staircase. The girls disappeared through the bedroom; Seixas, without so much as changing his position, said loudly:

"Come upstairs!"

This casual way of receiving guests might be cause for comment in such a well-bred young man, but no one called on Seixas at home except a sales clerk or people of a lower class.

The round, chubby figure of Mr. Lemos gushed—gushed is the proper term—into the room, and in a bat of an eye zig-zagged and unexpectedly pumped three handshakes onto the immobile Seixas, one after the other, crowned by the usual courtesies.

"Do I have the honor of speaking with Mr. Fernando Rodrigues de Seixas?"

Our writer stood up quickly. Adjusting the front of his robe with a rapid gesture, he assumed the air of supreme distinction that only he could adorn with such nobility and tact.

"Please have a seat," he told Lemos, indicating the sofa, "and forgive me for this disarray of someone who has just returned."

"I know. Did you arrive yesterday?"

Seixas confirmed this with a nod.

"Whom do I have the honor of receiving?"

From his pocket Lemos took a letter, which he handed to the young man, fixing upon him his keen gaze.

"The person who does me the honor of introducing you, Mr. Ramos, is worthy of every consideration. I am fortunate to have this occasion to prove my friendship to him; I am, therefore, entirely at your disposal, sir."

When Seixas pronounced the name *Ramos*, the old man bowed and corrected him—*Lemos*—with such alacrity and with such clearing of the throat that the man standing before him did not notice.

Here is the reason for the mistake. When Lemos arrived home to São José Street he had formulated a plan, as indicated by this monologue:

"What cannot be remedied must be considered remedied. Do not fool yourself, Lemos: with a girl like that, there is no use trying to play tricks because she will clip your wings. Therefore, the best a shrewd man like you can do is to take advantage of the situation."

Stepping off the tilbury, the old man entered the two-story building from which he promptly returned wearing a pair of green eyeglasses that he had used in the past when threatened by ophthalmia. Signaling for the coachman to follow him, he turned onto Quitanda Street.

A short distance away he went into a store:

"Hey, Commander, give me a letter of introduction to Seixas."

The businessman to whom he addressed these words racked his memory:

"Seixas—I do not know him!"

"You will have to force yourself to know him. Hop to it, write. In the name of Mr. Antônio Joaquim Ramos."

This was the letter that Aurélia's guardian had just presented to Seixas. He put his trust in two disguises: the eyeglasses and the name of the person recommended.

If, in spite of this, the young man recognized him, he would find a perfect way out of the predicament.

"Excuse me, sir, if I come to you on the day immediately after your arrival, when you must still be tired from the trip, but the purpose of my visit is most urgent in nature."

"I am ready to give you my full attention."

"It is an important matter requiring the greatest reserve and discretion."

"You may rest assured of it."

Lemos wriggled in the chair in his frenetic cheerfulness and proceeded:

"It is about a young woman, rather wealthy, attractive, whom the family wants to marry off as soon as possible. Suspicious of these rogues that roam about sniffing out dowries and fearing that the girl may unexpectedly fall under the spell of one these dandies, they decided to find a serious young man of good standing, even though he be poor, for it is precisely the poor who know best the value of money and understand the need to save it rather than throw it out the window as the sons of the rich do."

Lemos stared at Seixas with his small, lively eyes.

"This family, which honors me with its friendship, has charged me with the search for a desirable person, and my presence here, at this moment, means that I was fortunate enough to have found him."

"Your choice should flatter my self-esteem, had I any, Mr. Ramos. But you must understand that I cannot agree—"

"Forgive me. When it comes to negotiating I have a system. I make the proposal very straightforwardly, omitting neither the drawbacks nor the advantages, because I am not in the habit of bargaining. The other party considers it, and accepts, if it is in his interest."

"I can see this is truly a business deal you are proposing to me," observed Fernando with courteous irony.

"Undoubtedly!" affirmed the old man. "But I have not finished yet. The girl is quite rich and will endow the husband with one hundred thousand in cash."

As Seixas remained silent:

"Now, sir, you might tell me if I can convey good news. Your decision?"

"None!"

"What do you mean? You neither refuse nor accept?"

"Your proposal, Mr. Ramos—allow me the honesty—cannot be serious," said the young man with the greatest civility.

"For what reason?"

"First of all I should inform you that I am betrothed, after a fashion, and although there is no formal agreement, I could not free myself that easily."

"Engagements can be broken at a moment's notice."

"To be sure. Sometimes circumstances arise that nullify the most solemn obligations. But of the reasons that move one's conscience, self-interest is not one; it would make regret look like a transaction."

"And what is life about, after all, but a continuous transaction between man and the world?" observed Lemos.

"I do not yet see life from that perspective. I understand a man sacrificing himself for some noble reason, to make a woman or those dear to him happy; but if he does so for a cash price, it is not sacrifice; it is trade."

Lemos insisted, using all the resources of materialist dialectics that he so skillfully manipulated. He did not, however, vanquish the scruples of the young man who heard him politely but remained inflexible in his negative answer.

"Well," the old man summed up, "these are not matters to be resolved like this, based on intuition. Give it some thought, and, since I expect a favorable decision, please advise me. I will leave you my address."

"Thank you, but for this purpose, it is pointless," observed Seixas.

"Nobody knows what might happen."

The old man wrote in pencil the number and the street of his house on a sheet of paper he took from his notebook and left it on the console.

Half an hour later, Seixas was walking down Ouvidor Street looking for the Europa Hotel, where he usually dined lavishly about noon.

On his way, he ran into some friends and acquaintances who greeted him warmly, asking about his trip and providing him with the latest gossip about the court. They told him of Aurélia's début, some months earlier, but still the most talked about event of Rio's season.

That evening there was a performance at the opera house. Lagrange was singing in *Rigoletto*. Seixas, after his eight-month exile, could not miss the performance.

At eight o'clock sharp, his fine ivory binoculars in his left hand and sporting soft gray kid gloves and an elegant overcoat over his arm, Seixas climbed the stairs toward the even-side seats.

At the top of the stairs he met Alfredo Moreira with whom he had spoken briefly at the casino the evening before.

"Where did you run off to yesterday, Seixas? I gave up looking for you!"

"I was right next to you. You were just too dazzled," answered Fernando, smiling.

"That is true! What a woman, Seixas! You cannot imagine. You look from afar and see an angel of beauty who fascinates you and has you trailing at her feet, drunk with love. When you touch her, you find nothing but hard metal beneath the splendor. She does not talk; she jingles like gold. I was looking for you to introduce you. There she comes now!"

Alfredo let out this last exclamation as he saw a car stopping by the door at that moment. Aurélia emerged and, accompanied by Dona Firmina, walked toward her box in the second tier.

She was draped from head to foot in a white cashmere cape that revealed nothing but her beautiful face in the shadow of the hood and the hem of her blue dress.

Only one possessing Aurélia's grand elegance could liberate the form of enchanting grace from such a simple and soft wrap.

She stopped directly in front of the two men, turning her back to them, waiting for Dona Firmina who took some time to descend from the car.

"Isn't she beautiful?" Moreira asked of his friend, loudly enough to be heard.

"Magnificent!" answered Seixas. "But for me it is a ghostly beauty."

"I do not understand."

"She is the image of a woman I once loved, who died. The similarity repels me."

Aurélia remained impassive. Moreira, who moved closer to pay court to her, thought his friend was right. There was indeed something otherworldly in that pale and scintillating face.

Dona Firmina approached. The girl, acknowledging Alfredo's greeting with a friendly curtsy, walked by as if she had not seen Fernando and went up to the second tier.

ᘒ **VIII** ᘒ

Lemos returned satisfied with the results of his exploration. He had an optimistic spirit, though of his own kind. He trusted the infallible instinct with which nature had equipped the social biped to pick up the scent of his self-interest and ferret it out.

He therefore considered it impossible that a young man in his right mind, counseled by a man of experience, would reject a fortune that suddenly came through his front door, and a door on Hospício Street at sixty a month, to lead him by the arm and drive him by carriage, reclining on soft cushions, to a palace in Laranjeiras.

Lemos knew that writers, in order to elaborate dramatic actions and romantic scenes, maligned the human race by attributing this kind of folly to it; in real life, however, he did not admit the possibility of such an occurrence.

"No one refuses one hundred thousand," he thought, "without solid, practical reasons. Seixas has no reasons, because all his empty talk about trade and the market is nothing but nonsense. I would like the moralists to tell me, what is this life but a corner grocery store? From the day he is born, the poor wretch, until the day they haul him away, all a man does is sell and buy. To be born you need money, and to die, even more money. The rich rent their capital; the poor rent themselves, when they do not sell themselves altogether, save for the right to swindle."

Thus convinced that Seixas did not possess what he called a solid reason to reject the proposed marriage, Lemos saw only a ploy in the initial refusal, or perhaps the impulse of the timid resistance that scruples often oppose to temptation. He waited, consequently, for the salutary revolution which should take place in the young man's mind within a few days.

When he left Seixas's house, Lemos went to Amaral's, where he began other negotiations that should ensure the success of the first.

Once the young man became disillusioned with Adelaide and the thirty thousand, he would have no choice but to accept the consolation of the hundred; a consolation bearing the smart of a tiny vengeance.

I do not know what you will think of Lemos's social physiology; the truth is that the old man was not too surprised when one fine morning his agent came to tell him that a man by the name of Seixas was looking for him.

This agent was called Antônio Joaquim Ramos and was the same man whose name Lemos had borrowed. Ramos had been forewarned by his employer about this circumstance and was not surprised, for he was well versed in such prankishness.

"Let him wait!" shouted the old man.

On the ground floor of the house where he lived, Lemos ran something called an agency office.

It was a corridor that led to the street and stretched toward the back of the house, where the old man worked in a kind of cage, consisting of a wooden partition with rail posts.

It was from there that he answered. His habit, whenever he had to deal with an important issue, was to ponder it beforehand so as to avoid being caught unprepared. And this is what he did now.

"What does the man have in mind? Will he try to feel me out about the bride, suspecting that I want to foist some old hag on him? Ha, ha! No danger on that side. Does he want to bargain? The girl does not mind going up to two hundred, and I will bet that if necessary she would go even higher, for with women money is only temptation. But I will not allow it. I will stand firm at one hundred, and nobody will budge me. At most, twenty, as a bonus, to prepare for the wedding, but not a cent more!"

Having made his calculations, Lemos shouted from the door of his enclosure to the front of the house:

"Send him in!"

When Seixas arrived at the office, Lemos was already back on his stool, bent over the desk, and going about his business. Without raising his head, with his left hand he indicated the sofa to the young man.

"Please be seated. I will be with you shortly."

When he finished the letter and blotted it, Lemos put it in an envelope and addressed it. Only then, rotating on his stool like a figure on a weathervane, did he face the young man.

"You wish to speak to me, sir?" he asked.

"You do not remember me?" asked Seixas restlessly.

"Vaguely. You look somewhat familiar."

"We were together only three days ago," replied Seixas. "It is true that it was the first time we met."

"Three days ago?—"

And Lemos pretended to search his memory.

Since entering, Seixas had betrayed in his face and gestures, an uneasiness alien to his character. He appeared to be struggling with some force within that dissuaded him from the decision he had made; but if he could not escape these warning signals, he controlled himself enough to subordinate them to necessity.

However, Lemos's failure to remember unsettled that momentary firmness: on the young man's features one could discern an immediate wavering of the spirit. This change did not escape the old man who, leaning back on his chair so as to look at the other party in half profile, burst into interjections of surprise:

"Oh—Mr. Seixas! Please forgive me! Businessmen are like that—you must know! Our memory is in our notebook or on our desks. We get involved in so many things that only a head with two hundred pages like this one can manage it all!"

The old man emitted a cacophonic laugh and pointed to a ledger on his desk.

"This is mine, certified by the business tribunal, duly stamped, with all the legal formalities. Ha! Ha! Ha!—So, my friend, what can I do for you?"

"Sir, do you still stand by what you proposed to me the day before yesterday at my house?" asked Seixas.

Lemos pretended to give it some thought.

"A dowry of one hundred thousand at the time of the wedding, is that it?"

"I still need to meet the person."

"Oh! I thought I had been very clear about that point. I am not authorized to reveal her identity until the contract is signed."

"You did not mention anything about that."

"It was implied."

"What is the reason for this mystery? It makes me suspect she is handicapped," observed Fernando.

"I guarantee that it is not the case; if I mislead you, you are free from the obligation."

"Can you at least give me some information?"

"Certainly."

Seixas asked the old man a series of questions about the age, upbringing, birth, and other circumstances that concerned him. The answers could not have been more favorable.

"I accept," concluded the young man.

"Very good."

"I accept it on one condition."

"Provided it is reasonable."

"I need twenty thousand by tomorrow."

The old man leapt from his chair. This caught him by surprise.

"My friend, if it were up to me—But you know that in this business I am merely an honest broker. I have no authority to advance any amount at all. As to the dowry, once the wedding has taken place, yes, I guarantee it."

"Can you give me a loan against that guarantee?"

Lemos grimaced, but tried to dissimulate.

"You are right," observed Seixas, without becoming upset. "You do not know me, Mr. Ramos; and the position I placed myself in when I took this step is certainly not one to inspire trust."

"That is not it, man," the old man quickly replied, somewhat confused, "but it is always best to have these things in writing."

"I am sorry for the inconvenience I may have caused you," replied the young man, taking his leave.

The business man was so dazed and perplexed that he did not return Seixas's courtesy, and watched him leave his office, unsure of what to do.

"What the devil does this rogue want with twenty thousand? I will bet he has been hanging around the Alcazar. He must have fallen for one of those French girls, and they are like boa constrictors! Delicate as amber, but capable of swallowing a man! What will my ward say to this? Can she be willing to take all the risks and dangers of the transaction?"

At this point in his monologue, the old man, recovering his insolent agility, dashed to the front door, where he arrived in time to see the gentleman walking slowly away, pensive, his head lowered.

"Mr. Seixas! Please!"

"Did you call me?"

The business man advanced some steps onto the street to meet the young man.

"Just one question!" the old man said quickly so as not to nurture false hopes. "If you received the twenty thousand, would we then have a contract?"

"Certainly. I said so before."

"We would have no more objections, nor those petty considerations of honor and dignity with which some fellows around here hoodwink others. Have you made up your mind, without inspecting the property—rather, the girl?"

"If she is what you assured me—"

"Done! Listen, I cannot promise anything, but wait for me at your house tomorrow morning; I will be there around nine."

Lemos took care of some small business matters, picked up a sheet of paper stamped in the amount of twenty thousand, and after dinner went to Laranjeiras.

Aurélia was reading in the living room; but George Sand's style could not, at this moment, contain her thoughts, which would now and then take wings and flitter away into the blue of a peaceful catnap.

When Lemos was announced, she woke up startled, and the tremor of the pink sides of her nostrils revealed the agitation within.

"It is a slight difficulty with that arrangement that brings me here."

"What happened?"

"Seixas—"

"I have already asked you not to mention that name," said the young lady sternly.

"It is true! I apologize. It was the rush. *He* demands twenty thousand in advance, by tomorrow, otherwise he will not accept."

"Pay it."

The young lady uttered these words in the sibilant pitch that her voice acquired on certain occasions, which sounded like a diamond etching into glass.

Her countenance was overcome by a deadly pallor and for a moment it seemed that life had abandoned that magnificent figure, frozen into a marble statue.

Lemos did not notice that deep distress, occupied as he was, fumbling to remove from his pocket one of the stamped sheets of paper which he placed on the table, smoothing it with the palms of his hands. Then, dipping the pen, he presented it to the young woman:

"A small voucher!"

Aurélia sat at the table and wrote a few lines in a tiny slanted handwriting.

"Why is he asking for this money?" asked the girl as she wrote.

"He would not tell me, but I have my suspicions. And since this has to do with a union on which your future depends, Aurélia, I must keep nothing from you."

"It is a favor for which I am grateful."

"I am not sure, but I suspect he is sowing his wild oats. With his asylum, our José Clemente created a palace to house the crazy, but then along came those dear Frenchmen and invented a certain Alcazar, a house to drive people crazy, so much so that Praia Vermelha is no longer big enough for all of them."

Aurélia was biting the end of her pen, whose ivory darkened between her pearly teeth.

"It does not matter!"

And she signed the payment voucher.

The next day, at the appointed hour, Lemos arrived at Seixas's house.

"You are a lucky man. I bring you the jack pot."

The clerk took the second sheet of stamped paper from his pocket.

"First we will have to draft a small receipt."

"On what terms?"

After a short discussion in which Seixas's scruples balked at the imposition of such a requirement, he reluctantly signed this statement:

"I hereby acknowledge receipt from His Excellency, Mr. Antônio Joaquim Ramos, in the amount of twenty thousand as an advance against the dowry of one hundred thousand, and thus obligate myself to marry, within three months, the lady indicated to me by the aforesaid Mr. Ramos. As guarantee I pledge my person and my honor."

After verifying that the receipt was in accordance with the rules, Lemos, with the dexterity of a currency exchange clerk, counted the pack of bills he had brought and handed it to the young man, keeping one:

"Nineteen thousand nine hundred and eighty—plus twenty for the stamp."

Seixas received the money sadly.

"Lucky dog!"

With his collusive laugh, Lemos pirouetted twice, hopped three times, pinched Seixas's thigh and went bouncing down the stairs like a rubber ball.

∞ IX ∞

Seixas was an honorable man, but under the friction of his office and the heat of the rooms, his honesty had acquired the flexible nature of wax, which can be molded to the fancies of vanity and the claims of ambition.

He was incapable of stealing from anyone, or of abusing trust, but he professed that facile and accommodating morality much in vogue in our society these days.

According to this doctrine, everything is permitted in matters of love, and self-interest enjoys full latitude so long as it remains within the law and avoids scandal.

Early in the morning of the day after Lemos's visit, Dona Camila looked for a pretext to go to her son's bedroom.

"I have come to talk about family matters, Fernandinho. There is a gentleman down the street who loves Nicota. He is just beginning his career, but he already owns a small store. I did not want to decide anything before your return."

Dona Camila then told her son the details of the innocent courtship. Fernando happily agreed to the wedding.

"High time," sighed the good old lady. "I was quite worried about Nicota being left behind too, like my poor Mariquinhas!"

"Poor thing! But I still have hopes of finding a good man for her, Mother."

"May God hear you. Oh! I almost forgot. We will have to withdraw some money from savings for her trousseau."

"Already? The man has not proposed yet."

"He is only waiting for Nicota to accept, but she did not want to before making sure that you and I agreed. This very day—"

"All right. I will withdraw the money as soon as I can; but if you need any right now, I have it here."

"No. It is better to buy everything at once."

Fernando left upset. With the kind of life he led, his expenses continually mounted. His monthly earnings were spent on hotels, the theater, courting, gambling, gratuities, and the thousand other personal expenses of a self-indulgent young man. At the end of the year, when time came to settle accounts with the tailor, the cobbler, the perfumist, and the stable man, there was nothing left.

He turned to the savings account and had no qualms about doing so, for he went on punctually giving his mother the allowance of $150 each month, hoping for a windfall to restore to his reserves what he had appropriated. But instead of returning it he continued withdrawing, to the point that it was long since exhausted.

Where, then, was he going to find the money his mother had requested for the trousseau and, later, for the rest of Nicota's portion?

Fernando signed in at his office and, as usual, left for breakfast. Afterwards he went to the house of the correspondent charged in his absence with paying Dona Camila her monthly allowance, and with forwarding a few items to her.

He had counted on the balance of the remittances he had sent from Pernambuco, and some late payments he had yet to collect. Instead he found a deficit of over two thousand, to which the correspondent had begun to add 12% interest. Seixas understood the eloquence of this rate which signaled a court order for immediate payment.

At dusk, returning home to dress for a party he had to attend, he found three letters that had been delivered during his absence.

One was from Amaral. It was two pages long, said a lot, but came to no conclusion; it was a true epistolary puzzle, whose deciphering the author left to Seixas's wit. In fine, Adelaide's father had written to prepare the suitor for an impending rescission of the promise.

Anyone experienced in Lemos's ways would recognize in the prose his style, as foppish as his physique.

The other two letters were only bills, but not insignificant ones, that Seixas had left outstanding when he left for Pernambuco, and of which he had no longer had the slightest memory. They reintroduced themselves with the brutal laconism of this language: — *Amount of your bill, pending since last year. —Resp.*, etc.

Fernando crumpled the three letters into a ball which he then threw into the corner of the room. The breach of the nuptial agreement, which in any other circumstance might have pleased him by the restitution of his freedom and gratified a hidden desire, at that moment left him crushed. He saw therein overwhelming proof of the ruin that would swallow him up, of which the outstanding bills and accumulated debt served as documentation.

At the gathering where he went to pass the evening, one final disappointment awaited him.

When he accepted the commission to Pernambuco, Seixas had obtained the promise that upon his return he would continue with the sinecure of compiling laws; but that morning, when he presented himself at the office, there were some doubts. He trusted his protectors.

As soon as the minister, one of the guests, arrived, Seixas sent him, one after the other, his most loyal emissaries of both sexes. It was unheard of: his excellency remained inflexible. Perforce some intrigue was under way.

This meant a reduction of sixteen hundred in his income, just when urgent expenses loomed large. Decidedly, the hand of fate weighed upon him and was punishing severely the peccadilloes of his youth.

While Seixas was still under the power of this new adversity, Aurélia Camargo entered the room; she had just arrived. Her entrance was dazzling as always; every eye turned toward her, and a frisson of powerful sensations ran through the numerous and splendid society assembled there. It was as if those at the ball fell to their knees to greet her in ardent worship.

Seixas withdrew. The woman humiliated him. Since the evening of his arrival he had harbored this unpleasant feeling. He took refuge in feigned indifference, endeavored to enlist disdain to fight the baleful influence, but without success.

Aurélia's presence, her magnificent beauty, obsessed and oppressed him. When, as now, he removed her from sight by fleeing, he could not expunge her from his memory, nor escape the admiration she provoked and which pursued him in the acclaim he heard proffered around him at every step.

At the casino, Seixas enjoyed a place of refuge, a shelter from this cruel fascination. He had occupied himself with Adelaide, who at that time still treated him as her fiancé, and had outdone himself with attentions and gallantries, so as not to fall prey to his worries.

This evening, however, forced to abandon the young lady, with whom he no longer had a relationship, he did not know what to do, and considered leaving, terrified at the thought of becoming the laughingstock of that *femme fatale*, when he heard a voice that shook him.

As he turned around, he found himself facing Aurélia on Torquato Ribeiro's arm and Adelaide escorted by Alfredo Moreira. Seixas tried to withdraw, but was in a narrow room, with a group of older ladies blocking his way.

"I propose an exchange, Dona Adelaide."

"What exchange, Dona Aurélia?"

"Let us trade partners. Is that all right?"

Adelaide blushed, and observed shyly:

"They may be insulted."

"Don't be afraid."

Aurélia dropped Torquato's arm and took Moreira's, who was as delighted as could be.

"This exchange is in return for the other we made, or that others made for us; all right, Dona Adelaide?"

Letting out these words with silvery laughter, Aurélia ran her sarcastic and imperious gaze over Seixas's face.

Fernando left in despair. In his interpretation, Aurélia mocked the rebuff he had suffered, and had exulted with his misfortune. This contempt, after the economic setbacks, affected him like caustic medication applied to a wound.

He remembered the young woman with the hundred thousand that he had been offered the day before. To be able to flaunt his wealth in the salons, before this woman infatuated with her gold, made it worth getting married, even to someone ugly, perhaps a provincial. The rural areas are the breeding grounds of rich brides that provide the elegant young men of the court; hence Seixas's supposition.

The next day, after tossing with insomnia, Fernando, recalling the antagonism with which he had been received by his favorite court after a long absence, arrived at a painful conclusion: he was ruined. Impoverished, with no credit, reduced to a life of menial jobs, his career cut short—what kind of future awaited him? Nothing remained but to resign himself to the vegetation of civil service with the ridiculous hope of emancipation with a meager pension around the age of fifty.

This prospect horrified him. However, his position was anything but frightening. With a modicum of resolve to confess his mistakes to his mother, and a bit of perseverance in correcting them, he could, at the end of two years of a modest and thrifty life, restore his former wealth.

But this was precisely the courage that Seixas lacked. Give up his social life, not cut a figure among the gentility, not have Raunier as his tailor, Campas as his shoemaker, Cretten as his haberdasher, and Bernard as his perfumist? Not attend all entertainments? Not to dress at the height of fashion?

This he could not imagine. He could kill himself, but recognized that he was too cowardly for such degradation.

This terror of poverty seized Seixas, and after operating on him all day, led him the following morning to Lemos's house, where he effectuated the transaction that he himself had qualified, unaware that soon he would become the prisoner of this indignity.

Of one count, however, he should be acquitted. Had he foreseen the anguish he was to suffer during the execution of the transaction, and especially at the moment of signing the receipt, he might have repented. But dragged from one concession to the next, his weakened dignity could no longer react.

Three days after he received the twenty thousand, as he was about to retire, Seixas found a message from that so-called Ramos to this effect:

"Be prepared for the introduction tomorrow evening. I will pick you up at 7 P.M."

The next day, at the appointed hour, with a merchant's punctuality, a car stopped at the door of the small house on Hospício Street. Moments later Lemos was on his way toward Laranjeiras with the bridegroom he had negotiated for his ward.

During the short ride, the old man amused himself by making the young man apprehensive about his bride, to whom he slyly attributed certain flaws, under the pretext of forgiving them. He suggested, for instance, that she had a glass eye or hinted that she was a consummated provincial whom the husband, immediately after the wedding, should send to school.

As fast as he concocted these jests, he demolished them with his customary peal of laughter, slapping three times on his companion's leg.

"Scared you, eh, you old rascal! She is no provincial! Rest assured! She needs no schooling; she herself is an academy! Take my advice; you'd better do some studying, otherwise you will cut a pitiful figure! Ha, ha, ha!"

Seixas paid no heed to the old man's witticisms; his spirit at this moment felt oppressed by the painful conviction of the shame and debasement of his position.

Especially now, at the outset of the transaction to which he had committed his person, when he was about to meet the woman to whom he had bound himself sight unseen, for the price of a dowry; now all the humiliation of his behavior depicted itself in the richest of hues.

The car came to a stop. The old man got out agile and lightfooted, and stomped his feet on the ground to free his trousers, which had become wedged in his boots.

"I should warn you," observed Lemos, "that the girl knows nothing of this, nor even suspects. For the time being, do not give it away."

∞ **X** ∞

The gate was about thirty steps from the house, which rose in the middle of a vast English garden.

Every window on the lower floor was open, and from each streamed cascades of light that shimmered on the waters of the pond and on the green shrubbery stirred by the breeze.

The guests were led by a servant to the drawing room, where only Dona Firmina Mascarenhas and Torquato Ribeiro were to be found. The old man exchanged some words with Ribeiro by a window, while Seixas, sitting next to the sofa, awaited the terrible moment.

There was a rustle of silk, and Aurélia appeared at the door.

This evening she wore a noble opal dress that suited her magnificently, outlining like a glove her beautiful bust. The glimmer of silk, undulating in the reflection of the lights, further softened the harmonious inflections of her seductive figure.

It was as if this voluptuous statue were bathed in an opalescent, fragrant vapor.

Her abundant hair, clasped at the nape of her neck by an opal diadem, cascaded effusively over the roundness of her pure white shoulders with an elegant simplicity and a stateliness uniquely her own that no art can lend, though it may imitate it; nature alone can impart it.

One could easily see that this proud and gentle head did not carry the burden, perhaps the remains of a dead skull, the cruel yoke imposed by fashion on vain young girls. What she exhibited was a luxuriant head of hair with which nature had adorned her, as it did frondescent trees, the sovereign mane with which modern gallantry crowned the woman as an emblem of her royalty.

Her well-turned arm, which the pulled-up sleeve displayed, was encircled by a bracelet, also of opals, like her loosely hanging necklace and the long pendant earrings glimmering on her pearly ears.

As she walked, the stones of her bracelet and earrings made a silvery sound, music for the melodious laughter that effused from this graceful creature and lingered after her like arpeggios from a lyre.

She crossed the room swaying softly like a swan on a silent lake, as the goddesses once walked. Amid the rustling silk, it seemed it was not she who advanced but the others who came toward her, and space humbly gathered itself at her feet, that she not tire over the distance.

If Aurélia had expected her entrance to affect Seixas's spirit, her hopes were dashed, for the young man's eyes, blinded by a sudden awe, saw only the form of a woman cross the room and sit on the sofa.

But for her these theatrical illusions were not uncommon. That splendid entrance had become an everyday fact in her life, like the rising of the stars. If her beauty always burst forth resplendent in the East of the salons, it remained thus throughout the evening, at the height of its glory.

Lemos, as he saw his ward enter the room, went to meet her and escorted her to the sofa:

"Aurélia, I have the honor of introducing to you Mr. Seixas."

The young woman responded to Seixas's bow with a slight nod of her head and offered him her hand, which he barely touched. Even at this moment the young gentleman still could not bring himself to look straight at the person in front of him.

This unknown face instilled in him an unspeakable terror, because it bore the features of his humiliation.

Aurélia, to dispel the awkwardness of the introduction, turned to her uncle and initiated one of those drawing room conversations that take the place of a piano or a song, and which, like them, are merely a sonorous noise to entertain our ears.

Words danced volubly on her lips, contrasting with the severity of her always harmonious gesture, and with a rigidity that could be said to freeze the side of her profile that faced Seixas.

Meanwhile, the great agitation that had deeply struck this man's being from the moment Aurélia entered the room and numbed his senses had dissipated. A melodious voice penetrated his soul, awakening echoes there asleep. For the first time, he turned his eyes to the woman's face. Great was his astonishment as he recognized Aurélia Camargo.

For a brief moment he imagined himself victim of a hallucination. It was difficult to believe that before him was truly the woman from whom he thought himself separated for all eternity. The commotion was so overpowering that his reason for coming to this house and the devious position in which he found himself virtually disappeared from his memory. An inner sense of well-being absorbed him complelety, freeing him from the bitter concerns that had dominated him a moment before.

Aurélia had also recovered her aplomb, for she turned to him and asked unabashedly:

"Have you been to the North lately, Mr. Seixas?"

"Yes, madam. I arrived from Pernambuco last week."

"Where he carried out an important commission," added Lemos.

"Is Recife really as beautiful as they say?"

"I believe few cities in the world can compete with its charming views and magnificent location."

"Not even our Rio?" asked Aurélia, smiling.

"Rio de Janeiro is no doubt superior in terms of nature's majesty; Recife, on the other hand, excels in grace and elegance. If our court resembles a proud queen on her mountainous throne, the capital of Pernambuco would then be the gentle princess reaching toward the waves from the arbors of her gardens."

"That is why they call her the Brazilian Venice."

"I have never been to Venice, but from what I know of it, I cannot understand why they compare a heap of marble erected on the mud of a swamp with the beautiful banks of the Capibaribe, adorned with green palms in whose shade countryside and sea tenderly embrace."

"I can see that you found a muse in Recife," observed Aurélia playfully.

"You think me poetic? I merely repeat what some Pernambucan bard must already have said. As to my muse—it has become an angel. It died after seven days and lies buried in the dust of my desk!" answered Seixas in a similar tone.

Several guests had arrived, and their appearance interrupted the dialogue. Aurélia rose to greet the ladies, while the men spread around the room waiting for an opportunity to pay their respects to the lady of the house.

The total absence of Aurélia's declared suitors was noteworthy; if one had managed to be invited, he owed the favor to the circumstance of not having yet revealed his intentions.

Weary of the adoration bestowed upon her at the balls, adoration that turned into veritable persecution, Aurélia had made of these family gatherings a place of tranquillity where she found refuge from the world's obsession.

Taking advantage of the confusion, Lemos took Seixas to the window:

"So, did I deceive you?"

"Quite the opposite. I could never imagine it was she."

"So, now that you have met her, it is time to disclose that I am the fortunate guardian of this sweetheart, and that my name is Lemos, not Ramos. A

difference of two letters only. Until the contract was signed, I had to keep the
secret. Do you understand? Hm? You rascal!"

And Lemos pinched Seixas's arm, one of his most significant signs of
friendship.

Some time in the evening, the young girl, as she crossed the room on her
way back from bidding farewell to a lady, saw Seixas outside, leaning against
a window.

Under the pretext of smoking a cigarette, he had gone to the garden and,
so as not to isolate himself totally from the gathering, had taken that position, from which he appeared to follow with his eyes what took place in the
room. But it was as if he were not there, such was the apprehension centered at that moment in his being.

His mind made use of this, the first pause in social duties since Aurélia
appeared in the room, to impart order to the events that had just occurred
and to seek a cause or explanation.

The girl, pretending to look at the sky, came to lean out the same window:

"You are so detached! Do you also cultivate the stars?"

"Which? The ones in the sky?"

"Why? Are there others?"

"No one has ever told you?"

"Someone may have mentioned it, but as yet no one has convinced me,"
answered the girl, smiling.

Seixas remained silent. His spirit, not very given to this kind of verbal
jousting was, furthermore, held captive of a troublesome thought.

"Perhaps I have disturbed an enthralling vision?" insisted Aurélia.

"I do not have one. I was contemplating the vagaries of fate that brought
me to your house this evening. Is it a blessing or fortune's irony? Only you
can tell me."

Aurélia burst out laughing.

"I would have to be an intimate of that lady to know her intentions; and
although many consider me one of her favorites, believe me, deep down we
do not get along that well."

The girl said this somewhat coquettishly. But she soon turned serious
and continued:

"What I apprehend from these words is that Mr. Seixas regrets not having
made better use of his time."

"And I have every right to regret!" he said, almost in a whisper, as if
fearing to be heard.

"Heavens, how mysterious you are! You only speak in riddles. I confess
that I do not understand you. Does anyone lack the right to regret some-

thing as simple as a visit!"

"You are right, Dona Aurélia. I apologize. I have not yet recovered from the surprise. When I came to this house, I did not expect to meet you. It was the farthest thing from my mind—"

"Did the meeting so displease you?" asked Aurélia, smiling.

"If I still believed in happiness, I would say that it had smiled on me."

"And why did you lose faith?"

Seixas gazed at the girl's face wistfully:

"Of what interest can it be to you? It is a matter of temperament. Some never abandon hope, others lack faith altogether and lapse into despair at the least disappointment. And you, Dona Aurélia? I heard your allusion just now; surely it was in jest! Tell me, are you happy?"

"I believe so; at least that is what everyone says, and I cannot presume to know the world better than so many people more knowledgeable and experienced than my empty little head. So, in order not to contradict the general opinion, I consider myself the most fortunate woman in Rio de Janeiro. All my whims are promptly satisfied; there is not a wish I make that does not come true. Everywhere I am surrounded by praise and adoration I do not deserve, which makes them even more flattering."

"Then you do not lack anything."

"My guardian informs me that I lack a husband and took it upon himself to find me one."

"Anyone? It does not make any difference to you?" asked Seixas, smiling.

"It is understood that I will only accept one who pleases me; but I do not wish to bother with such matters."

"It is of so little importance to you?"

"On the contrary; I am so fearful of compromising my future through my own actions that I entrust it to Fate. God will provide."

Seixas scrutinized the girl's smiling countenance for traces of irony beneath that graceful volubility.

"And in the midst of your opulence, in the rare restful moments permitted by your elegant life, don't memories of other times ever come to you?"

"Let us not talk about the past!" exclaimed the girl curtly.

A warm smile, however, soon obliterated the fierceness of her gesture and the scintillation in her eye.

"We have met each other as of today, Mr. Seixas. The dead—let them rest in peace."

Spilling into the man's soul the emanations of her ineffable smile, Aurélia withdrew from the window.

∞ **XI** ∞

From that day on, Seixas met with Aurélia almost every evening, either at her house or in society.

The girl's courteous manner toward him had, if not totally dispelled, at least dulled his qualms of conscience about the bargain he had struck with Lemos. Not that he absolved himself from guilt, but he expected to redeem himself through love.

His conversations with Aurélia usually dealt with drawing room themes. Now and then, however, he found an excuse to talk to her in that tender and affectionate style, resembling a love song, which for this reason lacks not the idea, only the melodious vocabulary, to cradle the heart to the sweet harmony of its music.

Aurélia would then lower her head and retreat within herself to listen to the lyricism of the young man's inspired words; however, never did her face or her person reflect the least sign that she reciprocated these feelings. She opened her soul to love; but the love that filtered through Seixas's tender words evaporated like a fragrance that enveloped her for an instant without penetrating the inner reaches of her soul.

On one occasion, Seixas let escape another reference to the past. Just as the first time, she cut him short:

"That time does not exist for me. I was born a year ago."

When he met Lemos one afternoon, Seixas told him:

"I have a favor to ask of you."

"Ask me two."

"Tell me honestly, why did you choose me as the preferred husband for your ward when you did not even know me?"

The old man unleashed a snicker peculiar to him:

"Huh! Huh! So you want to know? Here it is. I do not mince words. It did not suit me to have the girl duped by the sweet talk of those mustached types out there sniffing after her dowry. Then I learned that in the past she had liked you; and since, based on the information I had, you suited my purposes, I went looking for you. Now the rest is up to you, you rascal."

This explanation appeased the young man's spirit and dissipated the uneasiness that at times still assailed him. Taking everything into consideration, the way he had arranged his marriage was no novelty; these marriages of convenience were being negotiated every day, in identical, if not more positive, terms.

Besides which, by a happy coincidence, fortune had turned this rational marriage project into a love bond, so the heart absolved and sanctified all that had been done toward the realization of its wishes.

Seixas persisted, therefore, with his sweet madrigals and the affectionate nocturnes in the corner of the drawing room.

After the evening of the introduction, Lemos left to his protégé, as he called him, the management of his affairs. One morning, however, he appeared before him:

"My friend, if you have nothing to do right now, let us complete the agreement. Marriage is like soup: you must not let it get cold."

Seixas was also eager to escape the situation in which he found himself. At every moment he feared that the sweet illusion with which his soul disguised the transaction he had accepted might be dispelled. He was tortured by the thought that Aurélia might see him as a fortune hunter.

He promptly accepted the businessman's invitation and followed him to Aurélia's house, in formal attire.

The lady, having been notified of the visit, awaited them in the drawing room, to which they were shown immediately. After the greetings and some small talk, Lemos assumed a more formal tone and said:

"Dona Aurélia, Mr. Seixas, of whose excellent qualities you are already aware, a person worthy of your high esteem, has asked me for your hand. On my part, I could not have made a better choice, in every sense; but all this is worth nothing if he has not the good fortune of meriting your approval."

Aurélia turned upon her suitor a gaze that belied the smile on her lips.

"Aren't you afraid of my whims and eccentricities?"

"But I adore them!" answered Seixas flirtatiously.

"Doesn't it seem difficult to you to bring happiness to a disillusioned heart such as mine, so afflicted by doubt?"

"I have faith in my love; with it, I shall overcome the impossible."

The smile vanished from Aurélia's lips, and an expression of passionate desire, emerging from the depths of her soul, swept over her countenance.

"Here is my hand; it is all I can give you. The woman you love and have dreamed of I do not possess. But if it is within your power to bring her into being, she will belong to you completely, as your creature. Believe me, that is the hope of my life; I entrust it to your affection."

The young girl, in a gesture of sublime abandonment, had offered her satiny hand to Seixas, who kissed it, murmuring effusively his joy and gratitude.

Lemos, who had discreetly withdrawn so as not to inhibit the couple, resumed the conversation, which once more took on the light tone of customary banalities.

The news of Aurélia's forthcoming wedding shocked Rio's high society.

No one could understand how this lady, pursued by the cream of Rio's eligible young men, who could choose as she pleased from among her innumerable worshipers, husbands of every type, had the poor taste of sullying herself with a scribbler for magazines.

Alfredo Moreira, when he met her after hearing the news, could not hide his contempt.

"So, you are to marry?"

"It is true."

"You finally found him. At a high price, no doubt?" replied the elegant man ironically.

"No," answered the young woman in the same tone. "He cost me next to nothing."

"Oh! I am glad to hear it. What was the price?"

"You want to know the price?"

"I am curious."

"It was the same as yours."

Moreira bit his lip and laughed. In spite of everything, he had not lost his final hopes. The wedding plans could be undone for any reason, and it was quite possible that the young lady might, from one moment to the next, regret her choice with the same fickleness with which she had all too suddenly made it, and on a whim.

Thus thought the rejected candidate, although all evidence seemed to reveal Aurélia's firm intention of persevering in her original decision, at which she had arrived only after great deliberation.

Once the wedding was announced, the girl appeared less often at social affairs, finally withdrawing from them completely, limiting herself to the small circle that met at her house, and in which she, so to speak, dusted her soul from a certain lethargy induced by her future husband's tender confidences and loving reveries.

Seixas, based on the words Aurélia had proffered from the depths of her soul when she offered him her hand as wife, believed he understood the secret of the strangeness and oscillations of the girl's character.

"She doubts I love her," he told himself. "She suspects I have my eye on her wealth. I must convince her of the sincerity of my affection. If she only knew! A wretch may sacrifice his freedom, but the soul cannot be bought!"

Steeped in this idea, it is not surprising that Seixas lent to his expansiveness an exuberance that lapsed into exaggeration. Quite often tired, if not overwhelmed, by these passionate remonstrations, Aurélia, who had tried in vain to allay through them the suspicions of her soul, observed half-coquettishly and half-ironically:

"Please, let me breathe! I have never been loved, nor did I ever dream I would be loved with such passion. I must accustom myself to it gradually."

The mansion in Laranjeiras had recently been refurbished with the luxuries commensurate with the heiress's substantial means, with the future union already in mind. There were but few preparations left to be done for the wedding, and these were expedited by money, that prime and most eloquent of improvisers.

Thus a wedding date had to be set. Lemos raised the question of the wedding attendants. He had given the matter some thought and, following the custom of our society, considered indispensable at least a baroness as matron of honor and two important figures, something between a senator and a minister, as best men.

He had no connection with people of that rank, but he assumed that even a nodding acquaintance or a letter of recommendation would suffice to ask such favors, which flatter the vanity of the great and exalt the presumption of the small.

Great was his consternation, therefore, when Aurélia declared that one of the best men must be Dr. Torquato Ribeiro.

"What a suggestion!" said Fernando involuntarily.

"Does it displease you?"

A sudden flash of light crossed the girl's visage. It might have been a reflection from the diamond on her ring, struck by the light as her hand smoothed a curl of hair that had come loose from her headdress.

"You could choose someone else, Aurélia."

"Isn't he your friend? Oh! I thought—!"

"He has no position in society."

"Right!" intervened Lemos. "Position is essential."

A mere attorney in no way corresponded to the old man's aristocratic notion of a millionaire heiress's best man. Furthermore, it thwarted his plan, for the high personalities he might invite would surely decline to stand next to a young lad who was not even a commander.

Nonetheless, Aurélia was unyielding.

On the following day they signed the prenuptial agreement separating their assets, insuring Seixas of a dowry of one hundred thousand.

The girl, who had always avoided any interference in financial matters, leaving them to her guardian and remaining aloof from such questions, once again managed to preclude discussion of material interests with her fiancé.

Lemos took Seixas to Fialho's notary office, maintaining that this was a demand of the Court of Orphans, which was not a total untruth, although it was actually the heiress's will that had determined this condition, so easily misinterpreted in a court of law.

Only later, when the notary brought the registry book to her house, did Aurélia sign. However, not a word about this was exchanged between her and the groom.

∞ XII ∞

Aurélia invited only a selected few to witness the wedding at her house in Laranjeiras.

The girl did not accept the suggestion of giving a ball for the occasion, but assumed that she should surround the act with some fitting solemnity, to leave no doubts about the spontaneity of her choice and the pleasure afforded her by the union.

Many of her friends recommended to Aurélia a wedding after the European fashion, with the romance of a trip immediately following the ceremony, a honeymoon in the countryside, and a spectacular ball upon their return to court.

She, however, refused all these suggestions; she chose to be married according to the customs of the land, in the evening, in a private chapel with a few ladies and gentlemen in attendance, who would comprise, for her, an orphan and alone in the world, the family she did not have.

The ceremony took place at eight o'clock. Lemos had found a baron to compensate for Ribeiro and a monsignor to officiate.

For matron of honor Aurélia chose Dona Margarida Ferreira, a respectable lady who had shown disinterested friendship from their first meeting in society.

When the moment arrived to kneel before the priest and pronounce the eternal vows that would bind her to the destiny of the man she had chosen, Aurélia, with the dignity that graced her every gesture and movement, bowed her head, modestly enfolding herself in the diaphanous shadows of her white bridal veil.

But in spite of herself, the happiness that filled her heart and poured forth from her glowing eyes and her smiling, dewy lips, raised her gracious countenance, bathed at that moment in a nimbus of joy.

In the proud distinction of her head and the ecstasy of her face, whose beauty was adorned by a splendid effulgence, was also manifest the sublime expression of triumph that exalts the woman who succeeds in making a fervid wish, long desired, come true.

The guests, who had previously admired her exquisite charm, this evening found her dazzling and understood that love had painted with colors from its unique palette that already bewitching beauty, imbuing her with irresistible fascination.

"How happy she is!" said the men.

"And with good reason!" added the women, turning their eyes to the groom.

Seixas's countenance also glowed with the smile of happiness. His pride at having been chosen by that fascinating lady enhanced his mien, already noble and genteel by nature.

Actually, in Aurélia's husband one could appreciate the fine flower of supreme distinction, that vaunts no pretentious gestures or artistic mannerisms, but emanates from within a fragrance that modesty seeks to restrain and yet streams from the innermost soul.

After the ceremony came the customary greetings to the bride, groom, and relatives.

Only then did people notice the presence of an older lady who had been there since the beginning of the evening. It was Dona Camila, Seixas's mother, who had come out of her obscurity to attend her Fernando's wedding and, feeling ill at ease among that society, left with her daughters soon after the ceremony.

To liven up the gathering, the young girls improvised some quadrilles and in the intermissions a renowned pianist who had been Aurélia's teacher played highlights from operas fashionable at the time.

Around ten o'clock the invited families departed.

Lemos then led Seixas to the part of the house taken up by the rooms Aurélia had set aside for her husband, which were furnished in great luxury and, above all, with a tasteful sense of innovation.

"My friend, you are now married, about which I have already congratulated you! However, I still have one duty to fulfill that falls upon me as your wife's former guardian and of whom this evening I still act as father."

"I have also awaited this moment to thank you for the care and devotion you have bestowed upon Aurélia, and to assure you of my true friendship."

"All I did was repay a debt to my good sister. I love this girl as if she were my own daughter; I witnessed her birth."

Removing a keyring from his pocket, the old man proceeded to open the various pieces of *érable* furniture, leaving them wide open. As he carried out this task, he continued to speak:

"I will have the pleasure of getting you settled into your new quarters. This is your work study; there is the dressing room; to this side of the garden is a bathroom and a smoking room with a separate entrance for you to receive your friends. Everything is very stylish."

"I recognize Aurélia's hand; I can sense in every object the perfume that comes from her beauty," said Seixas, intoxicated with happiness.

"Right you are, sir; she took it upon herself to do all this. But you have not seen all of it yet. Have a look at your personal effects."

Lemos then pointed out the drawers and shelves of the wardrobe and the dressers filled with various items of clothing, tailored from the best fabric and with extreme care. Nothing was lacking that a man accustomed to all the comforts of fashion might wish.

On the dresser, the marble top displayed all sorts of toiletries, and the drawers contained copious jewelry as befits an elegant gentleman. Some quite costly, like the ruby ring and full diamond cufflinks.

"All this belongs to you, sir," said the old man, concluding his inventory. "That is her doing; it is not part of our agreement."

Seixas experienced a sensation akin to that of a man who, in the midst of a pleasant dream, is cast into a swamp to awaken mired in some sordid reality. The word *agreement*, there, at the moment when he had just sanctified by his vows his eternal love for his wife, when he was absorbed in the recollections that impregnated every detail of the luxury and elegance the girl had lavished on these rooms—this word uttered unwittingly by the old man inflicted upon him the bitterest of humiliations.

Meanwhile, Lemos closed the doors and drawers he had opened and ended by presenting Seixas with the keyring.

"Here you are, my dear old friend. There is only one key I cannot give you. That one."

The old man indicated at the end of a short hallway a door covered by a blue silken portière with a golden arrow.

"When that door opens, there will not be in all of Rio a more fortunate rascal!"

And the old man, pealing his high-pitched laughter, returned to the drawing room, where he met five businessmen, old companions, who at his request had stayed on, and now found themselves somewhat confused by the story.

"Come, Lemos, tell us why we are still here at this hour. Listen, we all know you as a prankster."

"The scoundrel wants to close the deal in high style! Did you see that— the notary?"

"It is true. They have just called him. And we will serve as witnesses."

At this point the men broke into hearty laughter.

"You almost guessed it," said Lemos. "Come here and see what it is all about."

In the waiting room into which Lemos led his friends was seated at the center table a notary public who had attended the ceremony as a guest and who now seemed ready to assume an official role.

Aurélia had just entered through the main door, accompanied by Dona Firmina. Over her shoulders the girl wore a gray cashmere cape that concealed her wedding gown and covered her head with a loose hood.

The halo of joy that magnified her beauty as she knelt at the altar beside her groom had not dimmed, but was gradually fading. Now and again a sudden tremor ruffled her delicate form, and at these moments one could see an eclipse of her inner radiance, like the flickering of a lamp as it is about to expire.

She sat facing the notary; Lemos and the other businessmen sat at the sides of the table.

"I ask you to forgive the inconvenience and accept my gratitude for your kindness in complying with this whim of mine."

There were a few murmurs of protest.

"This is the last of my eccentricities!" replied Aurélia with a captivating smile. "I am still saying farewell to my single life and thus deserve some indulgence. Besides, on careful consideration, what I am about to do is not that extravagant, because a will is also part of confession. I want to take advantage of this moment, while I am still answerable to myself and to my wishes, to state the final one, which happens also to have been the first, of my life."

In spite of the joviality with which the young lady uttered these words, and the joyful charm that her magic smile always radiated about her, a feeling of vague and undefinable sadness afflicted those present, especially when Aurélia handed the notary the will she had written on a perfumed satin sheet with gilded borders and the monogram A.C. embossed in scarlet.

The association of such opposing actions, the dawn of existence and its departure; the idea of death intertwined with that youth, so rich with every gift; the bridal garland crowning a dying brow—this contrast could not but leave a deep impression in one's spirit.

The notary executed the record of confirmation with the time-honored formulae, and amidst the most profound silence returned the will to the girl; it was already bound with a silk cord and sealed with drops of golden wax whose perfume wafted through the room.

Never did the abstruse and antiquated gibberish of notaries seem so stylish. The document, albeit a will, did not gainsay the beautiful hand that had penned the text, or the gracious soul that might have enclosed therein, alongside her final wish, the perfume of unknown tears.

As he said goodbye to his ward, Lemos squeezed her hand.

"I hope you will be very, very happy."

"If I am not, it will be my fault, and only mine," answered the young girl, thanking him.

Dona Firmina offered to accompany the girl to her dressing room, to render the services of a lady-in-waiting of honor, a privilege customarily bestowed upon the mother, and in her absence, upon the nearest female relative.

Aurélia refused; embracing the older lady, she said, deeply moved:

"Pray for me!"

Left alone, the girl locked the door to the waiting room and whispered:

"At last!"

In that entire side of the house, there was no one but her and her husband.

❧ XIII ❧

Let us indiscreetly draw back a fold of the drapery that screens the nuptial chamber.

It is a square room, all in splendorous white that enhances the royal blue of the velvety carpet, decorated with embroidered stars, and the beautiful gold tone of the curtains and upholstery.

On one side, two golden bronze statues representing love and chastity support a delicately shaped oval dome, from which lambrequins of finest lace unfold to the floor.

Through the diaphanous clarity of these linen clouds can be seen the outline of an elegant silkwood bed, modestly enveloped in its nuptial veilings, covered by a camlet quilt also in golden tones.

On the other side is a fireplace, not for fire, unnecessary in the pleasant climate of our Rio even in the worst of winter. This chimney of pink marble is merely an excuse for a quiet conversation corner, since we cannot call it as do the French *coin du feu*.

Actually, the fireplace is nothing but a flower box that spreads perfume from its flowers, instead of heat from its glow, around the circle formed by low armchairs, a transition between chair and bed.

The room is illuminated by a large gas lamp whose opaque crystal dome filters a peaceful and sweet brightness that spreads over objects and infuses them as if in a creamy light.

A curtain was drawn aside and Aurélia entered the nuptial chamber.

Her feet glided over the blue velvet rug, dotted with golden artichokes, like the steps of the goddesses of the heavens who traversed the galaxy as they climbed the Olympus.

The beautiful girl had replaced her wedding gown with this other that might well be called a wifely garment, for the soft signs of immaculate purity that the virgin dons on her way to the altar were falling away like the petals of a flower in Autumn, allowing a glimpse of the chaste first fruits of sacred conjugal love.

Aurélia wore a green satin tunic, gathered at her waist by a gold twisted cord, whose tassels moved to her measured steps. Bursting through the folds of this simple robe appeared the ruffles of the transparent cambric that embraced the young woman's seductive shape.

The ample, loose sleeves were gathered at the bend of the arm and over the shoulders by a brooch that also held the shoulder piece, exposing the delicate arm whose flesh tinged with pink the cotton chemise buttoned at the wrist by a pearl.

Her magnificent black hair flowed down her shoulders, held only by a gold band that encircled her luxuriant tresses; the foot hid itself in a satin slipper that sometimes nipped at the hem of her petticoat like a mischievous hummingbird.

The girl's chaste garb shielded her graceful figure; however, as she walked and her ethereal body swam in waves of silk and cotton, one sensed, more in the soul than in the eyes, the silhouette of that statue trembling with emotion. With each movement of her undulating walk, one envisioned that the shoulder pin had opened and the zealous veils had fallen suddenly at the feet of that sublime woman, revealing a divine creation, though one of immaterial beauty, attired in celestial splendor.

Aurélia crossed the room and, approaching the door opposite the one through which she had come, lowered her head slightly, concentrating to listen; but she heard only the panting of her heaving breast.

She withdrew quickly, and fell into one of the armchairs, disheartened, crossing her hands and raising them to Heaven with an expression of deep anguish.

"My God, why didn't You make me like other women? Why did You give me such a demanding heart, proud and selfish? I can be happy like so many women in this world, and drink from the cup of love, which these lips may never again touch. It is not the divine nectar I dreamed of, no, but they say that it intoxicates the soul and makes you forget!"

Aurélia's spirit pursued the budding idea, and for a time seemed to cradle herself in a dream.

"No!" she exclaimed, rashly. "It would be the profanation of this sacred love that was and will be the whole of my life!"

She rose and walked around the nuptial chamber, caressing with her gaze the furniture and the ornaments she had chosen to decorate the sanctuary of her happiness and with which she could be said to have sculptured her fondest hopes.

Having thus reflected on the motives aroused by these objects, she looked at herself in the mirror, and directed to her charming image reproduced in the glass an indefinable smile.

She then went to the door where moments before she had listened, turned the key, and drew aside one of the curtains. Soon thereafter, Seixas pulled back the other curtain and, clasping his wife's body, sat her down on one of the chairs.

"You took so long, Aurélia!" he said querulously.

"I had a vow to fulfill. I wanted to become emancipated once and for all so that I could belong totally to my one and only master," said the girl coquettishly.

"Do not kill me with so much happiness, Aurélia! What else may I wish for in this world other than to live at your feet, worshiping you, since you are, for me, a divinity on earth."

Seixas knelt at his bride's feet, grasped her hands, which she did not withdraw, and intoned his song of love, that sublime ode from the heart, understood only by women, just as only mothers fathom the babbling of their infants.

The girl, reclining languidly against the back of the chair, her head leaning forward, her eyes brimming with tender affection, listened to her husband's speech; she found herself enraptured by the effusions of the love he showered upon her with fervent words, subdued gaze, and passionate gesture.

"So, it is true that you love me?"

"Do you still doubt it, Aurélia?"

"And that you have always loved me, since the day we met?"

"Have I not already told you?"

"And that you have never loved another woman?"

"I swear, Aurélia. These lips have never touched another woman's cheek, except my mother. My first kiss of love, I have kept for my wife, for you."

Rising to reach her cheek, Seixas did not notice the sudden change that had come over his bride's countenance.

Aurélia was livid, and her beauty, radiant a moment before, had turned to marble.

"Or for a richer one!" she said, retreating to escape her husband's kiss, pushing him away with her fingertips.

The girl's voice had assumed a crystalline pitch, echoing the severity and harshness of the emotion swelling in her breast, and seeming to resound on her lips like steel.

"Aurélia! What is this?"

"We are playacting in a comedy, in which both of us perform our roles with accomplished skill. We may be proud that not even the best actors could surpass us. But it is time, sir, to put an end to this cruel farce with which we have been taunting each other. Let us face reality, however sad it may be, and resign ourselves, each of us, to what we are: I, a woman betrayed; you, a man who sold himself."

"Sold!" exclaimed Seixas, wounded deep in his soul.

"Sold, yes; there is no other way to put it. I am rich, very rich, I am a millionaire; I needed a husband, a trinket that every respectable woman must have. You were in the market; I bought you. You cost me one hundred thousand; it was cheap. You did not place a high enough value on yourself. I would have given twice, three times as much, my entire fortune, for this moment."

As Aurélia spoke these words, she unfolded a piece of paper in which Seixas recognized the contract he had signed with Lemos.

One cannot describe the sarcasm that speckled the girl's lips, or the indignation that poured from that deeply rebellious soul into the pitiless look with which she flayed her husband's face.

Seixas, transfixed by the cruel insult, plunged from the ecstasy of happiness into this abyss of humiliation, was at first dumbfounded. Then, when the waves of anger rose from his soul, he held them at bay with that powerful sentiment known as respect for a lady, which rarely abandons the well-bred man.

Conscious of the impossibility of returning the offense to the woman he had loved, he listened wordlessly, wondering what he should do, whether he should kill her, kill himself, or kill them both.

Aurélia, as if guessing his thoughts, continued for a time to insult him with merciless scorn.

"Now, my husband, if you wish to know the reason why I bought you rather than any other, I will tell you, and I beg you not to interrupt me. Let me pour out what I have in my soul, which has embittered and consumed it for a year."

The girl indicated a nearby chair to Seixas.

"Sit down, my husband."

The girl uttered the phrase *my husband* in such an astringent and bitter tone that on her steely lips it became as sharp as a spear poisoned in caustic irony!

Seixas sat down.

This woman's strange fascination prevailed upon him, and even more so did the incredible situation into which he had been drawn.

SECOND PART

Redress

❦ I ❦

Two years before this unique wedding, there lived on St. Teresa Street a poor and infirm lady.

Known as Dona Emília Camargo, she lived in the company of a grown daughter, all the family she still had.

She represented herself as a widow, although there was no lack of malicious individuals for whom this widowhood was only a veil of decency hiding the fact that she had been abandoned by some lover.

There was some small truth to this unfair suspicion.

When she was young, Dona Emília Lemos became fond of a medical student who had fallen in love with her. Certain that his feelings were reciprocated, the student, Pedro de Sousa Camargo, gathered his courage and proposed to her.

Emília lived in the company of Mr. Manuel José Correia Lemos, her older brother and the family's patriarch, who undertook to seek information about the young man. He learned that he was the natural child of a wealthy landowner, who had seen to his education and treated him magnanimously. He had not acknowledged him, however, which was of utmost importance, for besides the fact that the landowner's mother was still alive somewhere in Minas, the fellow was still young and healthy and might well marry and sire legitimate children.

In light of this information, Lemos realized that he could not forego certain formalities, indispensable in case the young man were to become the necessary heir. Emília's brother was far from well-off, and the burden of the twelve people he carried on his shoulders was sufficient without risking the added weight of this new family in the making.

"On our part, there is no doubt, young man. Get your papa's permission, or a notarized statement of parentage; the rest, you can leave up to me."

It was a formal refusal, for Pedro Camargo would never dare confess his passion to his father who, with his harshness and ill-temper, had inspired in him from early childhood a superstitious horror.

"Your family rejects me, Emília, because I am poor and am not assured of my father's inheritance," said the student the next time he met the girl he loved.

Lemos's sister knew from her relatives' explanations that this was indeed the reason for the refusal.

"They reject you because you are poor, Mr. Camargo; but for that very reason I accept you."

"Do you still want to be my wife, Emília? In spite of your relatives' opposition? Even though I am only a penniless student?"

"So long as the reason for my relatives' opposition is just your poverty, I feel strong enough to resist. What better fortune can I desire than to share your fate, good or bad?"

"I would not dare ask for this proof of your love, Emília. You are an angel."

Two weeks later, Pedro Camargo stopped at Lemos's door in a car. It was tea time; everyone was in the dining room. Emília, who had retired pleading indisposition, went down the stairs without being noticed.

The next morning, Lemos opened the newspaper to read the announcements, his customary manner of beginning the morning, when he was handed a letter. The envelope was embossed, and inside was a sheet of satin paper with these words:

Pedro de Sousa Camargo
and Dona Emília Lemos Camargo
have the honor of announcing their wedding.
Rio de Janeiro, etc..

In Lemos's house no one could believe there had been such a wedding. For the family, the girl was nothing less than Pedro Camargo's mistress and therefore a fallen woman.

Nevertheless, the marriage had been solemnized at the Engenho Velho church, secretly but lacking none of the formalities, for the bride and groom were of age and had obtained the necessary dispensations.

Around this time, the landowner Lourenço de Sousa Camargo received word that his son was living with a girl he had taken from her family's house. The well-meaning friend added that the student already considered himself married; it should therefore come as no surprise if he decided to crown his initial folly with the madness of such a union.

The old man immediately dispatched one of his men, the most resolute, with a summons for his son to report to the farm within a week. The courier also had direct orders to bring him by force if he did not obey.

Pedro Camargo tore himself away from the arms of his Emília, promising to return soon, never to be separated from her again. Once the old man's initial outburst of anger had subsided, he would find an opportunity to confess everything. His father, who loved him, would not withhold forgiveness for a lapse beyond redress and sanctified by religion.

The young man, however, lacked the courage to rouse the landowner's wrath anew with the revelation of his marriage. He prepared himself, made firm plans, but at the propitious moment, the resolution deserted him.

Thus the days went by, and Pedro Camargo's absence grew longer. He wrote lengthy, tender letters to his Emília, full of love and promises in which he vowed to depart in a few days to bring her to the farm.

At the same time, while he could not summon her to his company, through a friend, he sent his wife means for her survival; he would send for her as soon as he confessed to his father their secret marriage.

Emília suffered greatly from his absence, less from the dubious predicament in which she had been placed than from the love she felt for her husband. She had, however, been created for self-denial; in her letters to Pedro she never let escape a single complaint. Far from reproaching him for his fears, which left her fate so uncertain, she tried rather to comfort him in the remorse engendered by his own timidity.

After a year, when the old man's suspicions had abated if not dissipated, he allowed his son a sojourn at the court.

The two lovers met again after the long absence and loved each other during those few days for all the time they had been apart.

Pedro Camargo returned to find his first child already two months old. He named him Emílio, in spite of the mother's entreaties, who insisted on Pedro.

"No, not Pedro; that's the name of a wretch," answered her husband tearfully.

This singular pattern of life continued, with the couple spending a few weeks together in their small house on St. Teresa Street, alternating with long months of separation.

These absences purified their love and gave it a vigor that later expanded with unsuspected passion. Blissful were the days Pedro Camargo spent at the court for these two hearts that found their own image in each other.

Emília resigned herself to the fate that Providence had destined for her; even so she considered herself quite fortunate with the love and tenderness of the man she had chosen.

She had concluded that if the old landowner learned of their marriage he might become angry and suddenly destroy these happy moments she and her husband were allowed to share.

Furthermore, Pedro Camargo was a natural son, not yet legally recognized, and his future depended solely on the good will of his father, who might abandon him as a stranger, leaving him destitute. This circumstance deeply influenced Emília's spirit—not for herself, for she was free of ambition, but as wife and mother.

By this time she had given birth to a daughter whom she named Aurélia, for this had been the name of Pedro Camargo's mother, an unfortunate young girl who had died from her shameful mistake.

Convinced that it would be dangerous to reveal the secret of her marriage, Emília condemned herself to an existence both obscure and suspect. Her virtue suffered, besieged by unjust disdain and vexed by scorn. She sought refuge in isolation and found comfort in the hope of reparation.

Both of Camargo's children grew, and both received an excellent education. The old landowner's largesse allowed Pedro to support his family with decency and abundance, especially as there was nothing to divert the money from this honorable use, except his unpretentious wardrobe.

Twelve years had elapsed since Pedro Camargo's wedding, and he was thirty-six years old when his weak and irresolute character was subjected to a cruel test.

On several occasions the landowner had shown an interest in seeing his son married; but these whims, devoid of a clear object, faded and the drudgery of rural life distracted the old man from domestic concerns. Pedro Camargo escaped the threat with only a minor fright.

At last, however, the father formally demanded that he marry, designating a person he had already chosen. The daughter of a rich farmer in the area, she had just turned fifteen. Before news of this seductive dowry reached the court, old Camargo decided to secure it for his son.

Pedro opposed his father's will with passive resistance. He never dared to say *no*, but neither did he move to fulfill the landowner's recommendations, or rather, his orders. His father raged, he bowed his head, and once the tempest had passed, he again lapsed into inertia.

When the landowner realized that, despite his upbraiding and screaming, his son never undertook to visit the girl, he became so angry that he threatened to drive him from the house unless he mounted a horse that very instant and went to the neighboring farm to see his bride and reiterate to her father the proposal made in his name.

Pedro Camargo said not a word. He went to the stable, saddled his horse, tied a pack behind it, and left, but not toward the nearby farm. He rode to a ranch where he had planned to stay while he determined what direction to give his life.

During this ordeal he continued to write to his wife but kept from her the hardship he was experiencing, so as not to distress her.

Resistance to the wishes of his father, whom he held in high regard, and the turmoil of his conscience against the fear of confessing the truth greatly weakened the sturdy body of this man, physically strong, but not meant for such moral convulsions.

Pedro Camargo fell prey to a cerebral fever and passed away at the ranch which had sheltered him, without medical assistance and nearly destitute. A muleteer on his way to the court was the only person with him during his final moments.

The unfortunate creature had on his person three thousand *mil-réis* he had been saving for some time with the intention of settling on a small farm where he could live peacefully with his family.

But fate did not consent. He trusted the money to the muleteer, asking him to deliver it to his wife in his name. But he begged him not to say anything of his desperate situation, to spare her further grief.

The muleteer carried out his task with the integrity still found among the uncultivated classes, especially in rural areas.

Emília draped herself in mourning clothes, which she would exchange only for a shroud. Blacker and sadder than her dress, however, was the wound in her soul, where never again would blossom a smile.

∽ II ∾

Widowhood rendered Emília's existence even more isolated and withdrawn, adding to it indifference and detachment from the world.

The only link binding her to this earth was her children, but her premonition was that she would not remain with them very long. Her husband summoned her; she yielded to the attraction that would bring her close to the being she had loved above all, and that little by little sundered her away from the earthly bonds that still kept her in this vale of tears.

Only one concern troubled her, as she pondered the oncoming end to her misfortune—the thought of the destitution her daughter Aurélia, already a young lady, blossoming at sixteen, would be left to face.

From her family Emília could not expect any support for the orphan. The relationship, severed at the time of her marriage, was never reestablished. Her relatives still considered her a fallen woman and avoided being contaminated by her reputation.

Her father-in-law had also disappointed the young widow. After her husband's death, as soon as her pain allowed her to consider other matters, she wrote Lourenço de Sousa Camargo, revealing the truth about the marriage and begging protection for his son's children.

The landowner, in a manner similar to that of Emília's relatives, disbelieved the reality of a marriage hitherto concealed and of which there were no documents or other proof.

The widow's letter merely revealed to him the continuation of a relationship he had supposed long dead.

Concluding that this woman's influence was the reason for his son's disobedience, he held her accountable for the misfortune that ensued, forgetting that no one had suffered as greatly as she, for in addition to widowhood, her husband's death had bequeathed her poverty and dishonor.

Even so, given his mental predisposition, Camargo was generous. He had one thousand *mil-réis* sent to Emília, cold and dry money unaccompanied by a word of comfort or hope. The bearer who delivered it to the widow left her with the feeling that such considerable charity should free the landowner from any future claims.

Emílio, who might have been his sister's natural support in the absence of their mother, was, unfortunately, incapable of assuming control of the demanding situation. To his father's irresoluteness he added a slow and thick-witted nature. Though he had attended the best schools, at eighteen he had achieved only the mastery of a twelve-year-old of average intelligence and diligence.

Realizing his ineptitude for any literary career, Emília had thought of preparing him for a life in business. Through her husband's correspondent, and soon after his death, the young man was hired as a salesman for a money broker.

However hard poor Emílio tried, he could not untangle the financial details of the trading of public funds and the fluctuations of the currency market. What any idler's son, whose mustache had not yet even sprouted, solved quickly—one, two, three—was for Emílio a science more abstruse than astronomy.

He brought home the interest tables, current quotes, exchange rates, and notes the broker had given him, sat at the table, prepared the inkwell and the paper but could not bring himself to begin. His spirit became entangled in those threads that he could neither weave nor unravel. Finally he cried with anger.

Aurélia, then, hastened to comfort him. She knew the reason for those tears; once, by dint of her love and tenderness, she had pried the explanation from him. She calmed his despair, urged him to make the effort, and in order to buttress his attempt, she aided his memory and guided his calculations.

Nature had bestowed upon Aurélia the lively and acute intelligence of the talented woman, which, if it does not attain a man's vigorous reasoning, has the precious malleability of lending itself to all matters, however diverse. That which her brother failed to master in months of practice was for her one week of study.

Thereafter, Emílio was the clerk who went to the trading center, received his boss's orders and brought him messages, but Aurélia was the broker who did all calculations and set the latest prices. Thus the sister spared her brother any grief and kept him in the position they had found at great pains.

It was quite obvious, therefore, that Emílio, rather than promising to be of support to his sister, would on the contrary, surely become, if not such already, an onerous sacrifice to the girl, who would be obliged to spend on him her time and the meager fruits of her labor.

Under these circumstances, the mother could envision for her daughter only the natural and competent support of a husband. Therefore, in conversation, she continuously touched on this point with Aurélia, regardless of the subject.

If the conversation veered toward her illness, which was progressing quickly, Emília would tell her daughter:

"What distresses me is that you are not married yet. Nothing else."

When they considered the money left by Pedro Camargo and that the alms from the landowner would come to an end one day, leaving them indigent, the widow would exclaim:

"Oh! If only I could see you married!"

The full burden of the household fell upon Aurélia. Her mother, debilitated by their misfortune and constrained by her infirmity, did what she could, making every effort to avoid becoming a cumbersome weight to her daughter. Though still alive, she wrapped herself in a shroud of resignation and dispensed with doctors, nurses, and apothecaries.

Domestic tasks, fewer in the home of the poor, yet nevertheless more demanding—laundry, bills from daily shopping, Emílio's accounts, and other needs—took up part of her day; the rest she spent sewing.

She hardly had time to glance out the window; with the exception of an occasional Sunday, when her mother managed to drag herself to Mass, or of a stroll in the evening accompanied by her brother, she never left the house.

This reclusion distressed the widow, who often suggested:

"Go stand at the window, Aurélia."

"I do not like to!" answered the girl.

Other times, faced with her mother's insistence, she found an excuse:

"I have to finish this dress."

Emília felt annoyed but said nothing. One afternoon, however, she voiced all that was on her mind.

"You are so pretty, Aurélia, that several young men, if only they could meet you, would fall in love. You could then choose any one you pleased."

"Marriage and shrouds are made in heaven, Mother," answered the girl, laughing to disguise her blushing.

Aurélia's heart had not yet opened itself; but though virgin to love, she had, notwithstanding, a vague sense of the overpowering feeling that fuses the destiny of two people into a single existence and, integrating each with the other, forms a family.

As all women of imagination and feeling, she found within herself, in the musings of her thoughts, that dawning of the soul called the ideal, which from afar gilds in its soft rays the horizons of life.

Marriage, when on occasion her thoughts turned to it, appeared to her spirit as something indistinct and confused, something akin to an enigma from whose center suddenly unfolded a magnificent sky that enveloped her, immersing her in happiness.

In her naiveté, Aurélia could not conceive of the idea of a rational, arranged marriage. But the insistence of her mother, ever fretful about the future, forced her to consider this aspect of real life.

She realized that she had no right to sacrifice to an imaginary dream, which might never come true, first her mother's tranquillity and then her own destiny; for what fate awaited her if she were unfortunate enough to be left alone in the world?

The blow she suffered about this time disposed her even further to sacrifice her aspirations.

Emílio, feeling very tired on an excessively hot afternoon, imprudently took a cold bath. As a consequence, he developed a fever of evil character that claimed him in a matter of days.

Aurélia, who loved her brother with maternal devotion, never left his bedside. The endless and extreme care she poured upon him, as well as the need to take responsibility for everything, was perhaps what saved her from being felled by this ill fortune.

Having barely survived the death of her son, the widow was now even more terrified at the isolation she would bequeath Aurélia. Although Emílio had been no hope of protection for his sister, he, in any case, afforded her some company and could at least provide her with material protection, if only by his presence.

She, therefore, intensified her pleas; and Aurélia, still in heavy mourning dress for her brother, complied with her mother's wishes and sat by the window every afternoon.

This public display of her beauty, with an eye to marriage, was a cruel torture for the girl. She overcame the repulsion at such a display of wares and endured the humiliation for love of the woman to whom she owed her being and whose only thought was for her happiness.

∞ III ∞

It took but a short time for the news of the pretty girl from St. Teresa to spread among a certain circle of young men who, never satisfied with the roses and daisies of the ballrooms, also passionately cultivate the violets and primroses of the window lattices.

The secluded and peaceful street was enlivened by an unusual traffic of tilburies and strollers, attracted by the beauty of this humble crawling flower, which some aspired to pluck and transplant into the whirlwind of the world, while others would be satisfied just to stain her purity, then abandon her to squalor.

The passionate and covetous looks of this crowd of suitors, the constrained smiles of the shy ones, the fatuous gestures and insinuating words of the bolder ones, were dashed by Aurélia's cold impassiveness. It was not the girl herself at the window, but a statue or, more appropriately, a wax figure from the showcase of a fashionable hairdresser.

The girl fulfilled to the letter the obligation she had imposed upon herself; she was on display to be coveted and to attract a groom. But she refused to go beyond this task of flaunting her beauty. The courtship artifices with which many girls enhance their charm, the tactics of dispensing smiles and sweet gestures or of denying them to quicken desire, Aurélia neither knew, nor would have the courage to use.

After spending an hour stationed at the window, she would retire to begin her evening of sewing; and of all the men who had passed before her in hopes of capturing her attention, she would remember no face, no word, no circumstance.

During the first month the assault of suitors was only a skirmish. Rounds on the sidewalk, tipping of hats, sighs in passing, symbolic gestures with handkerchiefs, some whispered flattery, and gifts of flowers that the girl declined: such were the methods of attack.

Shortly, however, the true assault began; and the one who served as example was an individual we know well by now, and from whom such familiarity would not be expected.

Lemos, always involved with a circle of young men, heard about the new minx on St. Teresa Street. The sprightly old man felt that, as her uncle, he had priority over this family possession.

He joined the line, and in the afternoon appeared at St. Teresa Street to speak for a second with his niece, to whom he had made himself known from the beginning.

Aurélia was very pleased to see her uncle. The affectionate tone in which he had spoken to her filled her with hopes of reconciliation with her family in the near future.

Fearing that her mother's wounded dignity would oppose it, she kept the fact from her.

During the next days her hopes flourished. Her stay at the window had ceased to be intolerable; there was now an interest that kept her there, looking ahead to the moment when her uncle appeared at the far end of the street.

She, who did not have for the most elegant gentlemen the faintest smile, found within herself, as a means to win over the old man, the secret of tenderness and coquettishness, much like the fragrance of a beautiful woman.

Aurélia was deeply interested in reestablishing relations between Dona Emília and her brother. In guaranteeing her protection for the future, this reconciliation would not only restore peace to her mother but also spare her this yearning for a marriage, a humiliation for the poor girl.

The mob of passionate street suitors was astonished and shocked to see the chubby old man leaning insolently every afternoon against Aurélia's window, talking and joking in great intimacy with the girl. Ignorant of the family tie, they attributed these liberties to an inexplicable matter of taste, for Lemos, notoriously poor, if not bankrupt, lacked the magic wand that dispenses with any virtue—money.

The shrewd old man decided to take advantage of his niece's willingness before any fortuitous circumstance arose to disturb this intimate relationship that he had skillfully woven.

One afternoon, after having flittered around Aurélia as usual, making her laugh with his wittiness, he bade farewell leaving in his niece's hands an elegant letter, decorated with flowers and sealed with forget-me-nots.

Aurélia received it with a slight surprise, but was soon struck by an idea and concealed the letter in her bosom, quivering with hope that inundated her soul.

The letter must contain the message of conciliation for which she had so fervently wished. As night fell, she ran to her room to read it.

At the first words, the smile that bloomed on her lips began to freeze and finally contracted into a gasp of anguish. When she finished, her face was mottled by that marble-like wanness that later would so often becloud her like an eclipse of her splendid soul.

She coldly folded the paper, which she locked in her small wooden case, and knelt by her bed before the crucifix that hung above the headboard.

As the swallow will not allow its feathers to be sullied by dust borne in the wind and, soaring, constantly dips its wings in the waves of the lake, so Aurélia felt the need to bathe in prayer and purify herself from being in contact with that maelstrom of vileness and infamy.

Lemos's letter was written in the commonplace style of a realistic courtship in which the simple vocabulary of passion carries a figurative meaning and expresses in slang not the impulses of feelings, but the seductions of self-interest.

The old man believed that his niece, like so many unfortunate girls caught up in the whirlwind, was merely awaiting the first one bold enough to snatch her from the obscurity where ravenous desires consumed her, to transport her to a life of luxury and scandal. He presented himself, therefore, quite overtly as the entrepreneur of such a metamorphosis, profitable for them both, and trusted that Aurélia was intelligent enough to understand.

When, the day following the delivery of the letter, he noticed that the shutters were obstinately closed whenever he passed by, Lemos realized that his first shot had gone awry, but he was not sufficiently disheartened to renounce his plan.

"The moment has not come yet!" he thought.

The old lad, like all positive men, had devised for his use a practical, if extremely simple, philosophy. Everything for him had a fated moment, an occasion; the great secret of life, therefore, could be summed up thus: watch for the occasion and grab it.

He calculated that his niece was not yet morally ready for a decision that would determine her future. Her woman's heart was still a bird without feathers; when her wings became fully grown, she would take flight and soar to the sky.

It behooved him, Lemos, to maintain a vigil over her during the transformation, so that he could intervene at the proper moment; and, he felt certain, at that time he would not miss his target.

The old man's example encouraged the braver ones. Trusting his audacity, one of them besieged the window, especially in the evening, when Aurélia sewed by the light of a gas lamp next to the sideboard.

Through the shutters, the suitor continually beseeched her with entreaties and protestations of love, with which he pursued the girl, insisting that she come to the lattice or at least accept his gifts and notes. After him, came the others.

Aurélia remained unmoved and so indifferent to these rivalries that she seemed not even to be aware of them. And indeed this was sometimes the case. Her cares diverted her attention and distanced her from the tumult in the street.

Nevertheless, those disturbances annoyed, and above all, offended her; since they would not stop, they finally led her to a decision that revealed certain impulses of her character.

One evening, when one of the more persistent suitors exhausted her patience, she rose, with perfect self-control, and went to the lattice, opened it, and invited the gentleman in. Taken by surprise, he hesitated and did not know what to do, but finally accepted the girl's invitation.

"Please sit down," said Aurélia, pointing to the old sofa by the far wall. "I will call my mother."

The *roué* moved to prevent her but did not succeed. He was beginning to consider the desirability of vanishing when Aurélia returned with her mother.

The young girl went back to her sewing, and Dona Emília sat on the sofa and engaged her guest in conversation.

The widow's ordinary and simple words convinced the would-be seducer, despite the layer of skepticism that lines this biped species, that his efforts were in vain. Aurélia's beauty was accessible only to those simpletons who still use the banal and anachronic means of marriage.

This incident signaled a desertion that was complete in less than a month. In its entirety, that pack of suitors retreated in full flight, from the moment they sensed the dangers and scandals of a matrimonial passion.

Thus Aurélia regained her peace, freeing herself from the torture inflicted by that insulting obeisance.

Now, when she sat by the window to gratify her mother, it was no longer such a bitter sacrifice. Her natural disdain sufficed to rebuff the inclinations of even the most intractable. These had not yet totally renounced hope of inspiring an irresistible passion, one capable of overcoming the strictest virtue.

❦ IV ❦

Seixas had heard about the girl from St. Teresa, but busy as he was at the time with some aristocratic dalliance, was not sufficiently curious to rush immediately to meet this new beauty.

However, he happened to be having dinner in the neighborhood at a friend's house, together with some companions. The conversation turned to Aurélia, still the talk of the town; they told anecdotes and made every kind of comment.

After dinner, toward the end of the afternoon, the friends left on foot, with the excuse of going for a stroll, but actually to show Seixas the girl they had mentioned and convince him that she was truly a masterpiece of exceptional beauty.

Seixas was of an aristocratic nature, though in politics he tended to flaunt some trappings of liberalism. As an artistic convention he admitted rustic and plebeian beauty, but true loveliness, the supreme feminine grace, the incarnation of love, this he could appreciate only in a woman enveloped in the aura of elegance.

The group stopped in front of Dona Emília's house and Seixas was able to admire the girl's bust to his heart's content. At first he examined her coldly, as an artist studies his model. He saw her through the expression of proud and sad indifference she wore like a veil protecting her beauty from insolent stares.

However, when Aurélia flushed and turned her face, and her large eyes clouded in a kind of translucent mist as she met the scrutinizing eyes sculpturing her profile, Fernando could not contain himself and exclaimed:

"Indeed—"

Curbing his initial excitement, however, he corrected himself:

"I do not deny it. She is pretty."

That evening, engaged in her sewing, Aurélia tried to recall the image of this gentleman who had gazed at her for some time in the afternoon; she was unable to do so. She had seen him for only a second; she had not retained any features of his countenance.

But amazingly, when she retreated into her innermost self, she found him there and saw his image, just as she beheld it that afternoon. It was an indistinct shape, almost a shadow; but she recognized him and she would mistake him for no other man.

Two days later, Seixas returned to St. Teresa Street; but alone this time. From afar his eyes met Aurélia's, which withdrew to return shy and submissive. As he walked by, he greeted her; she responded with a slight nod of her head.

Another week went by. Seixas did not come in the afternoon as usual; it was evening and Aurélia was about to retire, sad and forlorn. As she was closing the shutters, she caught sight of a figure and waited. It was Fernando. The gentleman took her hand and declared his love. Aurélia listened to him, trembling with emotion, enraptured by her happiness.

"And you, Dona Aurélia?" asked Seixas. "Do you love me?"

"Me?"

The girl uttered the monosyllable with an expression of deep surprise. She thought Fernando must be aware that, with his first look, he had taken possession of her soul.

"I do not know," she answered smiling, "You should know, sir."

Seixas did not understand how sublime were the girl's modest and simple words. The dalliance of the salons had inured his heart and dulled the delicate touch that might have sensed the timorous vibrations of that virgin soul.

Fernando visited the humble dwelling on St. Teresa regularly, spending there the first hours of an evening that usually ended at a ball or at the opera. When he left the unpretentious parlor where his passion bound him to his beloved's eyes, the elegant gentleman felt somewhat abashed. It seemed to him that he was derogating his aristocratic habits, and he was disturbed lest he should stain the perfection of his fine distinction.

For a month, Aurélia lived inebriated by the ultimate joy of loving and being loved. Enraptured in her friend's soul, the hours Seixas spent beside her were a time of ecstasy. The affection received sufficed to fill with dreams and reveries the periods of his absence. It would be difficult to say which the gentle girl loved more, on which her life depended more: the man who visited her daily at nightfall or the ideal her imagination had copied from that model.

Like Pygmalion, she had fashioned a statue, and, perhaps, like the mythological artist, she had fallen in love with this creature, of whom the man was only a rough sketch. And is this not the eternal legend of love, in souls illuminated by the sacred fire?

Among those in love with Aurélia was Eduardo Abreu, a twenty-five-year-old gentleman, from an excellent family, rich and renowned among the most distinguished in the court.

Although rather serious and not prone to adventures, Abreu was tempted by the fascination of an easy and ephemeral love affair. He joined the ranks of Aurélia's suitors, but kept himself to the rear, among the more timid.

When the professional wooers dispersed, he persisted without changing, however, his shy and reserved ways. An old cobbler who had given himself the task of keeping a logbook of the tollgate, continued to see the young man who rode by every afternoon on his Cape horse.

The impression Aurélia made upon his spirit grew deeper as the girl's purity became more evident. When he finally saw the audacity of Rio's most dangerous seducers dash against her virtue, Abreu's feelings overflowed with admiration and respect.

It is natural that this gentleman, whose standing allowed him to aspire to the best matches in Rio's society, should ponder at length before deciding. But once resolved, he did not hesitate to effect his plan. He went to Dona Emília and asked for her daughter's hand.

The widow, still reeling from this unexpected stroke of luck, spoke to Aurélia:

"God has heard my prayers. Now I can die in peace."

The girl heard without interrupting Dona Emília's exposition on the advantages of marrying Abreu. In her good mother's words she not only sensed extreme loving tenderness, but also recognized the prudence of her counsel.

Nonetheless, her answer was a formal refusal.

"I had decided to accept the first proposal my mother considered desirable to appease her spirit and dispel the worries that consume her. My young girl's dreams, as petty as they once were, I would gladly sacrifice to see her happy. Now everything has changed. I cannot give that which does not belong to me. I love another."

"I know—Seixas. And are you sure that he will marry you?"

"I have never asked him, my mother."

"But we must know."

"I will not talk about this with him."

"Then I will."

In fact, that evening, when Fernando arrived, Dona Emília guided the conversation to the delicate matter. At the first opportunity she questioned him about his intentions. She stressed the formidable argument of the shadow that a highly visible courtship casts on a young lady's reputation when not perfumed by budding orange blossoms. She also reminded him that the exclusive preference drove away other suitors, with no guarantee of a future.

Seixas was disturbed. However prepared a gentleman of high society is for this confrontation, he still is moved by the need to choose between affection and advantages. Even more so when, to escape this dilemma, such a man has defined a sinuous path along which he creeps like a reptile, snaking between love and self-interest.

"I assure you, Dona Emília, that I have the purest intentions. If I had not expressed them yet, it was because I was awaiting the moment when I could execute them immediately, as befits such a matter. My career depends on events that should take place this next year. Then shall I be able to offer Aurélia a future worthy of her, enviable for the most elegant ladies in the court. Prior to this I dare not bind her to my uncertain fortune, which might turn out to be rather meager. I honestly love your daughter, madam; and this love strengthens me against the selfishness of passion. I would rather lose her than make a sacrifice of her."

"That is a very noble attitude on your part, Mr. Seixas. Truly you could give no clearer indication of your regard for Aurélia than to renounce her rather than stand in the way of a union that will make her happy."

Once she had spoken these words, the ailing lady, to whom the conversation had been extremely tiring, retired. Fernando remained in the parlor, dazed at the outcome the conversation had led to, so unlike his expectation.

He had believed in fact that Dona Emília, lulled by the hope of the brilliant future rendered golden by his touching words, and moved by the tenor of his passion, would allow him to sweetly cultivate the forget-me-not right there, in this flowerbed of a humble, shy parlor, poorly lit by a dim gas lamp.

Rising at last, he went to the corner of the room, where Aurélia worked totally absorbed in her own thoughts, removed from the scene that had just taken place—of which, nonetheless, she was the subject, and perhaps the victim.

What was the reason for the girl's inexplicable indifference at that moment? She herself might not have been able to express it. Possibly the consequences of the conversation weighed more heavily on her spirit than the words exchanged by her mother and Seixas.

"What does this mean, Aurélia?" asked the young man.

"She is a mother, Fernando, and is entitled to worry about her daughter's future. As for me, you know my love is unconditional, and never have I asked you where this love was taking me. I know it means my happiness, and for me that is enough."

The following day Dona Emília told her daughter the result of her conversation with Seixas and reiterated her advice with the usual reasons.

"Should I have the misfortune of losing you, my mother, your daughter would not be alone anymore. She would be stayed not only by your memory but also by a love that will never abandon her."

The widow let slip a gesture of doubt.

"Believe me, Mother, the wish to remain worthy of the man I love would protect me more than a husband chosen at random."

Dona Emília did not insist further. She recalled that she too had sacrificed herself for a similar love and could not demand of her daughter more courage than she had once had to resist an impulse of the heart.

Seixas, who had left Aurélia the evening before, moved by the girl's innocent selflessness, upon learning that she had unceremoniously rejected a match for which many a noble young lady pined, could not restrain the impulses of his generous soul.

He presented himself at Dona Emília's house and asked for Aurélia's hand: it was granted.

When he learned that his niece's marriage had been agreed upon, Lemos recognized that his plans had been defeated. However, as he was not the kind to abandon a good idea easily, he pondered a way not to lose the contest.

The only idea that occurred to him was rather trite; but it happens that it is precisely these kinds of plans that produce the best results in matters to be resolved by social interests.

On his way to Aurélia's house, Seixas used to notice, at a window on Mangueiras Street, a young girl deemed among the elegant in the court. To our journalist, it had always been an unqualified act of rudeness to cross paths with a beautiful and distinguished lady without directing to her a glance and a smile that bore testimony to his admiration.

Seixas belonged to that class of men, engendered by modern society, for whom love has ceased to be a feeling and has become an obligatory act of attentiveness between well-bred gentlemen and ladies.

The girl belonged to the same school. Like Seixas, she was engaged to be married; nonetheless, she was delighted to receive the gallant compliment. If by chance they met each other in some drawing room, absent from those to whom they were betrothed, they would, with no qualm, weave an inno-cent idyll to bring amusement to their evening.

In this house on Mangueiras Street lived Tavares do Amaral, a customs clerk. Lemos, who often visited an old friend in the neighborhood, perhaps with the intention of maintaining an observation post already in mind, noted the exchanges between Fernando and Adelaide.

The first time he met Amaral on Ouvidor Street, the old man wormed his way into his confidence and under the pretext of congratulating him, stressed the advantages of a marriage between his daughter and Seixas.

"If you play your cards right, you will catch the rascal!" he concluded as he bade farewell.

Amaral did not look with favor on his daughter's close relationship with Dr. Torquato Ribeiro, who, besides being poor, was experiencing financial trouble. Lemos's idea pleased him. He found a way to introduce Seixas into his home, and to the young man the new acquaintance was a powerful tonic.

Once the first effusions of pure and deep-seated contentment occasioned by the generous impulse of proposing to Aurélia had dissolved, Fernando began to consider the practical effect such a marriage would have on his life.

He calculated the material responsibilities to which he must subject him-self in order to furnish a new home and maintain it properly. He recalled the extent of the wardrobe expenses of a lady who attends social functions, and realized that as yet he could not afford to marry a beautiful and elegant lady, naturally prone to luxury, the flower of those butterflies of silken and lace wings.

To enclose himself in obscure but sweet domestic warmth; to live on placid, intimate affections; to devote himself to creating a family where souls united by conjugal love are revitalized and multiply—this supreme happiness Seixas could not understand. Seen from this perspective, marriage seemed to him an exile that inspired in him an indefinable terror.

He could never live far from society, withdrawn from this elegant world that was his country and the cradle of his soul. Superior natures obey hidden forces. It is predestination. With some, it is glory; with others, money. With him it was—gallantry.

Sometimes, Seixas, fearing for his health under relentless exposure to the action of noxious habits and the influence of an enervating climate, would visit the farm of a friend in Campos, intending to stay perhaps two months, merely vegetating, waking with the sun and retiring with it.

If it happened to be the party season and there were dances and games in the countryside, mimicking life at the court, he might stay two weeks, time enough to create a gentle pastoral romance with some spirited country girl, which would end like one of Lamartine's stanzas.

When, however, the farm was peaceful amid the sweet monotony of rural tasks, Fernando would give himself with unflagging zeal to what he called the country life. He would rise at the break of dawn, bathe, wander about the plantation, and return for lunch with a nosegay of various kinds of orchids and bromeliads. When the sun was high, he would visit the mills to watch coffee beans being hulled or cornmeal being made.

This enthusiasm for the bucolic would last three days. On the fourth Fernando would find some excuse for a hasty return, and within a week he was reintegrated in the court. The first evening at a ball or a party was a resurrection.

Of a man thus organized by the molecule of luxury and gallantry, one could not expect the enormous sacrifice of renouncing a life of finery. This was beyond his powers; it was an aberration of his nature. It would have been easier to renounce life itself at the apex of his youth, when fortune smiled on him, than to subject himself to this moral suicide, to this annihilation of his ego.

When Seixas became convinced that he could not marry Aurélia, he reviled himself. He could not forgive his indiscretion of falling in love with a poor girl, virtually an orphan, an indiscretion climaxing in a proposal of marriage. To him, breaking off this ill-conceived engagement was inevitable, fated; but his conduct vexed him.

This contradiction between Seixas's conscience and his will entailed a psychological abnormality far from rare in today's society. The distortion of certain moral principles, dissimulated by breeding and social interests, engenders these deformities in men of integrity.

Who has not read Otávio Feuillet's novel in which he glorifies with the title of honor the final hesitations of a deeply corrupted soul?

Seixas was far from being a Camors; but the deadening of his moral sense had already begun, for the impact of an advanced civilization, if one is surrounded by a society just as corrupted as Paris's, will in the end give rise to such monsters.

To the *roué* of Rio de Janeiro, lying to a lady, implying hope of marriage, betraying a friend, seducing his wife, were maneuvers in a social game permitted by the code of a fashionable way of life. Schoolboy morality had nothing to do with how classy people amused themselves.

To go back on one's word, however, to rescind without cause a formal pledge of marriage, was, in Seixas's mind, an act unbecoming to a gentleman. In his particular case, this breach of promise was even more serious.

Aurélia had no one except her mother, consumed by the illness that left her only a short time to live. With Dona Emília gone, her daughter would be left an orphan, without shelter, unprotected. Abandoning a poor girl, known to be betrothed to him, in this plight, would surely create a scandal.

Apart from the disapprobation this would cause in his circle, his own conscience warned him of the impropriety of such behavior, which he did not consider overly severe to label as underhanded.

These anxieties wore down Seixas's congenial and pleasant spirits. His features did not lose their affable expression, which constituted the best of his noble and intelligent countenance; nor did the smile that seemed the matrix of his persuasive speech fade from his lips; but beneath this display of good spirits lurked a hint of sadness, which must have been deep, for it settled in that changeable and carefree nature.

Aurélia noticed immediately the change that had occurred in her fiancé and inquired as to the reason. Fernando dissembled; the girl did not insist and even seemed to forget her observation.

One evening, however, when Seixas seemed more preoccupied, as they were about to part, she said:

"Your promise of marriage troubles you, Fernando; I give it back to you. For me, your love is enough—I have already told you once. After you gave it to me, I have asked for nothing more."

Fernando weakly objected to Aurélia's words and formulated a question whose intention the girl did not grasp:

"Do you believe, Aurélia, that a girl can love a man she has no hope of marrying?"

"The proof is that I love you," answered the girl innocently.

"And the world?" said Seixas, things unspoken in his eyes.

"The world is entitled to demand of me the dignity of a woman, which you, more than anyone, know I respect. As for my love, I am answerable to none but God, Who gave me a soul, and to you, to whom I surrendered it."

Fernando left even more unhappy and disheartened. Those deep and passionate feelings of sublime abnegation, by flattering his self-esteem, bound him even more to the beautiful girl from whom his aristocratic instincts and the panicky terror of toil and mediocrity were wrenching him.

When he had suggested to Aurélia the matter of his ambiguous position, he hoped to arouse misgivings that might provide him an excuse to end once and for all this sweet, yet dangerous relationship. The girl's response baffled him.

It was in this situation that Seixas received Amaral's offer and, ceding to his kind entreaties, began to frequent his house.

Without this incident, he would have gone on debating this conflict visited upon him by circumstances, hoping that time would offer the solution that his indolent nature would never move to advance.

That slight deviation, however, had launched him from the maelstrom, subjecting him to a new current that was to overpower him and bear him far away.

Torquato Ribeiro loved Adelaide dearly. The girl's inconstancy offended him, and he withdrew from the house, leaving an open field to his opponent, who scarcely had need of this advantage. Amaral, following Lemos's advice, attempted, as the old man said, to strike while the iron was hot.

Seixas, invited to dinner at the clerk's house one Sunday, smoked a delicious Havana as he rose from the table covered with fine delicacies, while tracing with languid eyes the graceful contours of Adelaide's shape; she smiled at him from the piano, lulling him with the softest of nocturnes.

Amaral sat beside him and, without preamble or circumlocution, offered him point-blank his daughter with a dowry of thirty thousand.

Seixas accepted. At that moment this marriage project was a foretaste of the delights conjured by his fantasy, stimulated less by the champagne than by Adelaide's seductiveness.

The main reason for Seixas's decision was, however, quite different. He acted as do debtors who escape their obligations by going bankrupt.

Concerned that he lacked the courage to recover his freedom, he mortgaged himself to others, who might lay claim to and defend him as their property.

∞ VI ∞

Aurélia's evenings were now lonely.

Fernando would show up only rarely, offering an excuse to justify his absences. The girl, who would not think of questioning him, did not contest these pointless fabrications either. On the contrary, she tried to keep the unpleasant subject out of the conversation.

The young woman realized that Seixas was withdrawing his love, but the pride within her heart allowed her no complaint. Furthermore, she had unique ideas about love, perhaps inspired by the special position in which she found herself as she became a young woman.

She did not believe she was entitled to Seixas's love, for whatever affection he had for her, whether much or little, was a gift he bestowed upon her. When she considered that this love had saved her from the humiliation of a marriage of convenience, a name used to give decorum to the matrimonial market, she felt impelled to worship Seixas as her God and redeemer.

This fervent passion may seem strange, so rich in heroic devotion, yet observing calmly, almost impassively, the ebbing of affection on the part of the man she loved and allowing itself to be abandoned, offering no protest, and making no effort to deter happiness as it flees.

This phenomenon must have had a psychological basis, research into which we will forego, because the heart, especially a woman's, which is her all, represents the chaos of the moral world. No one knows what wonders, or what monsters, may emerge from those limbos.

I suspect, however, that the explanation for this uniqueness has already been made manifest. Aurélia loved more her love than her lover; she was a poet before a woman, preferring the ideal to the man.

Those who do not fathom the power of this motivation should ask themselves why some admire the stars with their feet on the ground while others, having climbed to the summit, stoop to pick up coins from the rug.

Since obligating himself with Amaral, Fernando had considered breaking the ties that still bound him to Aurélia. So disposed, he resumed his visits.

At first the girl, thinking that Seixas had returned to her, was filled with joy, but the illusion was short-lived. She quickly understood that it was not the wish to see her or to be with her that brought the gentleman to her house, for during the few moments he lingered he was completely inattentive and seemed perplexed.

"You want to tell me something but fear hurting me," observed the girl one evening with angelic resignation.

Fernando took advantage of the occasion to resolve the crisis.

"My most fervent wish, Aurélia, my life's golden dream, was to attain a brilliant position and place it at the feet of the only woman in the world I have loved. But the fate that weighs upon me has shattered all my hopes, and it would be selfish of me to prevail upon your feelings and tie you to an obscure and troubled existence. The sanctity of my love has given me the strength to resist its very impulses. Foreseeing this cruel situation, I once told your mother that I would be less wretched renouncing your hand than accepting it and bringing you unhappiness, condemning you to the humiliations of poverty."

"Those I already know," answered Aurélia with a touch of irony, "and they do not frighten me; I was born to them, and they have accompanied me throughout my life."

"You did not understand me, Aurélia; I was referring to a favorable match that will certainly appear as soon as you are free."

"Do you think, then, that a word from you is enough to restore my freedom?" asked the girl, smiling.

"I know that the fate that separates us cannot sever the link that joins our souls and which will reunite them in a better world. But God has presented us with a mission in this world and we must fulfill it."

"Mine is to love you. The vow that afflicts you, you may withdraw as spontaneously as you made it. I have never asked you for even the simplest indulgence towards my feelings; nor will I now that it disquiets you."

"Listen, Aurélia! Bear in mind your reputation. What would they say if you accepted the courtship of a man with no hope of marrying him?"

"They would perhaps say that I sacrificed a brilliant match to a scorned love, which would be—"

The girl cut the irony short, withdrawing:

"But no. They would fall short of the truth. I have not sacrificed any match; to sacrifice is to renounce a benefit. What I did was to defend my affection. Let us be honest: you no longer love me; I do not blame you, nor am I complaining."

Seixas muttered some excuse and took his leave.

Aurélia remained for a moment at the window, as she always did, to follow her lover with her eyes to the end of the street. Had Fernando not been so enraptured by the satisfaction of having regained his freedom, he would have heard the echo of a sob as he turned the corner.

The following day, Dona Emília received from Seixas one of those letters that explain nothing, but express everything by their calculated ambiguity. Upon finishing the epistolary riddle, the widow understood that the projected wedding had been abjured, and she estimated the consequences. The good mother still nurtured hopes of persuading her daughter to accept Abreu's hand.

Around this time Torquato Ribeiro began to frequent Dona Emília's house.

He had heard how Seixas had acted toward the widow, and the circumstances of adversity attracted him. He mentioned Adelaide's inconstancy to Aurélia and attributed it to his poverty.

The young woman listened to him tenderly and comforted him; but despite the intimacy that developed between them she never spoke of her own feelings. Modesty about her sadness did not allow her to confide in anyone. It may actually have been pride; but she draped it in modest and frank privacy.

Ribeiro's remonstrations about the betrayal of which he had been victim had cast a bitter suspicion into Aurélia's mind. Could Fernando have been attracted to Amaral's wealth rather than to Adelaide's love?

The girl constantly rejected this idea, instilled by Ribeiro's feelings of resentment; but the moment came when they finally wrested away the comforting doubt.

She received an anonymous letter. It said that Seixas had abandoned her for a dowry of thirty thousand. When she finished reading the words, she raised her hand to her breast to sustain her faint heart.

Never had she felt such pain. With resignation and indifference, she had suffered disdain and rejection, but the debasement of the man she loved was an unending torture, divined only by those who have seen their soul's spark extinguished, leaving them only nothingness.

In vain Aurélia took refuge in her first dreams of love. Seixas's degradation intruded on the ideal the girl had engendered in her imagination, stigmatizing it. She had forgiven her faithless lover everything, save his being unworthy of her love.

What a poignant dilemma! Either banish from her heart this fallen love, and leave life forever barren of affection, or humiliate herself by worshiping this defiled being and linking herself to his shame.

The news of the behavior attributed to Seixas was nothing but an anonymous accusation, which might have been maliciously inspired.

Nevertheless, Aurélia believed it implicitly; a voice within told her that it was the truth.

A few hours later, approaching the gate to open it for the maid, through the lattice she saw Lemos pass by, looking at the house with roguish eyes.

The thought that he was the author of the letter crossed her mind; and it was confirmed when, in the course of the next days, she noticed the old man's maneuvers vainly attempting to catch her at the window.

As Dona Emília expected, Eduardo Abreu returned as soon as he learned of Seixas's withdrawal. Aurélia received him, filled with appreciation for the tender feelings she had inspired in this young man and with admiration for his noble character.

"I do not belong to myself, Mr. Abreu; if one day I freed myself from this ill-fated love and recovered possession of my being, believe me, I would proudly share your destiny."

Three days later a ship was leaving for Europe. Abreu booked passage and went to be flustered in Paris, where he shed the illusions of his youth and some tens of thousands, but not the memory of Aurélia.

Meanwhile Seixas was beginning to feel the weight of the new yoke to which he had submitted himself.

Marriage, unless it afforded him a brilliant position and wealth, was nothing short of disaster.

The expenses of maintaining just his own personal level of ostentation fully absorbed his annual income, as well as the supplementary credit. What would become of him when, in addition to his own, he must provide luxury for an elegant woman, who consumes in silk alone more than enough to feed a very large family? Not to mention the house, which, if as a bachelor he had successfully reduced to mythical status, would acquire, for the husband of a fashionable lady, an expensive reality.

The promise to Adelaide's father was explicit and formal. Under no circumstance could Seixas negate it or shamelessly go back on his word; but as he had not committed himself to wed by a certain date, he hoped that time, the great problem solver, might bring about some lucky accident to free him.

Around this time, things took a favorable turn for the candidacy of which our writer had long dreamed, and as it coincided with the departure of that certain northern star, it occurred to Fernando to take an eroto-political trip to Pernambuco, at state expenses.

He would have never decided on this year-long exile, however, had he not hoped that the postponement might exhaust Adelaide's patience.

Both the girl and her father pressed to celebrate the wedding before his departure, but Fernando, having learned as part of his apprenticeship for government office the craftiness of ministers of state in preparation for emulating them in a not too-distant future, offered *raisons d'état* to counter his bride's demands.

He had received orders from the government to depart immediately. If he refused, he risked dismissal.

∽ VII ∽

One day, in the morning, there was a knock at Dona Emília's door.

When the widow and the daughter went to the living room, they found, seated on the sofa, an elderly man, tall and husky, whose clothes revealed him to be from the provinces or the backlands. He had a ruddy face, with hard, prominent features.

He fixed his steady gaze on Aurélia, without rising at the ladies' approach. Having thus examined the young girl with uncommon insistence, he turned to the widow. He noticed her worn black housedress and again turned his forbidding eyes to the girl.

Dona Emília, frightened by this behavior, exchanged an unspoken signal with her daughter. Both feared they were in the presence of a madman or drunkard. Convinced that they were being subjected to some form of disrespect, they did not know what to do.

In the meantime, tears began flowing copiously from the old man's eyes. Rising suddenly, he ran to Aurélia and lifted her in his arms before she could evade him.

"What is this, sir? Are you crazy?" said Dona Emília rising to her feet to defend her daughter.

At the widow's words and Aurélia's scream, the old man stepped back and tried to speak, but a sob choked his voice:

"Don't you recognize me, my daughter? I am your husband's father!"

"Mr. Lourenço Camargo?"

"Precisely. Will you allow me to embrace my granddaughter?"

It was Aurélia who threw herself into the old man's arms, and he, after holding her close to his breast for some time, moved away abruptly and sat on the sofa, wiping his face with a large silk handkerchief rolled into a ball.

"You are the very image of my Pedro. The poor boy!" muttered the old man.

After some questions about Aurélia's name and age, the farmer explained the reason for being there at that time to reconcile himself with his daughter-in-law, filled with remorse at the way he had treated her.

At the inn or ranch in which he had died, Pedro Camargo had left his bag. The innkeeper had kept it with the intention of taking it to the farm or sending it with the first bearer. There it remained for years until one day an antman, the name we give the expert who kills the harmful insect that destroys our harvests, happened by.

The aforesaid was on his way to Camargo's farm to offer his services, and agreed to take the bag. When he received it, the old farmer once more felt memories of his son being rekindled; he dried his eyes and ordered a fire to be started in the yard to burn the objects that had belonged to the deceased.

As his order was being carried out, he opened the bag and removed one by one the soiled items, a small toiletry kit and other things of everyday use. At the bottom there was a volume wrapped in paper and tied with a black ribbon.

It contained photographs of Pedro Camargo, his wife and his two children, the marriage certificate and the baptismal certificate of the two children, and finally a letter without envelope addressed to the farmer.

This letter, dated long before his death, indicated that Pedro Camargo had first considered committing suicide and had prepared himself to carry out his plan, writing to his father to beg forgiveness for his shortcoming.

After confessing the marriage he had concealed only for fear of grieving his father, he beseeched him to protect his widow and the innocent orphans who were his grandchildren and who would replace him, Pedro, in love and reverence.

As he read this letter, Lourenço Camargo became aware that he had received his son's last words and recalled his injustice at questioning the reality of a marriage of which he now had before him the irrefutable proof.

His was a crude, but upright soul.

That same evening he left for the court. Through his correspondent he asked for information about the neighborhood and learned that the widow still lived in the same house.

After these explanations, which elicited tears from the two ladies, especially when they read Pedro Camargo's letter, the old man paced about the living room and, picking up his hat, said:

"Cry as much as you like. I will be back later."

Indeed he returned every day while he stayed at the court. He would have loved to shower Aurélia and her mother with gifts, but the two ladies were loath to accept from his excessive generosity and he was annoyed:

"All right. I will not give you anything anymore. When you need something, ask for it."

Two days after this incident the old man called upon them, bearing a sealed packet of paper. As he took it from his jacket pocket, he frowned playfully at Aurélia:

"Do not think it is a present, no madam! Rest assured. I want you to keep this paper here, until I come back."

"If it contains money, I think you had better—" Aurélia began.

"No money! You seem to feel that my cash is dirty!"

"No, not that, Grandfather. You can see that two women in a house like this cannot offer much security."

"Well, you should know that this is a piece of paper—a document I have registered, and so as not to lose it on my trip, I leave it in your hands."

On the cover were these words written in a round, carefully scribed calligraphy: "For my granddaughter, Aurélia, to keep until I, her grandfather, request it. L.S.Camargo."

The old man departed for his farm, having sent ahead masons, carpenters, and painters to transform, as quickly as possible, the old and dirty countryhouse into something worthy of receiving Pedro Camargo's family, with a certain pomp that the farmer thought essential as reparation for his former indifference.

In addition to the building itself, there were also in the household routine some ingrained habits that tend to become established on some farms, especially when the owners are unmarried. Camargo needed at least a month to suppress certain familiarities formerly tolerated and to abolish a kind of skirt or loincloth that lent the female slaves the appearance of dancers, albeit without the stockings and the gauze ruffles.

Camargo realized that these details, innocent as they might seem to a grizzled old man like him, might be jarring to courtly scruples. But even if this idea had not crossed his mind, it was enough to have seen Aurélia and breathed the atmosphere of proud chastity surrounding the beautiful girl to not dare to defile her by contact with such indecencies.

Soon after Camargo's departure, Dona Emília suffered another attack of her chronic illness; but it was so grave that the doctor was seriously concerned. The paroxysm yielded to powerful medication, but the widow never again left her bed, where she agonized for almost two months.

This was the most trying period of Aurélia's life, for to the bitter sorrows of having been deceived by love was added the pain of her mother's suffering. And as if this blow were not enough to crush her, poverty appeared with its retinue to aggravate the situation.

When Camargo, sent by Providence, arrived to acknowledge his daughter-in-law and granddaughter, the two ladies' existence had already become quite difficult. Once the money the muleteer had brought them was exhausted, they lived on Aurélia's sewing and on the income from some jewelry, gifts remaining from Pedro.

But these meager resources were not enough, and they would have suffered hardship were it not for the credit they obtained at the store and the grocery where they bought their supplies.

The widow paid these debts with part of the money the landowner had left her, and the rest she gave to her daughter for their expenses.

While this sum lasted, Aurélia had the means to face her expenses; but these grew larger with her mother's sickness, and soon there was nothing to take to market to buy a chicken for the ailing woman's broth.

Only under these circumstances did Aurélia finally yield to Dr. Torquato Ribeiro's entreaties, and borrowed fifty *mil-réis* from him. Until then she had always refused his offer and attempted to conceal the hardships she faced.

It is true that Aurélia expected to receive at any moment the help she had requested of her grandfather. She had written him as soon as her mother's illness had worsened, and she was surprised at the lack of an answer, or of news from the farm.

Only later would she discover the reason. Upon his return to the farm, Lourenço Camargo found a mob of idlers, who claimed to be his nephews, and with them their wives and the pack of louts and minxes that comprised the brood of those kinsfolk.

Camargo could not stand them. To get rid of them, he allowed them to sponge off him once a year, but did not permit them to linger in his house more than one night, and then only if the weather was bad.

You can imagine, then, how the old man felt when he found them all there at once, with their appurtenances, making themselves very much at home.

But Camargo's rage knew no limits when the intruders had the effrontery to confess the reason they had gathered there.

They had been informed by a reliable source that the old man had made his will at the court, and surmised that he had bequeathed his entire estate to a girl, the daughter of some fallen woman, a former mistress of Pedro Camargo's.

In view of this, they had come together to inform their uncle that they would not tolerate such robbery. If, as they expected, he did not rectify his mistake, for which purpose they had brought a notary, he should be warned right away that they would have the will nullified on the basis of his designating an unqualified heir. On this point they trusted the word of a shyster, whom they had taken the caution to bring with them.

Old Camargo controlled himself during this exegesis, but as one controls the torrent that rises to burst the dam, and the storm that gathers until it erupts.

When the shyster, snuff box open, advanced the two tobacco-stained fingers to grasp the pinch meant to distill in his nose mucus and eloquence, they caught nothing. The tortoise-shell snuff box flew out of his hands at Camargo's punch. He then snatched a mule harness hanging on the veranda and lashed out at his kin, dispersing them with blows of leather and iron.

Men, women, children, everyone was driven away. At the same time, the farmer called out for his blacks and arming them with fetters and whips, scourged from his house the plague that had invaded it. Only after he had seen them to the road with their bundles and luggage did the old man return.

But the sturdy body, which in spite of its seventy years had summoned this portentous physical effort, could not resist the impact of the stupendous rage that had undermined his soul. When he had no one left on whom to vent his indignation, it rose to his brain and dealt him a mortal blow.

The attack paralyzed him completely; the vital force of his system struggled almost two months within that lifeless body, until it finally faded away. Throughout this time he was unconscious. Aurélia's letters remained in the drawer, where the manager had placed them.

Within a few days Dona Emília also passed away, leaving Aurélia totally orphaned. During the cruel ordeal, Dr. Torquato Ribeiro did not leave the girl's side, and it was because of his entreaties that Dona Firmina Mascarenhas took the orphan into her home.

With the exception of this relative, no other person from her family appeared or sent word to Aurélia's house during her mother's illness or after her demise. Lemos and his people remained distant.

ಎ **VIII** ಎ

In accepting Dona Firmina's company, Aurélia had no intention of becoming a burden to her relative.

When the week of mourning was over, she placed through Dr. Torquato Ribeiro an advertisement in the newspaper offering, under satisfactory conditions, her services as schoolteacher or tutor in a family's home. She was willing, however, to descend to the more modest level of seamstress or even nursemaid to an elderly lady. More than a month went by without any serious offer. The only ones interested were a few libertines seeking some cheap adventure at one hundred *réis* per line. Dona Firmina, however, recognized their insidiousness and dismissed them from the steps without allowing them to see the girl.

Aurélia was contemplating placing another advertisement when she was sought out by a business man looking for her new residence. He was the late Camargo's correspondent, come to apprise the young lady of the farmer's death.

"You have in your possession a document that my friend asked you to keep, advising me that in case anything happened to him I should tell you to open it. It is as if he had a premonition."

The document was Lourenço de Sousa Camargo's will, in which he recognized and legitimized as his son Pedro Camargo, who had married Dona Emília Lemos, and named his granddaughter Dona Aurélia Camargo, born to a legal marriage, as his sole and universal heir.

With the will, the old man had enclosed a detailed list of everything he owned, in his own handwriting, with various explanations concerning some minor business matters still pending and advice about the future management of the farms.

Camargo's estate was calculated in the neighborhood of one million. No sooner had the news spread of Aurélia's inheriting such a large fortune than all her relatives rushed to her house, and at the head of the pack was Lemos with his coterie.

While his wife and daughters smothered with self-serving praises and tenderness the orphan whom they had failed when she was poor, Lemos, shrewd in his dealings, arranged with the Court of Orphans to be appointed his niece's guardian.

Aurélia's first impulse was to object to this appointment and show the judge the disgraceful letter her uncle had written her; but, besides loathing the scandal, she delighted in the idea of having a guardian she could dominate.

She therefore accepted her uncle, but with the proviso that we have already seen—that she would live in her own house and would have nothing to do with a family whose presence reminded her of the wrong done her mother. This was precisely what she told her aunt and cousins while they did their utmost to shower her with endearments.

The wealth she came into unexpectedly, raising her suddenly from indigence to eminence, effected in Aurélia a quick transformation. It was not, however, in her character, or in her feelings, that such a revolution took place; possessing as they did the fine temper of her heart, these were immutable. The change occurred only in her attitude, if thus we may speak of that soul in the presence of society.

With a peaceful existence and a joyful love, Aurélia would have been an affectionate wife and a devoted mother. She would have gone through life like so many other women, wrapped in that innocent bliss of illusions that are the pure alb of the angel, a pilgrim on earth.

But the flower of her youth she saw bloom amid the squalid environment of the vulgar seductions that pursued her. Without the inborn pride that protected her chastity, the shameful breath of vice might have stained her bosom. But she was strong enough to retract, like a cactus from the blazing heat, and to live on her own dreams.

When she compared her beautiful ideal with the sordid aspect that society presented to her, it was natural for her to begin to despise it and to view the world as a rotting swamp, yet covered with foliage dotted with bright flowers that cannot be picked without stepping into the mud.

Hence her horror at the proximity of this abyss of degradation and the isolation to which she wished to condemn herself. Quite often, her soul was appalled by the indignities to which she was subjected, and even by the villainies whose echo reached her obscure retreat. But what could she, a fragile young girl about to face orphanhood and abandonment, do against the formidable thousand-headed beast?

When fortune took her by surprise, a woman who no longer had anyone with whom to share it, her first thought was that it could be a weapon. God was sending it so that she could do battle with this corrupt society and avenge the noble feelings scorned by the mob of speculators.

She therefore prepared herself for the fight, spurred perhaps above all else by the idea of the marriage she later effected. Possibly it was Fernando Seixas's ignominy she was punishing by mocking and humiliating her every admirer.

On the first days following the opening of the will, Aurélia repaid her mother's debts and compensated all the poor neighbors who had rendered services during Dona Emília's illness. In this endeavor she had the help of Dr. Torquato Ribeiro, whose advice she sought, especially concerning the guardianship. The attorney did not practice law, but he consulted with his colleagues to satisfy the girl and offer proper guidance.

"We also have a debt to settle between the two of us," said Aurélia. "But we will take care of that later. I will not pay you back now."

"A trifle," answered Ribeiro.

"Oh! I did not know you were so rich."

"I am poor, as you well know, Dona Aurélia."

"I know; if you were rich, I would not owe you anything. You must be needing the amount that you spent to pay for my mother's funeral."

"Forgive me, it was not me."

"Who was it then?" asked Aurélia, taken aback.

Ribeiro took out his wallet.

"I never mentioned this for fear of causing you distress. On the day Dona Emília passed away, I went out, as you know, to make the funeral arrangements; I had already made several trips in vain, when I received a letter with no signature. I accepted because there was no other way; I did not have twenty *mil-réis* of my own."

The letter contained only these words: "This is to inform Dr. Torquato da Costa Ribeiro that the funeral of Dona Emília Camargo has been arranged and paid for by one of her relatives."

Aurélia read the letter, written in a handwriting she did not recognize and put it away.

"So I owe you only fifty *mil-réis*, which I will pay upon coming of age. For now, I ask you to accept this small gift."

The gift was a picture of the girl, in a solid gold frame studded with diamonds, whose total value, aside from the labor, was one thousand.

The lawyer understood the girl's intention, which was to give him, in this extremely delicate way, the financial help that he surely must need.

He thought for a moment and decided to accept it honestly and without false humility.

"I thank you for the gift, Dona Aurélia. Above all, even more than the picture itself, I appreciate what you have hidden in it. Your features are merely a copy of beauty; your intent reflects the soul God bestowed upon you."

Only after the six-month period of mourning did Aurélia appear in society.

She had rehearsed her role. From the first moment she appeared in the salons, she established her empire there and took possession of the enslaved throng whose destiny it is to flatter those of imposing reputations.

We find her dazzling the crowd with her beauty and exciting the gold lust among the gentlemen in the high-stakes matrimonial game. She delighted in dragging them behind her, trailing them in the dust, and flogging them with sarcasm, these associates and emulators of Fernando Seixas's, like him eager to sell themselves, albeit for a higher price.

She had therefore reduced them to merchandise or trinkets, assigning them a price as had been the custom in the past with bands of slaves.

The high-priced husband to whom she referred was none other than her former love, who had scorned her because she was poor.

Amid this bitterness that society inspired in her, Aurélia had not totally lost her belief in nobility of soul, and she respected it wherever she found it.

Hence, if some honest man courted her sincerely, seduced by the qualities of her person and not by the glitter of her wealth, she behaved toward him in a completely different manner. She welcomed him with friendliness and grace, but would take the first opportunity to disabuse him of any hope.

Only with the dowry hunters was she coquettish, if such a term can be applied to subjecting to constant mockery and humiliation those who pursued her.

Once, Aurélia met Eduardo Abreu, now back from Europe, at a social gathering. She had learned that he had dissipated his inheritance and was reduced to poverty. As he avoided speaking to her, the girl approached him and urged him to frequent her house.

Abreu paid her a formal visit. The girl invented some excuse for an urgent letter and asked for an inkwell. Suddenly she turned to the gentleman and asked him to write a message to a certain store.

Aurélia examined the handwriting and muttered to herself.

"Just as I guessed!"

She said nothing about it to Abreu. In a few days someone took care of the young man's outstanding debts at several stores on Ouvidor Street no longer willing to give him credit.

The first time the young lady ran into Abreu after the incident, she asked him:

"Do you still love me?"

He blushed.

"I no longer have that right."

"Remember what I once told you. If I redeem myself from my captivity, my hand belongs to you. Should you not want it, no one else in this world shall have it."

Dr. Torquato Ribeiro could not resist the passion he harbored for Adelaide Amaral. With time and the absence of his rival, the earlier resentment began to dispel; and since Seixas's behavior was already arousing suspicion, the reconciliation was not long in coming.

Aurélia watched the attorney's passion grow with each passing day. It was a true reversion. At first she marveled at his indulgence:

"And I? Don't I love a man who not only left me for another but also debased himself?"

She then had the idea of fostering Ribeiro's courtship, which she accomplished, contributing to the realization of the project she so cherished and whose execution we have witnessed.

These were the events that occurred before we first met Aurélia Camargo in the salons.

∽ IX ∾

Let us return to the nuptial chamber, where the opening scene of the original drama, of which we know only the prologue, is being acted out. The two actors are still in the same position in which we left them. Fernando Seixas, automatically obeying Aurélia, had sat down and was staring dumbfounded at the girl. She pulled up a chair and sat opposite her husband, singeing his face with the heat of her breath.

"I need not tell you of my love and my soul's devotion from the moment I first met you. You know it, and if you do not, your presence here on this occasion has revealed it to you. For a woman to sacrifice her entire future as have I, life must have become for her a desert, holding only the corpse of the man who has devastated her for life."

Aurélia pressed her hand against her breast to hold back the surge of emotion that threatened to overwhelm her.

"You did not return my love, or even understand it. You assumed I gave you preference over other suitors, and chose you as the hero of my fantasies, only until a marriage came along, which you, sir, young and honorable gentleman that you are, would find agreeable in order to reap, at your pleasure, the fruit of your poetic flowers. As you see, I distinguish you from the others. They offered bluntly, but honestly and without mincing words, a life of shame and ruin."

Seixas lowered his head.

"I realized you did not love me as I wished and deserved to be loved. But it was solely my fault, and not yours, that I did not know how to arouse in you the same passion that I felt. Later you withdrew from me the consolation of your affection and transferred it to another, in whom you could not find what I had given you, a virgin heart full of passion with which to adore you. Nonetheless, I still had the strength to forgive you and love you."

The girl shook her head in a proud gesture:

"But you abandoned me not for Adelaide's love, only for her dowry, a trifling dowry of thirty thousand! That you had no right to do, and I could never forgive you! You could even have scorned me, but you should not have lowered yourself from the height to which I had raised you in my soul. I had an idol; you swept it from its pedestal and flung it into the dust. Debasing the man I loved, that was your crime; society has no laws to punish you, but with it comes remorse. One cannot murder in this way, infusing with disbelief and hatred a heart that God created for love."

Seixas, who had lowered his head, raised it again and gazed into the girl's eyes. His features remained tense and beads of perspiration bubbled at the roots of his lustrous black hair.

"The wealth God has given me came too late; it did not even afford me the pleasure of illusion that betrayed women enjoy. When I received it, I was already acquainted with the world and its miseries; I already knew that a rich girl is a business arrangement, not a wife; very well then, I said, this fortune will provide me the only satisfaction I can still enjoy in this world: to show this man, who did not understand me, what kind of woman had loved him, and what kind of a soul he has lost. Yet, I still harbored some hope. If he nobly refuses the shameful proposal, I will throw myself at his feet. I will beg him to accept my fortune, to squander it if he so wishes, but to allow me to love him. This final consolation you snatched away. What was left me? In the past, they would lash the corpse to the murderer, to expiate his guilt. You have killed my heart; it was only fair that I should bind you to the remains of your victim. But do not despair; the torture cannot last long. This ceaseless martyrdom to which we are condemned will finally snuff out my last breath; you will be left free and rich."

When she had uttered these last words, in a tone beyond contempt, she removed the paper she had placed in her waistband and opened it before Seixas's eyes. It was a check for eighty thousand, drawn on the Bank of Brazil.

"It is time to conclude the sale. Of the hundred thousand you have estimated as your worth, you have already received twenty; here is the balance of eighty. We are quits, and I can call you mine—my husband, since that is the conventional term."

The girl held out the paper, which was being crushed in her convulsively trembling hand. Seixas remained as motionless as a statue; only two deep lines were etched in his face from the corner of his eyes to the corners of his mouth.

Finally the paper slipped from the girl's tremulous fingers and fell to the rug at Fernando's feet.

There followed a moment of silence, or rather of stupor. Aurélia grew angry at Seixas's unassailable muteness, which perhaps she attributed to a cynical moral insensibility. Hoping she might strengthen the noble instincts of a man still capable of rehabilitating himself from the debility into which he had been dragged, she found an individual so apathetic and shameless that he did not respond to even the greatest humiliation.

From Aurélia's lips came not a smile, but a shrill sound.

"Now we can proceed with our comedy, for our own amusement. It is better than staring speechlessly at each other. Take your position, my husband; kneel here at my feet, and give me your first loving kiss—for you do love me, don't you, and have never loved any woman but me?"

Seixas stood up; his voice, calm but faltering, finally escaped his lips:

"No, I do not love you."

"Oh!"

"It is true that I did love you; but you have just crushed that love beneath your feet, where it will lie buried forever, in the abjection into which you have cast it. I could love you now only if I wished to insult you; for what greater offense can a wretch inflict upon a lady than to stigmatize her with his passion? But never fear; even if I were overcome with rage, which is not the case, there is one act of revenge I would not have the strength to commit—loving you."

Aurélia rose impetuously.

"Then I was wrong?" she exclaimed in a strange exaltation. "You do love me sincerely and did not marry me for my money!"

Seixas's eyes lingered a moment on the face of the girl, who hung on his every word.

"No, madam, you were not wrong," he said finally in the same cold and inflexible tone. "I sold myself; I belong to you. You had the bad taste to purchase a debased husband; here he is just as you wanted him. You could have molded his character, perhaps warped by his upbringing, into that of a man of integrity, ennobled by your affection; instead you chose a white slave. You were within your rights; you paid for him with your own money, and generously. That slave is here before you; he is your husband, but nothing more than your husband!"

Aurélia's face flushed at the sound of that word underscored by Seixas's sarcasm.

"I settled for a hundred thousand," Fernando continued; "it was not much, but the agreement has been concluded. I received twenty thousand as down payment; I was still owed the balance, and you have just paid me."

He bent down to pick up his check. Carefully he read the figure; then, slowly folding the paper, he put it in the pocket of his sumptuous blue cotton robe.

"Would you like a receipt? No, you trust my word. It would not be safe. After all, I have been paid. The slave can go to work."

Uttering these words with amazing lightheartedness that seemed to indicate the magnitude of his impudence, Fernando again sat facing his wife.

"I await your orders."

Aurélia, who to that moment had listened anxiously to everything, eagerly scrutinizing her husband's face and words for some sign of indignation disguised under that aloofness, covered her face, burning with shame.

"My God!"

The girl stifled the sob that filled her breast and, taking refuge in a corner of the sofa, as if fearful of any contact with the man to whom she was joined for all eternity, sank into the vortex of her turbulent conscience.

After a long while, Aurélia, as if awakening from a nightmare, raised her eyes, and once again meeting those of Seixas, who observed her with scornful calm, felt a powerful surge of repulsion, or rather, of repugnance.

"Does my presence disturb you? It is as you wish. Is it not, my lady? Do you not have the right to give orders? Do so, and I shall leave."

"Oh, yes! Leave me!" cried Aurélia. "You disgust me."

"You should have examined the item you were buying so as to avoid regrets!"

Seixas crossed the nuptial chamber and disappeared through that same door by which he had entered an hour earlier full of life and happiness, swelling with joy and emotion, and through which he now passed bearing death in his soul.

When Aurélia heard the sound of his steps fading in the hallway, she ran, impelled by horror, and turned the key. Attempting to flee, she took a few faltering steps and fell unconscious to the carpet.

THIRD PART

Possession

∽ I ∾

Arriving in his room, Seixas did not even have time to sit down. Like a drunkard, he clutched the dresser next to the hallway, and stood there in a stupor, his soul shaken violently by that terrible crisis. As if struck by a mortal blow, he seemed about to gasp his last. His anguished breath hissed through his lips like the throes of the dying—the only sign of life in that young and vigorous being.

Suddenly he broke loose from his torpor, but only a monumental effort wrenched him from the insanity that was penetrating him. In his face could be seen the terror that possessed him at the realization that life was abandoning him, or at the very least that the light of his soul would soon fade away.

"God, do not take my life at this moment! Now more than ever I need my reason."

Seixas dashed about the room in hasty steps, bumping against the furniture, running into the walls, hallucinating and at the same time driven by the desire to tear himself away from the obsession that had destroyed him.

He ran his eyes anxiously around the house, searching for some object onto which his spirit could grasp, like a shipwrecked man clutching at the smallest fragment amid the waves in which he struggles. The elegant dressing table, lighted by twin crystal candleholders with pink candles, boasted of luxury of the highest order.

It was then that a spark ignited in this vanquished soul. The instinct for elegance was certainly the strongest chord in his poetic and aristocratic temperament.

Seixas approached the dresser, moved by an undefinable impulse, and began to contemplate in detail the objects on the marble top: ivory carvings, vases and groups of mat china, wine glasses of cut crystal, jewels in the finest taste.

As he became absorbed in this examination, his former existence began to reemerge, the one he had lived until the moment of the disaster that had overwhelmed him. He sensed a rebirth to that fine and delicate materialism which attracted his aristocratic spirit with such powerful seduction and gentle voluptuousness.

All this finery seemed strange and stirred in him obscure emotions—such was the abyss separating him from his recent past. And with childish eagerness he examined the objects one by one, uncertain which to cling to. He held the diamonds to the light to see them sparkle and inhaled the perfumes from the vials with unutterable delight.

In this meaningless activity, he remained absorbed for some time. Perchance drawn by memories aroused by objects similar to these, he retraced in his mind the course of his life, and, following it, was led at last to this ill-fated evening and to the bitter reality of this moment.

He drew back in a gesture of repulsion. The artistic refinements that a moment before had soothed his imagination now inspired only repugnance. He withdrew from the dresser and went to the window.

It was a peaceful and calm night. The sky was adorned with stars and a breeze caressed flocks of clouds white as heron feathers. A flickering wave swept over the marble pool covered with water lilies that raised their large white dew-sprinkled calyxes. The trees that stood out grotesquely against the bright horizon resembled a Gothic relief, swaying in the soft rustle of the breeze that scattered the perfume of roses and magnolias.

Seixas stood for a moment contemplating the sweet serenity of nature. The peacefulness of the night settled within him. The sinews of his soul relaxed.

His forehead pressed against the window frame, he released the tears overflowing from his bosom.

When these sobs had eased the pain, Seixas went to the elegant hardwood desk and opened it. He took out the scarlet camlet portfolio. On the upper flap, in a white rosette, was his monogram, the intertwined letters FRS, outlined in gold embroidery.

He stared mechanically at those letters that represented an enigma to him. As in the ancient fable, the sphinx left him confused. What meaning could this have after the event that moments before had cast him into the depths of degradation?

Finally he made the decision that had taken him to the desk. He placed a sheet of paper over the portfolio and prepared to write a letter.

But the pen was stuck in the mouth of the inkwell. Seixas pulled it out briskly and anxiously examined the nib. Noticing that it was undamaged, he stood up and paced about the room.

After some time he returned to the dresser in a decisive mood. He had changed his mind.

Opening the drawers, he carefully placed in them all the expensive objects in the room. This done, he locked the dresser and did the same with all the other pieces of furniture that Lemos had shown him some hours earlier.

In spite of advice from Aurélia's guardian, in the morning Seixas had sent over a bureau, into the bottom drawers of which he had put his best clothes, both undergarments and outerwear.

He looked for that old item of furniture and, finding it in an adjoining room where it had been placed, verified that his clothes were indeed there; he was quite pleased to find them. He removed the expensive silk robe, the velvet slippers, and put on less pretentious clothes from those he had brought.

There were cigars in the bureau. He lighted one and sat by the window. He felt strong enough to face the situation into which he had been drawn and the crisis confronting his life.

Amid these bitter reflections, rekindled by memories of the recent scene, of the long-repressed rebellion of his dignity against the pride of the woman who humiliated him, hovered a feeling that finally broke free from the turmoil of his thoughts and came to dominate him.

This feeling was the intense admiration inspired in him by the energy and power of Aurélia's love. In the passion that had just offended him lay a fierce beauty that instilled in him an enthusiasm filled with awe.

"I did not understand this love—and how could I understand it? If anyone were to tell me what has just happened to me, I would receive such a story with an incredulous smile. Long ago, when the family isolated women from society, passion could reach such heights, to the point of absorbing the whole of one's existence. There was time, then, for only a single love, and love exhausted the soul. But nowadays when a woman lives surrounded by admirers and all suitors, no matter how distinguished, kneel before her beauty, love is nothing more than a whim, a sweet preference and a tender fancy, until it becomes a conjugal friendship. This is how I always imagined it, this is how I have experienced it and how it was reciprocated. When Aurélia told me of her affection, I could not imagine that she harbored a passion capable of such extremes. I thought they were romantic fancies. Didn't I feel them too? Didn't I often swear eternal love, only to have it vanish the next day in the whirl of a waltz? This love that I assumed to be a poet's illusion, a dream of the imagination, is here in its splendid reality. Its fiery wings have brushed against my soul and singed it for evermore!"

For a moment Seixas stood ecstatic before the image etched in his mind representing the figure of Aurélia, when, magnificent in her rage and indignation, she had inveighed against him in bitter reproach.

"A passion like hers had the right to be unforgiving. And this woman who gave herself to me in sublime self-sacrifice, this woman to whom fate has linked me forever, this unique woman, I admire her, and I can never again love her! I found her along my path, and I have lost her forever! But I will love no other. Having met her, I cannot defile my soul with the affection of any other woman."

The blush of dawn could already be seen on the horizon. A cooling breeze diffused through the air, and the first twitter of birds mixed with the disordered sounds of the city, which was awakening beyond the walls of the country house.

Seixas went down to the garden and walked through the winding paths of the artificial meadow covered with fine grass and clipped in English fashion. Beds of daisies and periwinkles, open to the first rays of the sun, adorned with their colorful crowns the green carpet of the lawn. Fuchsias and begonias spread through the latticework composing sweet lambrequins like thyrsi of fanciful flowers.

The buds of camellias and begonias filled with sap inbreathed from the night's coolness awaited the warmth of day to blossom, while yesterday's flowers, having sealed their bosoms in the evening, reopened, but pale and languid, to bid farewell to the sun that had given them life and then, like a capricious artist, singed them.

As a man of society, Seixas knew nature only by tradition or, at most, by viewing it at a distance. To him, trees, flowers, and panoramas were decorations which became confused with tapestries, draperies, knickknacks, gilded objects, and the entire range of adornments created by luxury.

By dint of living in a world of convention, these men of society had become artificial. Nature for them was not the true one, but that fictitious one, ingrained by habit, which some bring from the cradle, for there convention awaits to make them its prey, transforming their mothers into mere childbearers.

Quite often in his poems Seixas spoke of stars, flowers, and breezes, from which he drew images to express the gracefulness of women and the emotions of love. Mere imitation—as is usually the case of poets bred by civilization, he took these images not from reality, but from wide reading. The only wit that is original is that infused by nature, an inexhaustible muse because she is divine. For such, one must be either born in primitive times or disdain society and take refuge in solitude.

At that moment, however, watching the break of day there in the garden, Seixas felt that besides the bright colors, the graceful shapes, and the scents of the countryside, there was something immaterial beating in the heart of this wilderness that permeated his being. It was the soul of creation enveloping him and sharing with his soul the unutterable serenity of the clear, cool morning.

With the calm that flowed into his spirit, the decision just adopted grew even stronger. It became filled with the cold resignation that renders the soul obdurate.

He was startled out of his train of thought by a sound close by. He turned and realized he was near the outside fence, hidden at this spot by leaves. He pushed aside the branches and approached to discover the source of the noise. Perhaps he feared he was being watched, or perhaps he was motivated by the idle curiosity that overcomes a man violently shaken from his usual concerns.

A peddler of trinkets had laid on the pavement the box he carried over his shoulders, and sitting on the ground, leaning against the wall, was counting his money and taking stock of his goods. He had either gotten up early to extend his rounds or, which seemed more likely, caught far from home at sunset, had spent the night in some hostelry and was now getting ready to return.

On the cover of the inverted case, held by pieces of string, could be seen several objects that especially caught Seixas's attention.

He moved forward as if to call the peddler but pulled back, somewhat chagrined. It seemed that he was about to act precipitously but was warned in time by his reason.

In any case, after some hesitation he overcame his earlier distaste, but not his discomfiture at the action he was about to take. He scrutinized the surroundings and, verifying that the street was deserted, extended his arm outside the fence and tapped the peddler on the shoulder.

"*Chi va—!*" exclaimed the peddler, turning around.

He did not see Seixas, who had retreated from the fence and was hiding behind the branches; but he noticed a two *mil-réis* bill floating above his head, and it certainly held more enchantment for him than his customer's face.

"A comb and a toothbrush," said Seixas quickly. "Hurry!"

"*Questo?*" asked the peddler, taking a buffalo comb from the cover.

"Yes, any. I cannot wait."

The peddler handed over the objects; he collected the money and, wishing to return the change, realized that his customer had disappeared.

"*Che birbone!*"

The peddler assumed that money thus thrown away with such indifference was stolen, and as a precaution packed his things and left before complications arose.

Meanwhile Seixas returned to his apartment afraid that someone might see him in the garden at that hour of the morning and suspect what had taken place. The house, however, showed no signs of its daily activities. Everyone was no doubt still sleeping as a result of the wedding celebration.

As he made this observation, Fernando remembered the situation in which he had left Aurélia the evening before and wondered what she had done during that long night of agony. She had probably spent it enraptured by the joy of the humiliation she had inflicted upon him and, finally satiated by this savage revenge, had fallen asleep in feverish pride.

If while crossing the garden he had cast a furtive glance at the windows on this side of the house, he might have partially satisfied his curiosity. One of the white diaphanous muslin curtains behind the panes was darkened by a shadow inside outlining the delicate shape of a torso.

The sun was already high when Seixas heard the sound of the doorknob that connected his apartment to the interior of the house. It must have been the manservant arriving to prepare the dressing table for his morning toilet. Finding the door locked and realizing that it was unnecessary to knock at that hour, he left.

There was water in the Sèvres pitcher that adorned the rich white quebracho wooden washstand. Seixas hesitated, but considering that the utensil would not lose its shiny newness if he used it once, decided to wash his face in the luxurious set. However, for the rest of his morning toilet he made use of the comb and brush he had bought.

When he finished, he dried the sink and the washstand with a towel from his own wardrobe; he locked in his desk the objects that might expose him, and, dressed and ready in his usual careful way, opened the connecting door and sat on the couch, waiting—for what, not even he could say. After the disappointment that had cast him from the pinnacle of happiness into this incredible circumstance, how could he know what unexpected turn of events yet awaited him in this drama in which his life now moved?

In a short while the manservant appeared.

"I see you are already dressed, sir. I came to prepare your dressing-table, but the door was locked."

"There was no need," answered Seixas.

"Do you wish to have the newspapers brought to your study, so that you can read them as soon as you wake up, or do you prefer them to remain in the sitting room?"

"Where have they been kept until now?"

"In the sitting room."

"It is better that way."

"As you wish, sir. Those are the orders I received."

The manservant looked about the room, surprised at the neatness of all the objects, including the toiletries.

"The coachman would like to know whether you wish to go out before breakfast. By car or on horseback?"

"No, thank you."

"*Diana* has already been saddled. But we can change the harness to *Nelson* in a moment, or prepare the victoria."

"That will not be necessary."

"At what time do you wish to have breakfast?"

"At the usual time. There is no need for change."

"At ten then."

The servant left, returning an hour later.

"Breakfast is served."

"Who asked you to call me?"

"The mistress."

Seixas nodded his head and let the servant lead the way.

❦ II ❦

At the center of the room was a table where the finest crystal sparkled in the light, altering the sheen of the fine china and the color of the fruit heaped in silver baskets.

Breakfast was a banquet, not of quantity, which would have been in poor taste, but in variety and exquisiteness of the delicacies.

Through the windows opening onto the garden came the morning breeze and the brightness of a magnificent summer day, the perfume of the flowers, and the warbling of the canaries in an elegant aviary.

Aurélia and Dona Firmina were in the room.

The girl was reclined in a rocking chair by the glare of a window, her graceful shape fully immersed in the light. Seeing her radiantly beautiful and smiling, one would assume that she deliberately challenged the day's splendor to display the immaculate purity of her face and her unchangeable grace.

She was wearing a dazzling white linen robe; the ribbons in her hair and her belt were blue, as was the satin of the flat shoes that molded her feet like the setting of a pearl.

Fernando stopped momentarily as he entered the room; afterwards, firm in his resolve, he advanced toward his wife to greet her. Nevertheless he had not considered in what manner he would carry out this task.

Aurélia noticed the movement. Her husband's morning greeting would rouse Dona Firmina's suspicion.

Seixas came forward. The girl rose and extended her hand; tilting her head toward her shoulder with a slight turn, she presented him her cheek to receive a chaste wifely kiss.

Her hand, however, was icy and rigid, as if made of jasper. Her face, smiling and coquettish just moments before, had suddenly contracted into an indescribable expression of indignation and scorn.

Fernando only noticed this transformation when his lips brushed the cold skin whose down was raised like the rough nap of felt. He retreated involuntarily, though at this point the caresses of this woman, to whom he was husband, were more humiliating than her rejection.

"Let us have breakfast!" the girl said, walking toward the table and motioning her husband and Dona Firmina to come closer.

No longer could be seen on her lovely face the slightest trace of the sarcasm that had transformed it; nor could one conceive that this splendid beauty could change into the satanic image that Fernando had seen moments before.

Aurélia sat at the head of the table. Fernando sat on her right, across from Dona Firmina.

At first the girl busied herself with serving; then, nibbling a red piece of lobster meat with her white teeth, she enlivened the conversation with animated and sparkling words.

Never had she displayed the gracefulness of spirit or the brightness of imagination that she did that morning, nor had her bubbly smile blossomed so on her lips, nor her beauty so overflowed with joy.

Seixas listened to her with amusement. Absorbed in her sweet prattle, he even managed to forget momentarily the unhappy predicament in which fate had placed him beside this woman.

In the pauses that appetite allowed for reflection, Dona Firmina marveled at the poise exhibited by yesterday's bride, which might more fittingly be a chaste shyness.

But accustomed to the changes that our habits have been undergoing with the invasion of foreign ways, the widow assumed that the latest Parisian chic must be this of newlyweds exchanging roles, the tuxedos assuming feminine bashfulness, while the gowns boasted the cheek of the *roué*.

"That's what comes of women's emancipation!" she thought.

"Would you like me to serve you the salad or the meat pie?" Aurélia asked, noticing that Seixas had stopped.

"Nothing else, thank you."

Seixas had eaten a steak with a slice of bread, and had drunk half a glass of the wine closest to him, without bothering to read the label.

"You did not eat!" the girl replied.

"Happiness takes away the appetite," Fernando observed smiling.

"In this case I should fast," Aurélia answered jokingly. "On me it has the opposite effect; I was famished."

"Even so, you did not eat much," Dona Firmina interjected.

"Try this lobster. It is delicious," Aurélia insisted.

"Is that an order?" Fernando asked agreeably, but with a particular inflection in his voice.

Aurélia laughed.

"I did not know that wives had the right to order their husbands around. In any case, I would never use my power for such insignificant trifles."

"That shows your generosity."

"Appearances can be deceiving."

The turn of this conversation did not gainsay the budding familiarity typical of happy newlyweds; nevertheless there were tones of voice and glances that strangers did not notice, but which they felt prick like pins hidden among satin ruffles.

When he finished his breakfast, Fernando went from the dining room to the sitting room where Aurélia joined him shortly. Dona Firmina, so as not to disturb the couple's tender moment alone, left on the pretext of running some errands.

Seixas had mechanically opened one of the day's newspapers found on a lacquer tray with gilded bronze feet beside the sofa. When Aurélia came in, he offered her the page he was holding and the others for her to choose.

"Thank you," said Aurélia, sitting on the sofa.

The manservant presented Seixas with a rose-pod cigar box with silver inlays filled with genuine Havanas, and a lamp, also of silver, at whose tip flickered the bluish flame of spirits of wine.

"Thank you. I have my own," said Fernando refusing with a gesture the proffered cigars, and taking out his case.

"And whose are those?" Aurélia asked vivaciously, pointing to the cigars offered by the servant.

Seixas was about to answer but, remembering they were not alone, drew back:

"I was referring to the ones I brought with me," he said, emphasizing the last words.

"They may be better."

"Quite the contrary; but I am used to them. Does the smoke disturb you?"

"The lady who these days displayed such repulsions would show poor taste; besides, I must adjust to my husband's habits."

"No, not for that reason. As your husband I have no habits, only obligations."

Aurélia cut the thread of this dialogue, asking indifferently:

"Is there anything new in the newspapers?"

"I have not read them yet. What are you interested in? The news and the serials, of course—"

As he said this, Seixas opened the pages, one after the other, and running his eyes over them, read aloud to Aurélia whatever he found most interesting. She pretended to be listening; but she was reviewing in her mind the recent events of her life, and wondering about the uncertainties of the future that she herself had partially designed.

However, the manservant's presence made her aware that Seixas still had not lighted his cigar.

"Aren't you smoking?" she asked her husband.

"May I?"

"I already told you it does not bother me," she replied with a surge of impatience.

"I am sorry; not having been given formal approval, I feared annoying you."

"Certain fears seem more like desires!" she observed ironically.

"Time will convince you of my sincerity."

"Time! Oh! If only one could have all one's hopes of it come true!" Aurélia remarked with bitter scorn.

Freeing herself from the sarcastic impulse that had provoked her aggrieved soul, the woman took refuge in triviality:

"It is best not to trust in it and to live for the present. The true book is the newspaper, with yesterday's stories and today's announcements."

Seixas went on perusing the newspapers, as if acceding to Aurélia's wishes. He quickly scanned the headlines to see if any one of them had the power to arouse the girl's curiosity.

"These pages are so interesting!" Aurélia said, searching for an excuse to vent her inner irritation. "When I remember to open them, which I do not do very often because my arms are not long enough for that difficult task, I always think I am reading a paper from last year."

"It is not the fault of the paper, but of the city where it is published, and of which it must be, as you just said, the diary, or the history of the preceding day."

"Forgive me, I forgot you were also once a journalist."

As Aurélia fell silent and the pages offered no further subject matter for conversation, Seixas took advantage of the criticism often directed at the press in our country to elaborate on a few variations on the theme, in order to pass the time.

Naturally, he addressed the question from an amiable point of view intended to win a lady's attention. Aurélia listened to him attentively for some moments, but realizing that her husband spoke in the monotonous tone and with the calculated pauses of one carrying out a duty and who, far from freely expressing his thoughts, on the contrary, petitions the rebellious spirit, she interrupted his discourse by rising from the sofa.

She walked about the room, running her eyes over it, looking at the wallpaper, the furniture, and the decorations as if she had never before examined them, or was wondering if something was missing. She then stared at the porcelain figurines and other knickknacks on the consoles, taking them from their places and changing their positions.

Next she went to the piano, which is to the ladies what the cigar is to the gentlemen, a friend for all hours, a pliant companion, and an ever-attentive confidant. As she opened the instrument, she remembered that it was improper for yesterday's bride to enjoy this kind of amusement when neighbors and servants, everyone, must believe her at that time to be enveloped in the joy of loving and being loved.

Oh! She had not known that mystic dawn of conjugal love, which for her had become a vigil of agony and despair. But she could imagine the mutual transfusion of two souls and she understood that in their longing for each other they would not distance themselves with such extraneous diversion.

Abandoning the piano, she dissimulated by looking over the music sheets arranged on the appropriate piece of furniture, a small stand with vertical partitions. She stood there, merely leafing through a few sheets, singing her favorite passages softly to herself, perhaps searching for one that might reflect her innermost thoughts, or rather, might translate the unutterable feeling harbored in her soul at that moment.

Apparently she at last found this sympathetic note, for her voice gave out a heroic allegro; then she remembered she was not alone. She turned to the sofa, where she had left her husband, who perchance might be observing her, surprised at her mimicry.

As the young lady moved away, Seixas had found on the table a photograph album, and was amusing himself by looking at the pictures.

"Are you looking at celebrities?" asked the woman, who had sat down again on the sofa.

Fernando sensed that the question was only a thread with which to weave a conversation and decided to gratify his wife's wish.

"That is true—European celebrities, since we do not as yet have any Brazilian ones. In photographs, that is; otherwise we have plenty. It is odd that in this land, so inclined to speculation and charlatanism, that no one has yet thought of bringing out an album of national celebrities. I am sure it would make a lot of money, not only from the sale of albums, but especially from candidates wishing to join the list of celebrities."

"Roll would be a better word."

"It is more expressive."

"This proves," Aurélia observed, "that literature has advanced further in our country than art; for, if I am not mistaken, there are, both here and abroad, firms exploiting biographies."

"You are right."

"You missed marrying an *illustrious contemporary*," Aurélia added, underscoring the last words with a subtle smile.

"Oh! I did not know! It's a shame that I cannot add this to the many other honors I have received."

"Well, I was threatened with having my face in some magazine or newspaper, as a distinguished Brazilian. It is my belief that my claim to celebrity came as my grandfather's legacy. I had to take about ten subscriptions to protect myself from the conspiracy against my obscurity and free myself from the glory these gentlemen wished to inflict upon me."

The two spent quite some time on this conversation and on the magazine of photographs.

The pendulum clock had just struck one o'clock. The servant opened the dining room door noisily, as if to warn of his approach, and, Lusitanizing the English term *luncheon* as was the custom, announced:

"*Lanche* is served."

"Shall we go?" asked the girl, standing up.

Seixas closed the album and followed his wife.

The servant who had caught the newlyweds bending over the album smiled mischievously.

Fernando noticed the smile and flushed.

∽ III ∾

Fruits in season—pineapples, figs, and navel oranges vying with imported apples, pears, and grapes—were the main ornament of the midday meal that foreign habits had substituted for the Brazilian afternoon snack enjoyed by our good forebears.

There was also an abundance of baked items such as meat pies, stuffed shrimp, and oysters, along with cheeses from various countries and crystallized candy and fruit preserves. The best dessert wines, from Sherry to Setubal Moscatel, from Champagne to Constance, were there tempting the palate, some with their eloquent label, others with the topaz that sparkled through the facets of cut crystal.

"I really do not feel like it!" said Fernando, obeying Aurélia's gesture and sitting at the table.

"Well!" said the young lady capriciously. "To sample fruit and sweets you do not have to be hungry; do like the birds. What do you prefer—a fig, a pear, or some pineapple?"

"Do I have to eat anything?" Fernando asked sternly.

"It is mandatory."

"In that case, I will have a fig."

"Here you are; a fig and a pear; it is merely a couple."

Seixas lowered his head. Positioning the plate in front of him, he ate both fruits, slowly and coldly, like a man performing a mechanical act. Nothing in his features revealed the pleasant sensation on his palate.

Aurélia, crushing muscatel grapes between her crimson lips, followed Fernando's automatic movements with her eyes and, if she did not guess it, she vaguely sensed somehow the motivation operating in her husband.

She stood up from the table and went outside, toward the edge of the house, where there was already some shade. There she amused herself by feeding the canaries and song thrushes who greeted her with a magnificent overture of warbles and trills.

Thinking that her presence might intimidate her husband, Aurélia found this excuse to absent herself from him for a while so he might feel more at ease. This idea fled from her spirit, however, when, peeking through the window, she saw Seixas standing motionless, his eyes fixed on the wall before him, totally lost in thought.

After the luncheon, Aurélia invited her husband for a stroll through the garden; but there were ladies at the neighboring windows, and she did not want to expose herself to curious glances. She was not the happy and beloved bride, but others took her to be such, and this was enough for her modesty to shield her from the gaze of strangers.

They returned to the sitting room.

There they flittered from topic to topic, but in spite of their wish to prolong their conversation, or perhaps precisely because they were anxious to do so, they could not find a topic to discuss at length.

Finally they fell back on photographs. This time it was the album of acquaintances that provided the subject matter. One of the first cards depicted Lemos, whose appearance brought forth this observation from Aurélia:

"I keep the album of friends to myself. These others are living room albums, like the signs that photographers have at their doors."

"But they do not show the odd antitheses of their signs. Those gentlemen seem to do it on purpose; it could not be more democratic."

Seixas, a distinguished connoisseur of Ouvidor Street, began to enumerate some of the contrasts he recalled; we will, however, refrain from reproducing his observations, as they showed the effects of extraordinary mordacity.

This caustic tone was not natural to the young man, whose benevolent and friendly disposition never went beyond a few touches of cold irony. He himself had already noted the change in his character, and took a special delight in allowing himself to become saturated with the bile he found in his heart.

After a while Fernando noticed that Aurélia often raised her eyes to the clock, and dissimulated, because he also frequently and furtively consulted the dial, eager to see the day slip away.

At one point, their eyes met while searching for the clock. Aurélia blushed lightly:

"I did not realize it was so late," she said.

"How rapidly time flies!" remarked Fernando. "Almost three o'clock."

"There is still a while before that. It is only a quarter past two."

"Oh! That is true."

"It may be slow," observed Aurélia. "Check your watch."

There was a difference of one and a half minutes between Seixas's watch and the living room clock. It was a good excuse to use up the rest of the time. Aurélia wanted to set the clock; she took the opportunity to wind it; this was followed by a discussion over the desirability of moving it to another console.

"Three o'clock, already!" remarked the young woman at last. "It is time we got dressed for dinner. Good-bye."

Aurélia gave her husband a graceful nod of the head and disappeared through the door that led to her dressing room.

When she entered this room and closed the door behind her, she had no time to unfasten the bodice of her dress; she forced her hands through the eyelets, and, hurting her delicate fingers on the hooks, tore the seams to keep from suffocating. The heart she had so long restrained finally rebelled and burst into sobs that wracked her breast.

For his part, Fernando, finding himself alone, breathed like a man resting after arduous and tiring labor. He wished he could leave this dwelling, rid his sight of this house, go far away from this place to enjoy those moments of solitude and recover his freedom for an hour. But a stroll, especially alone, was not advisable on the day after a marriage for love.

The servant asked permission to enter the room.

"Do you need me, sir?"

"No, thank you. At what time do we dine?"

"At five, sir, unless you give orders to the contrary."

"Fine."

"I know it is not proper on the first days of a marriage, sir, but those are the orders I received—that you should want for nothing."

"Who gave these orders?"

"The mistress."

This consideration which in other circumstances would have deeply pleased him, in his current position humiliated him. He felt the influence of tutelage weighing upon him and reducing him to the condition of a nuptial ward, if not worse. But he was resigned to the ordeal to which his error had subjected him.

On this same occasion, Seixas revealed another change in his character, or at least in his habits.

He had the noble appearance of artless elegance, which is nurtured not by the vanity of admiration but by inward personal satisfaction. Getting dressed had once been a pleasure; the feel of a new suit would give him a delightful sensation, like a cool bath in a peaceful moment.

That day, however, when his wardrobe and dressers overflowed, he barely noticed a slight untidiness, and gave the morning outfit a new look by changing his tie. When he entered the sitting room, Dona Firmina was already there, and Aurélia followed shortly.

She was dressed in green. She had those daring moments, permitted only to truly beautiful women, of challenging the monotony of one color. Her lovely face, harmonious neck, and well-turned arms bloomed from the silken foliage like waterlilies lightly pink from the morning blush.

When the door opened to admit her, Seixas thought he was observing the metamorphosis of nymph turned into lotus. But immediately, admiring the grace radiating from this exotic elegance like the glow from a star, he realized that it was more as if flower had become woman, given life by a divine breath.

Dona Firmina brought much news from the street: greetings from some of Aurélia's friends, a thousand questions from others about the wedding, praises for the bride and groom, and the entire assortment of banal pleasantries that to a great extent make up life in large cities.

With this repertory she managed to fill the half-hour before dinner.

"The general opinion is that one could not find a more perfect couple," said the widow in conclusion.

"As you can see, we married because of unanimous popular acclamation," observed Aurélia, smiling at her husband. "We lack nothing to be happy."

"Impossible to be more so than I am," Seixas replied.

"That privilege is mine, and I shall not yield it to you!"

Dona Firmina applauded this refutation that revealed the extreme love the newlyweds felt for each other.

Dinner went by just as had lunch. Free from the confusion, or rather the oppression, that had restrained her when she found herself alone with her husband, Aurélia recovered in the presence of Dona Firmina and the servants her charming volubility, in which a dispassionate observer might notice a certain nervous irritability, skillfully concealed by a coquettish gesture and a graceful smile.

Seixas did not depart from the sobriety he had exhibited in the morning, except to accede to his wife's wishes; and she, more than once, exercised that feminine tyranny which, like some royalty, takes delight in minutiae.

As they rose from the table, Fernando walked toward the garden door and, gazing idly at the trees, waited for the others to decide the fate of the rest of the afternoon. Aurélia approached him while Dona Firmina was occupied with the train of her fluted dress, a fashion to which she had not yet become accustomed.

"What a beautiful afternoon!" remarked the young lady at her husband's side.

Immediately, though, lowering her voice, she whispered close to his ear, in a curt, sharp tone:

"Offer me your arm!"

Then, extending her comment, she went on pointing toward the horizon at some beautiful red streaks in the sunset, in which the most delicate of hues were changing over the soft white mass of a large cirrus cloud that was suddenly ablaze like a string of fiery gems.

"Look; even the skies are celebrating our joy. Who has ever had such fireworks as these the sun has prepared for our pleasure?"

"It is unfortunate that we cannot—that I cannot enjoy the party up closer, to appreciate it better."

Aurélia turned quickly to give her husband a cold inquisitive look; but Fernando was gazing upon the gradations of light in the sunset and turned only to offer his wife his arm, obeying the admonition he had received.

He did so, however, more through the gesture, for his barely murmured words could scarcely be heard.

"Light your cigar," the woman said, seeing he had forgotten this detail, although the servant had offered him fire.

Aurélia led her husband to a pavilion in the middle of the orchard, whose thick vines hid them from Dona Firmina's eyes and from the gardeners who were about their business.

Seixas had some superficial knowledge of orchids that he had acquired during a summer in Petrópolis, at a time when the cultivation and study of this species of plants had been fashionable and had for some degenerated into an obsession. As one of Rio's *roués*, he had to submit to this new whim of the empress and at a gathering it was his task to give the scientific name of the flower in vogue that decorated a grotto in the garden or a vase in the living room.

Just under the pavilion was a magnificent collection of orchids, which the gardener had protected from the sun. Fernando took advantage of the theme to display his botanical knowledge.

Aurélia listened to him attentively; only when her husband seemed to have exhausted the subject did she interject a reflection.

"Like everyone else, I have always loved flowers; but there was a time when I could not stand them. That was when they tried to teach me Botany."

"Does that mean that I have been unfortunate enough to bore you with my conversation?"

"That is what prejudice does! You have succeeded in reconciling me with Botany. There is nothing better for the nerves."

It was already dark when Aurélia returned from the garden on her husband's arm. Dona Firmina awaited them in the sitting room, which was already alight in a sweet artificial dusk filtered through the opaque crystal of the chandelier.

The widow, seated at the coffee table to devour the serials in the newspapers, was discreet enough to turn her back to the sofa where the newlyweds had taken their place.

Aurélia, weary of the comedy she had acted throughout the day, leaned against the cushion and, closing her eyes, became absorbed in her thoughts. Fernando respected this meditation; so much more since his spirit was also yielding to an irresistible concern.

The evening had aroused in him an indefinable disquietude that now grew stronger as the time to retire approached. He did not know what he feared; it was something vague, shapeless, unknown, that filled him with dread.

Thus, each at a corner of the sofa, separated even more by total alienation than by the space between them, she lost in thought, he agitated, they spent the first evening of their wedded life.

Dona Firmina, now and then, when a part of the serial was less interesting, listened carefully; and that suspicious silence made her smile thinking of the hugs and kisses she would catch by surprise should she suddenly turn toward the sofa.

Discreetly mischievous, on the pretext of looking for a handkerchief, she

started to turn around to enjoy the pleasure of startling the lovebirds. She
then sensed a slight rustle, and imagined that they were moving apart, when,
quite the opposite, they pretended to pay attention to each other, so as not
to betray their mutual indifference.

Around mid-evening, Aurélia left the room. After a short absence during
which noises could be heard inside, she returned to occupy her corner on
the sofa.

Finally the clock struck ten. Dona Firmina folded the papers and took
her leave.

Aurélia followed her slowly as if to make sure that she had gone; then she
closed the door, walked twice around the room and approached her husband.

Seixas saw her draw closer and was astonished by the strange expression
animating her face.

It was a cruel and lascivious sarcasm that emanated with a satanic glow
from the woman's face and gestures. She lacked only the crown of vine over
her scattered braids and the thyrsus in her hand.

However, as she faced her husband, this fever abated as if by magic and,
once more, from the delirious bacchante's body emerged the chaste and coy
virgin.

Aurélia held two similar objects in her hand, one wrapped in white paper,
the other in colored paper. She offered Seixas the first, but took it back,
replacing it with the other.

"This is mine," she said, keeping the one in white wrapping.

While Seixas looked at the object he had received, not fathoming what it
might mean, Aurélia said with a nod of her head:

"Good night."

And she withdrew.

∞ IV ∞

Seixas headed toward his apartment with such precipitation that he forgot
the object enclosed in his hand; only in the dressing room, when it fell to the
floor, did he realize he had it.

He then opened the paper. Inside was a key, and attached to the ring a
label in Aurélia's handwriting: *key to your bedroom.*

As he read these words Seixas turned pale; and he glanced in confusion
at the portière of the room he had entered the day before pulsating with love
and which he could never again penetrate except intoxicated with shame
and branded by infamy.

Moving about, he noticed a change in the room. Somebody had pushed aside the wardrobe that had concealed a door now fully visible and covered only by a curtain of blue silk.

The key was to this door, which led into an elegant alcove furnished with a narrow *érable* bed and other accessories. It was the most garish bachelor's bedroom imaginable.

Seixas guessed by the wave of fragrance wafting about the room that Aurélia had just been there. She must have left at the sound of the key in the lock.

"God!" exclaimed the young man pressing his skull between his hands. "What does this woman want from me? Can't she see I am already humiliated and disheartened enough? She is gorging herself on vengeance. Oh! She has a perverse instinct. She knows that gross insult either hardens the soul, if it is vile, or removes its last vestige of dignity, if any pride remains. But this courteous offense, so full of attention and consideration, which is nothing but scorn of another kind; this ostentatious generosity with which at every moment one wreaks supreme contempt; cruel flagellation inflicted amid smiles and with distinctions that the world would envy—there is no comparable torture for a soul not yet totally lost. Why am I not what she thinks I am, a wretch, devoid of honor and without noble instincts befitting a man of integrity? Then she would have someone to fight!"

Seixas dropped his head at the weight of this thought.

"The strength of resignation—that, however, I will have. It shall not abandon me, no matter how cruel the provocation."

The following days, that waxing phase of the honeymoon, went by like the first one. The bride and groom then entered a second phase, in which the rapture of belonging to each other now permits, especially for the man, a return to normal activities.

On the fifth day, Seixas appeared at the office, where he was resoundingly congratulated on his success. His coworkers saw this early return as a mere visit. If when poor his presence was perceptible only in the time book, now that he was rich or almost a millionaire he would surely leave his job or, at best, keep it as an honorary position like some ministerial scions.

Therefore, Seixas's assiduous work habits greatly surprised everyone. He would come in punctually at nine in the morning and leave at three in the afternoon, and all this time he worked steadily; in spite of the continuous temptations posed by his companions, he did not, as in the past, spend the greater part of his work day chatting or in the smoking room.

"Look, Seixas, this is a way of life, not of death!" said one of his colleagues, repeating this commonplace for the twentieth time.

"I lived many years at the state's expense, my friend; it is only fair that it should also live some at mine."

There was another noticeable change in Seixas. It was a certain sobriety which, without affecting the politeness of his manners, elegant as always, converted him into an even nobler and more distinguished gentleman. His lips still smiled often; but the smile bore signs of meditation and was not, as before, a mere habit of gallantry.

Marriage is often considered a young man's initiation into the realities of life. It prepares for a family, the greatest and most serious of all responsibilities. Nowadays this solemn act has lost some of its meaning; there are individuals who marry with all the awareness and serenity with which a traveler sojourns at an inn.

That is why Seixas's colleagues were amazed by that behavior, so unlike what it had been before, in his single days; and, refusing to accept that marriage had so suddenly changed the man's nature, they attributed the transformation to his wealth; and his humility they deemed an imposture.

To arrive on time at the office, Seixas had to have breakfast early and by himself, which spared him, and Aurélia, close to half an hour of torture inflicted on each other by their presence.

"You have been going to work very diligently!" Aurélia told her husband one day. "Are you seeking a promotion?"

Seixas overlooked the sarcasm and answered honestly:

"You are right. There is an opening, and I would like to be chosen for it."

"How much does the job pay?"

"Forty-eight hundred."

"Do you need it?"

"Yes, I do."

Aurélia burst out into a silvery laughter, mean and poisonous.

"Well, why don't you become my employee? I will guarantee you the promotion."

"I am already your *husband*," answered Seixas, with heroic calmness.

The girl went on trilling her sarcastic laugh; but she turned her back to her husband and left.

Seixas went on foot to catch an omnibus on the way; the stop was a considerable distance from the office. One day his wife questioned him about it:

"Why do you refuse to take the car when you go out?"

"I prefer to exercise by walking. It is healthier; it does my body and spirit much good."

"It's a shame you did not concern yourself with studying health while you were single."

"You cannot imagine how I regret it. But it is never too late to learn, and these few days I have made good use of the time."

"It seems to me that you have unlearned. In those days you knew I was rich, very rich; today, you take me for a wife whose husband rides an omnibus."

Fernando bit his lip.

"Wealth has its decency, too. You married a millionaire; you must subject yourself to the burden of the position. The poor believe we have only pleasures and delights, and hardly imagine the servitude this golden piece of land imposes on us. Does it bother you to take the car? And isn't this luxury that surrounds me a form of torture? Is there any hair shirt that can compare to these fine lace and silk hair shirts that I wear over my flesh, which debase me at every moment because they remind me that in the eyes of the world, I, my being, my very soul, is worth less than these rags?"

The last words seemed to escape the girl's lips moistened with tears. Seixas, forgetting the bitter affront he had suffered a moment before, stared with compassionate eyes; but she had already recovered her aggressive ironic tone:

"Thus will the *world* find in me its creature—the woman it celebrates, upon whom it lavishes adoration. I shall be for it what it has made me."

That *world*, Fernando understood to be the pronoun for her unhappiness and ambition. Restored to the reality of his situation from which a sudden agitation had been slowly releasing him, he said:

"Do you believe, then, that the decency of your house demands that your husband ride in a car?"

"I believe I married a distinguished gentleman who knows how to use his wealth, and not a common man."

"You are right. You claim what belongs to you; I would be a scoundrel if I denied you what you have rightfully acquired."

Dona Firmina's arrival put an end to this dialogue.

When he returned from his office, Seixas would find his wife in the sitting room. If Aurélia had company, Seixas would embrace her waist and brush a stiff kiss over her peach-like face which would become taut under his cold breath. After dinner came the walk through the garden. It was then, hidden by the trees, as they were supposedly exchanging tender gestures, that Aurélia would pepper her husband with pointed remarks and derision. Ordinarily Seixas responded to this steady fire with patient indifference that would eventually tire his wife.

Now and then, however, it happened that Seixas returned the sarcasm, which would aggravate Aurélia's already fierce mood; her utterances would then turn relentlessly vitriolic.

If there were guests, the couple would spend the evening in the living room. When they were alone, they stayed in the sitting room, Seixas would open a book while Aurélia pretended to be listening to the passages her husband read aloud. Other evenings they would improvise some game in which Dona Firmina would participate, and whose futile monotony would kill the time.

They had been married for almost a month; during this period, seeing and talking to each other every day, they had not once pronounced each other's name. They used their verbs in the formal mode of address, respecting between them this tacit anonymity, underscoring the word with the gesture.

On one occasion, the living room was crowded. Aurélia approached her husband while he, a short distance away, chatted with several people. Seixas did not answer; she tried to draw closer to catch his attention, but his friends were all around him.

"Fernando!" she said, making an extreme effort.

Seixas turned, amazed; he saw on his wife's lips a smile that saturated with gall the sweetness of her voice.

"Did you call me?"

"To accompany Dona Margarida who is leaving."

The change in character that Seixas had undergone after his marriage could be felt equally in his elegance. The fine distinction of his manners and the fastidiousness of his attire were untarnished, but the dandyism that had glittered on him before had vanished.

His clothes had the same faultless cut as before, but no longer boasted the fashionable refinements; the fabric was superior, but the colors were subdued. Bright hues and artistic combinations of colors were no longer seen in his wardrobe.

Aurélia not only noticed this change, which lent a masculine tone to Seixas's elegance, but another particular as well, which piqued her curiosity even more. Of the objects that she had offered as part of his effects, she could not recall having seen her husband use even one.

Meanwhile the gossip among the slaves warned her of a circumstance of which she was unaware and which was linked to the other one.

It was her custom to have her personal slave distribute among the others various used adornments and dresses.

"Miss, you waste too much!" observed her servant, with the liberty that favorite slaves would sometimes take. "You do not know how to save things like Master; he keeps everything locked up, even the soap!"

"It is not your concern, neither yours nor the others', what your master does," Aurélia said, cutting her off severely.

She felt the impulse to question the slave but resisted the strong desire in order to maintain the decorum of her position and not lower herself to familiarity with the servants.

She sent the slave away, but decided to verify for herself what had gained Seixas this reputation as a miser that the public opinion of kitchen and stable had bestowed upon him.

∞ V ∞

The next day, after lunch, Aurélia remembered the decision she had made the day before.

At that time her husband was at his office, and the servant would have finished cleaning the rooms; she could therefore carry out her wishes without arousing attention.

She turned the key in the door that had been closed a month before between herself and her husband; she slowly drew aside the blue silk portière to ascertain that no one was in the room; trembling and excited by an agitation that seemed childish to her, she entered that part of the house to which she had not returned since her wedding.

What wonderful moments she had spent there on the days preceding the ceremony, when she had busied herself preparing and decorating these rooms destined for the man to whom she would be joined forever, only to be separated from him by a moral divorce, perhaps eternal!

The sentiment that overcame Aurélia and dominated her in those days she herself could not define, so unique were the feelings of affection generated in her soul.

While she caressed with bitter refinement the requital for her betrayed love, and foretasted the enjoyment of this man's humiliation, this man who trafficked her, there were moments in which she distanced herself completely from this concern with revenge and surrendered to pleasurable illusions.

She longed for love; and since she did not find it in reality, she drank of it in long, deep swallows from the golden cup offered her by fantasy. These hours she spent with her ideal; they were inebriating, delightful hours.

It was during that time that the girl took great care in decorating her rooms and studies. She dreamed that they would be occupied by the only man she had ever loved, and who returned her love with equal passion. She wanted this beloved being to find, as if it permeated the elegance of these chambers, her throbbing soul, which would embrace him and enclose him within it.

When she again saw the place and the objects that had been companions during those thoughts and ardent emotions, Aurélia yielded momentarily to the magical influence of her memories, which unfolded like pearled clouds dimming the sunlight and mitigating its heat.

Pulling herself out at last from the enchantment of this past, which was not even real and existed only as sweet chimera, she walked about the room, perusing it.

She noticed something that was in fact quite evident. The dressing table was totally stripped of the tasteful items with which she had decorated it with her own hands. It looked like a piece of furniture just delivered from the store. The wardrobes, dressers, desks, all locked, and likewise bare, announced lack of use.

"That is why!" she murmured to herself. "The servant does not suspect the reason and attributes it to stinginess."

One of Aurélia's most moving puerilities, when she dreamed of her marriage to the man she loved, was that of identical locks to all doors and pieces of furniture of each one's special use. Two souls that come together, she thought in sweet abnegation, have no secrets and should possess each other completely.

When she assembled the two sets of absolutely identical keys on golden rings, she smiled and imagined that on her wedding night when her husband knelt at her feet, she would raise him in her arms and tell him:

"Here are the keys to my soul and to my life! I belong to you; I have made you my master; and all I ask of you is the happiness of being yours forever!"

In what abyss of pain and shame all these tender visions had drowned, we already know. No one ever suspected, nor did she reveal, the vortex of despair hidden within that magnificent bosom, which seemed to heave only with the gentle emotions of love and pleasure.

Aurélia opened the furniture with her keys; and her assumptions were confirmed. Everything—jewelry, dressing table utensils, clothes—everything was put away in there, just as it had come from the shop.

"What does this mean?" murmured the girl to herself. "It seems a lack of interest. But no! It cannot be. In any case there is a plan, a fixed idea. The other day the car; now this!"

She pondered a bit longer and concluded:

"I do not understand."

Aurélia was right. If by this obstinacy Seixas wished to show his indifference to the wealth he acquired through marriage, he was cutting a ridiculous figure; for the personal effects were merely an insignificant accessory to the dowry for which he had exchanged his freedom.

The door to the bedroom was shut. Aurélia opened it with the duplicate key on her ring.

There she found the desk, which served as Seixas's temporary dressing table, and some very cheap combs and brushes.

"Now I understand. He wants to mortify me."

After dinner, they strolled in the garden; Aurélia who had picked up a rose, stroked her cheeks, purer than the flower's hue, with the soft petals.

"I was in your dressing room today," she said, simulating indifference.

"Oh! You did me the honor?"

"A lady of the house, as you know, has the obligation to see everything."

"The obligation and the right."

"The right here would be the wife's; and not only that one, but others as well."

"I understand," said Fernando.

"Fortunately. I can see we shall understand each other."

This dialogue, to any outsider who might overhear it, would never betray the slightest hostile or aggressive expression. So accustomed had the two actors of this unique drama become to dressing their irony with pleasantries and gallantry that they completely obscured their intention.

Quite often Dona Firmina would approach in the middle of one of these skirmishes of wit, and assume, as she listened to them, that they were cooing with courtesies and endearments, when they were peppering one another with biting allusions.

The girl hesitated a moment but, suddenly fixing her gaze on her husband's face, she asked him:

"What did you do with the objects that were on your dressing table?"

Seixas repressed a wave of noble resentment and smiled disdainfully:

"Do not worry; they are locked in the drawers, as untouched as you left them. Did you think that perhaps I had taken them to the pawn shop?"

"Those objects belong to you; you can do with them as you please, without answering to anyone. That was the response I expected and I would have no grounds to reply, for I recognize your right and I respect it."

"You put me in your debt with such generosity," said Seixas, feeling the sting of the allusion.

"Be not so quick to thank me. If I respect your right to dispose freely of what belongs to you, I too, for my part, insist on the guarantee of what I acquired at the sacrifice of my happiness. I married Mr. Fernando Rodrigues de Seixas, a distinguished gentleman, honest and liberal, and not a miser, for this is how the servants think of you, as will soon the whole neighborhood, if not the entire city."

Seixas listened with forced calmness to his wife's words and then replied briskly:

"Some days ago, this question arose between us because of the car; now it comes back over the issue of the dressing table; and it may be renewed at any moment. The best thing therefore is to put an end to it."

"Let us put an end to it."

"Give me your arm; here comes Dona Firmina."

Aurélia passed her hand through Seixas's arm. Strolling along beds of different kinds of fuchsias and admiring the flowers, they held the following interview, certainly one never before entertained between husband and wife.

"You bought a husband, and therefore have the right to demand from him respect, fidelity, companionship, all the attentions and honors that a man owes his wife. Until today—"

"You forgot to mention one, perhaps an insignificant one—love," interrupted Aurélia, playing with a cluster of fuchsias.

"It was understood. There is only one reservation to be made about this kind of product. Suppose you did not have this beautiful and rich head of hair, this sumptuous tiara the likes of which is not owned by any queen, and that you did like the other young women who buy their knots, their tresses, and their curls. You certainly would not pretend that those purchased hairs grew on your head, nor would you reasonably demand anything but false ones. Love that is sold is of the same nature as those wigs: wool nap or other people's scraps."

"Oh! No one knows better than I what kind of love this is, which is used in society and can be bought and sold in a commercial transaction called marriage! The other kind, the one I had dreamed of in the past, that one I well know that all the gold in the world cannot give! For that, for one day, for one hour of such bliss, I would sacrifice not only my wealth, which is worth nothing, but my life, and, I believe, my soul!"

Aurélia, choking on these words that sprang from her troubled bosom, had withdrawn her hand from Seixas's arm; when she finished she turned around quickly to hide the passionate feelings that had ignited her eyes and cheeks.

Seixas followed this movement with a gesture of profound grief, which for a moment afflicted his face but quickly vanished. He was busy threading some longer shoots of honeysuckle through the green trellis when Aurélia approached him.

"Do not take this foolishness too seriously. They are the final bursts from the past. I thought it was completely dead; it is still breathing, but in a few days we will have buried it. Perhaps then I will succeed in becoming the woman you needed, one of the many the world celebrates and admires."

"You will become whatever you wish to be; in any case, you will meet my needs provided you do not become poor."

This sarcasm brought Aurélia back to the reality of her situation.

"That is true. I forgot that there is only one link between us."

"May I continue?"

"I am listening."

"The obligations and respect I owe you as your husband, I have not yet failed to fulfill; nor will I fail to do so, whatever the humiliation they may impose upon me."

Aurélia felt a strange repulsion as she heard these words; her cheeks flushed.

"Madam, you also assume you did not buy just any husband, but an elegant one, of good background, and well-mannered. Although it does violence to my humility, I agree. Everything needed to flaunt a rich woman's vanity, I will do and I have been doing. With a few slight alterations that come with age, I am the same man I was when I received your proposal through Lemos. Am I mistaken?"

Aurélia answered with a gesture of extreme indifference.

"As you can see, I am precise and scrupulous in the execution of our contract. Grant me at least this merit. I sold you a husband; you have him at your disposal, as owner and mistress that you are. However, I did not sell you my soul, my character, my individuality; because this a man cannot alienate from himself, and you, madam, knew perfectly well that you could not purchase it at the price of gold."

"At what price then?"

"At no price, obviously, since money was not enough. If it is my whim that I should pretend to be sober, economical, industrious, I am fully within my rights; no one can forbid me this hypocrisy, nor impose upon me certain social skills and force me to behave like a glutton, an indolent, and a wastrel."

"Skills you had when you were single."

"Precisely, and which gained me the honor of being chosen by you."

"That is why I wish to revive them."

"When it comes to that, I am free, and you have not the slightest power over me. The magnificence of your house requires that you have a palace, a sumptuous table, expensive cars and horses, that you live amidst luxury and grandeur. I do not oppose you in the minutest detail; I live in that house, sit at that table, will ride those cars to accompany you; in your splendid salons I will not be a wretch who clashes with the other pieces of the furniture. As for the rest, to feel, for instance, appetite for your delicacies and pleasure at your parties, to that I did not commit myself. And, by chance, is boredom or the habit of walking a shortcoming that lowers a man in his social position, in his merits?"

"By chance, let me ask you, is it pleasant for a lady to have a husband who becomes a laughingstock for the servants and is known to lock up his soap? And you can see how out of control they are, if their mockery has already reached my ears."

"I understand that this wounds your pride. But there is a solution: let them steal those objects, or give them away on some pretext, as long as I do not have to use them."

Aurélia made an impatient gesture.

"I do not argue the right you say you have over what you call your soul and your character. You have contrived this ingenious way to irritate me; I will not deprive you of the pleasure; but if you wish to know how I feel—"

"I am committed to it. Your opinion is for me a beacon; it points out the shoals."

"But it did not prevent your running aground. However, let us not waste time on witticisms. What need have we of these plays on words when we are each the living satire of the other? There are certain sinners in the world who, after having obtained the means of enjoying the pleasures of life, find a few virtues to flaunt, with which they bargain for their absolution and thus avoid having to restore their soul to God."

Seixas's face betrayed the anger welling in his soul and on the verge of erupting. But this time he still managed to contain the rebellion of his self-respect.

"Finish."

"I had already finished. But to satisfy you, I will dot the i; your economy and sobriety belong to the official virtues of those timorous sinners."

"Your sagacity is amazing! No wonder you are Mr. Lemos's niece."

Aurélia, who had moved forward, turned around as if a snake had bitten her heel. So eloquent was the access of insulted dignity that the girl's forehead trembled, and such was the hauteur of her queenly look that Seixas regretted his words.

"I am sorry!" he said gently. "Sometimes your irony is unforgiving."

Aurélia did not answer. Walking ahead of him, she went into the house and retired to her dressing room.

This was the first evening since they were married that she did not return from the garden accompanied by and on the arm of her husband.

☞ VI ☜

It was a magnificent moonlit night.

Seixas was talking to Dona Firmina on the front marble walkway which was shaded by leafy trees.

To the right of her husband Aurélia reclined in a low chair with the back dropped down, a comfortable lounge chair for the body and for the spirit that wishes to daydream.

Since the afternoon of the explanations concerning the dressing table, the relationship between the two companions of these matrimonial fetters had been altered.

As if they had at that point exhausted their store of bitterness and gall, accumulated during the first month of marriage, beginning the following day their words corresponded to the amenity and refinement of their manners and lost the ironic edge with which, like wasps with their subtle and poisonous barb, they had previously always been armed.

They spoke less about themselves; conversing about things that were trivial or indifferent, they sometimes forgot, for hours on end, the calamity that had united them in eternal conflict for them to mutually lacerate their souls.

Seixas was at that moment describing to Dona Firmina the beautiful poem by Byron, "Parisina." The theme arose from a passage of the opera Aurélia had played before she came outside to sit on the walkway.

After the poem, Fernando turned to the poet. He missed those bright fantasies that had once cradled the most cherished dreams of his youth. Just as a butterfly numbed by the cold unfurls her wings to the sun's first ray, imagination reveled about those flowers of the soul.

He was not addressing Dona Firmina, who perhaps did not understand him, or Aurélia, who certainly was not listening to him. It was for himself that he unfolded the riches of his spirit; the audience was merely an excuse for this monologue.

Sometimes he would repeat the translations he had made of the English bard's blank verse, those literary gems, exquisitely attired, enhanced even more by the sweet language of Rio and by coming from the lips of Seixas, who recited them like a troubadour.

Aurélia, in the beginning, surrendered to the enchantment of that Brazilian evening, which reminded her of a dream of her soul painted on the diaphanous blue of the sky.

Sometimes she took refuge in the deeper shade, as if fearful that the indiscreet moonbeams would spy in her eyes her most secluded thoughts. There, in the darkness that disguised her, she amused herself looking at the trees and the buildings floating in the brightness that flooded them like a serene lake.

Other times she would fearfully and slowly turn her head until her eyes met a strip of moonlight shining through two palm leaves and adumbrating the wall. This vein of light would then fall upon her forehead and bathe her in white splendor.

She remained in this position for a moment, her eyes engulfed by moonlight and her lips slightly parted to imbibe the celestial emanation. Later, satiated with light, she once again withdrew into the shade; and, like a tree that blossoms with the sunlight, her soul transformed the night's effulgences into dreams.

Nearby, the corymbs of mignonettes, swaying in the breeze, perfumed the air, and it was through this reverie of light and fragrance that Seixas's resonant voice penetrated Aurélia's musings and became so entwined with them that she imagined hearing not her husband's conversation, but a voice from her dream.

In order to listen, she had supported herself on the arm of the lounge chair and, impassively reclining her head, rested against Seixas's shoulder in a graceful, languid movement.

"One of Byron's most beautiful poems is 'The Corsair,'" Seixas was saying.

"Tell it," the girl whispered in his ear with a voice that sylphs would have if they could speak.

Fernando surrendered at this moment to a very sweet influence, against which he wished to react but lacked the strength to do so. The pressure of that beautiful head produced in him the effect of a fairy's magical touch; prey to the enchantment, he no longer remembered who he was or where he was.

Words flowed from his lips quivering with emotion, but words rich, inspired, colorful. He did not recite the English bard's poem; he embroidered a different poem on the same web, and anyone hearing him at that moment would have found the original cold and pale next to the eloquent plagiarism. For in this one there was a soul throbbing, whereas in the other remain only the silenced songs of the bygone genius.

"You should translate this poem. It is so beautiful!" said Dona Firmina.

"I do not have the time," answered Seixas. "Nor the desire. I am a public employee and nothing more."

"You do not need the job now; you are rich."

"Not as much as you think."

Aurélia stood up so impetuously that she seemed to repel her husband's arm, against which she had been leaning just a moment before.

"You are right. No, do not translate Byron. The poet of doubt and skepticism; only those who suffer from that cruel disease, a truly apathetic heart, can understand him. For us, the fortunate ones, he is an insipid visionary."

After hurling at Seixas these words, enwrapped in sardonic laughter, the girl left the walkway. She had just entered the zone of light that turned the fine sand into silver when she felt a chill. That splendid moon, a gentle wave in which she had voluptuously bathed some moments before, cut through her like a vein of ice.

She turned hastily and went to the drawing room, where there was only the dim glow of two gas burners in their lamps. She herself had ordered it thus, so that the artificial light would not disturb nature's celebration. Now she rang the bell, calling to the manservant to do exactly the opposite. The lighted chandeliers poured forth dazzling torrents from the gas and expelled the moonlight's niveous reflections.

"Are you spending the whole evening there?" asked Aurélia.

"We were enjoying the moonlight," said Dona Firmina, coming in with Seixas.

"There are those who admire moonlit evenings! I find them unbearable. The spirit drowns in that blue sea like a wretch thrashing in the ocean. For me, there is no sky or meadow equal to these evenings in the drawing room, full of comfort and warmth and light in which we feel alive. Here there is no risk of drowning one's thoughts."

"No, but one asphyxiates!" observed Seixas.

"I prefer that."

Aurélia sat at the mosaic table, turning her back to the garden to avoid seeing the beautiful evening that had displeased her. However, as the mirror before her reproduced with the scintillation of crystal a corner of the garden where the silvery brightness of the moon seemed to coalesce on the lilies and the cacti, the girl called the manservant once more and ordered him to close the window that admitted that obtrusive sketch of the superb nocturnal canvas.

On the table there was a game box, from where Aurélia took a pack of cards and amused herself telling fortunes.

"Shall we play?" she asked, addressing her husband.

He took a seat across the table from Aurélia, who handed him the pack and took another one from the box.

"*Écarté.*"

Seixas made a gesture of consent or obedience. Once the cards had been prepared for the game and it was his turn to deal, he handed her the cards to cut.

"Ten thousand a game!" Aurélia said, ringing the bell.

Seixas's eyes searched for Dona Firmina, who was leaning against the window, not paying attention to the game. At that moment, the manservant walked in.

"Have Luisa bring my purse. We may continue."

"Forgive me," corrected Seixas, in a low voice. "I do not play for money."

"Why not?"

"I do not like it."

"Are you afraid of losing?"

"That is one reason."

"I shall lend it to you."

"I have also outgrown the bad habit of counting on other people's money," replied Seixas, smiling and emphasizing the words. "Since I have become rich, I only spend my own."

"Don't I deserve this kindness?" retorted Aurélia, also sharpening her smile. "Please be, at least for this evening, a gambler and wastrel to satisfy my whim."

The girl received her purse from the slave, removed from it a pound sterling, and placed it on the table.

"Are you not tempted?"

"It is very little!" replied Seixas with an embittered smile.

This smile annoyed Aurélia and she put away the coin and the purse. She continued for a while to shuffle the cards absentmindedly and then uttered some disconnected words resembling a monologue:

"They say that water and wine make two excellent beverages into one that is terrible. The same happens to the mixture of virtue and vice. It makes man a hybrid being. Neither good nor bad. Neither worthy of being loved nor so vile that one avoids contact. I understand what a woman must feel— what a friend of mine felt when she realized that she was in love with one of these dubious men, the products of modern society."

"This friend of yours, whom I suppose I know, would she rather her husband be, instead of one of these equivocal creatures, purely and simply a slave?" Seixas asked.

"Certainly. If her husband were a slave, she would immediately break the shackles that bound her to him and would walk away with death in her soul. But I—"

"You, madam?" asked her husband, noting her hesitation.

Aurélia's fringed lids raised, revealing the large brown eyes that dazzled Seixas. Her torso extended with her movement to draw nearer, and her voice sounded deep and vibrant.

"I? I would not care if he were Lucifer, so long as he was able to deceive me to the end, convince me of his passion and intoxicate me with it. But to worship an idol and see him at every moment turn into something that derides and repels us—that is the torture of Tantalus, more cruel than thirst and starvation."

Having spoken these words, Aurélia stood up and, crossing the room, went into her apartment.

"Where is Aurélia?" asked Dona Firmina when she turned away from the window.

"She has already retired. The evening was cool. The damp air disagrees with her. Good night."

The next day was a Sunday.

At dinner, Aurélia said to her husband:

"We have been married for over a month. We should make our calls."

"Whenever you wish."

"We shall begin tomorrow. At noon; is that a good time?"

"Would it not be better in the afternoon?" offered her husband.

"Do you object to the morning?"

"I do not want to miss going to work."

"Well, then it really is going to be in the morning," the girl replied smiling. "I will not admit this lack of gallantry. Don't you agree, Dona Firmina? Preferring his work to my company?"

"Certainly!" confirmed the widow.

Seixas did not argue. It was his duty to accompany his wife when she wanted to go out, and he was determined to fulfill all his obligations scrupulously.

∞ VII ∞

Seixas wrote a letter to his employer justifying his absence for a serious reason and sending him some papers he had dispatched the day before.

As he entered the sitting room, he found Aurélia examining the weather.

"It is such a hot day! Perhaps we had better postpone our calls. What do you say?"

"Make up your mind because there is still time for me to go to the office."

"Let us have breakfast. I shall decide afterwards."

When they rose from the table, Aurélia still had not decided. Seixas, realizing that his wife's intention was to annoy him and that she relished it, resigned himself to a wasted day.

At one o'clock, the girl approached him:

"We shall have an early dinner today and leave at five o'clock. Would that suit you?"

"Any time you choose suits me," Seixas replied.

"Perhaps you dislike going out in the afternoon. In that case, it will be at eleven."

"So let it be tomorrow."

"Will you miss work again?"

"If I must."

"No, we will go out this afternoon."

Aurélia called the servant and gave her orders. As she had determined, dinner was earlier, and at five o'clock she descended the steps of her mansion; at the gate the elegant victoria drawn by a team of Cape horses awaited her.

The girl wore a blue grosgrain dress interwoven with silver threads which endowed her pure complexion with mellow and translucent tones. Her movements as, lightly resting the tip of her boot on the step, she elevated herself from the ground to recline on the yellow upholstery of the carriage, resembled a soaring butterfly, fluttering its large wings and nestling in the calyx of a flower.

Aurélia's dress filled up the carriage and submerged her husband; what remained visible of his face and chest was obfuscated by the young lady's beauty. No one could see him; all salutations, all eyes were for the queen who emerged from her brief retreat.

The car stopped by several houses, indicated on the note the coachman had received. Seixas would offer his hand to his wife to help her alight and lead her by the arm to the steps, which she would ascend by herself, for she needed both hands to swim in the deluge of silk, lace, and jewelry, that these days comprises the woman's *mundus*.

There, as on the street, all attentions were for Aurélia, surrounded by eager ladies and by men fascinated by her loveliness. Seixas was afforded only a pale reflection of this consideration, whatever was demanded by strict civility. In some houses, in the zeal to welcome his wife he was left behind, as unnoticed as a servant.

In different circumstances this annihilation of his individuality might not have bothered him. Perhaps, should he notice it, he would have taken pride at being the favorite of this magnificent woman, surrounded by general admiration and contested by so many admirers. All this worship the world bestowed upon her, all the homage society paid her would in his eyes be only a tribute offered him by his wife's love.

But the circumstances in which he found himself must completely alter the disposition of his spirit. The higher his wife was elevated—this wife to whom he was bound not by love but merely by a monetary obligation—the more debased he felt. He exaggerated his position; he even compared himself to one of the lady's accessories or adornments.

Had Aurélia not said on that cruel evening that a husband was a trinket every respectable woman must have and that she had bought him for that purpose? She was right. There, in that car, or in the drawing rooms they entered, it seemed that his position and his importance were like unto, if not less than, the fan, fur, jewelry, and car in the dress and the luxury that were Aurélia's.

When he offered his hand to his wife to help her alight, or carried her cashmere shawl on his arm, he compared himself to the coachman who drove the car and the footman who opened the step. The only difference was that those were services gentlemen customarily offered ladies; only in their absence do they receive them from a higher ranking servant.

One of the last visits was to the family of Lísia Soares, who had considered herself Aurélia's closest friend when she had been single.

After the greetings and congratulations, when the conversation wavered in search of a theme, Lísia, who was mischievous, remembered to breathe upon a spark. There was no greater pleasure for her than to goad Aurélia, whose wit had many times nettled her.

"Do you remember, Aurélia, when you used to quote the price of your suitors?" said the spiteful girl, raising her voice to make sure she was heard.

"Do I? Of course!" replied Aurélia, smiling.

"And what you told me one evening about Alfredo Moreira? That he was worth at most one hundred thousand, but that you were wealthy enough to pay for a more highly priced husband?"

"And did I not speak the truth?"

"So, Mr. Seixas? . . ." inquired Lísia with an obnoxious ellipsis that arrested the words on her lips, only to sprinkle malice in her smile and in her eyes.

"Ask him!" Aurélia said, turning toward her husband.

Never, after finding himself enslaved by this woman or before the ill fortune that subjected him to her whims, had Seixas so needed the resignation he had draped about himself to avoid succumbing to the shame of such degradation. The first shock produced by the dialogue between the two friends was terrible, yet they took no notice of it because, at the moment, the general attention converged upon Aurélia.

But he controlled himself. When the eyes that followed his wife's gesture turned toward him, they found him calm, naturally serious, and courteous, although still left with a slight paleness that no one saw.

"So, Mr. Seixas, is that correct?" insisted Lísia.

"What, my lady?" asked the young man in his turn, with extreme politeness.

"What Aurélia said."

"Can't you see it was in jest?" observed Lísia's mother.

"She has always been like this; she loves to play!" one of the cousins said.

"You do not believe me!" replied Aurélia rather indifferently.

"Is it true, Mr. Seixas?" Lísia asked again.

"Answer!" said Aurélia to her husband, with a smile.

"On my wife's part I do not know, and only she can tell you, Dona Lísia. As for me, I assure you that I married only for the dowry of one hundred thousand that I received. I assume my wife changed her mind about paying for a more highly priced husband."

The seriousness with which Seixas proffered these words and perchance also a certain asperity of tone noticeable in his harmonious speech, as one feels the iron springs beneath satin upholstery, left those present perplexed as to the meaning and the credit they should lend to this assertion.

At this point the crystalline sound of Aurélia's laughter rang out.

"This is what you wanted, Lísia, for Fernando to become suspicious. Do you want to know if I bought him and for what price? I make no secret of it; I bought him, and paid dearly. He cost me more, much more than a million; and I paid not in gold but in a different currency worth far more. He cost me my heart; that is why I no longer have it!"

These words and the expression resounding in them convinced everyone that Aurélia had indeed been joking about her marriage. The reply to Lísia was nothing but a disguise to provoke that inopportune confession about the passion with which she and her husband loved each other.

Thus, when the guests had left, the theme of the conversation was the mutual delight of the newlyweds who, a month after their wedding, walked down the street cooing like a pair of lovebirds. Lísia attested to having seen Aurélia so entangled in her husband's arm that he could not even walk.

Meanwhile the car drove around Catete, and Aurélia, swaying to the gentle movement of the cushions, seemed to have completely forgotten Seixas seated beside her, when he addressed her:

"Since we have been married, not once have I questioned your intentions. I respect them, as is my duty, and comply with them when I can, however strange they may seem. But to satisfy your wishes I at least must know them, even though I may not understand them."

Aurélia turned her face toward her husband. No longer in fear of being seen because of the twilight, she allowed her visage to assume the expression of haughty disdain that came upon it in these moments of implacable annoyance.

"What do you have in mind with this prologue?"

"At first I thought you wanted to hide the reality of our position from strangers. I confess that I could never fathom the reason for this peculiarity. To deliberately create a situation just for the pleasure of denying it at every moment—"

"It is absurd, is it not? I feel the same way."

"I will not probe your thoughts. You must have had a reason, of which I am unaware."

"As am I."

"I would like to know, however, whether you changed on purpose, as indicated by the scene you have just performed, or whether you have decided, henceforth, to make a scandal from what yesterday you kept a mystery."

"And why do you want to know this?"

"I have already told you, to comply with your wish and attune myself to the same key. The duet will win more applause."

"Doubtless, but on my part, I did not marry to turn my life into a musical score. I may be flighty and inconsistent, I may have these flaws, but what I do not have, you may rest assured, is the talent for scheming. Allow me my eccentric temper. Now, at this moment, do I by chance know what I shall be doing this evening? What extravagance might tempt me? How could I, then, formulate a marital program for our use? I can make of our marriage either mystery or scandal, as I fancy. But you, sir, you do not have that right."

"As much as you, madam!"

Aurélia contested with cold impassiveness:

"You are wrong. Mr. Seixas cannot discredit my husband and expose him to public ridicule."

"But the wife of the wretch can; she has the right."

"You gave it to her."

"No, use the proper term: I *sold* it!"

Aurélia did not answer. Resting her body against the cushions and turning her face to watch the outline of the trees and farms on the sunset-illuminated screen of the sky, she allowed the conversation to lapse.

They made further visits. It was past eight o'clock when the car stopped at the door of their house. Dona Firmina had gone out. Aurélia, complaining of fatigue, took leave of her husband and retired.

In his room Seixas recalled the words that had escaped Aurélia during the afternoon conversation. "Do I by chance know what I shall be doing this evening? What extravagance might tempt me?" his wife had said. And he knew what these enigmatic phrases meant on her lips.

Ever since the moonlit evening and the poetic reveries about Byron, Aurélia displayed continuous irritability. What could be the resolve, inspired by that fever in her soul, already so given to whims and eccentricities?

Seixas spent a moment mulling over this point, conjecturing. He tired of the task, however, and abandoned it, believing there could be no worsening of the unbearable situation in which he found himself.

He had ceased thinking about it when, suddenly, an idea crossed his mind and made him shudder.

Dominated by an impulse of curiosity, he rushed to the door that separated him from the nuptial chamber and his wife's apartment. He raised his hand to knock, began to utter Aurélia's name, but did not muster the strength to execute his original intention. He placed his ear to listen. In that part of the house reigned absolute silence. What could he do?

Troubled by the terrible idea that had assailed him, he paced about the room aimlessly, in cruel perplexity. His eye, unwilling to leave the door, noticed a jet of light at the end of the dark corridor and realized that it came from the keyhole.

He approached, carefully and quietly. Through the opening for the key he could see on the opposite wall an illuminated portrait that stood out in the twilight of the nuptial chamber. It was the mirror placed over the marble flower stand, which reflected obliquely through the open door a narrow band of the other room.

This area comprised a couch where, at this moment, amid the green brocade, stood out the statue of Aurélia, reclined like the high relief that in times past decorated the tombstones of nobles. The girl's body was wrapped in a cambric robe whose pleats fell onto the rug like gushes of white foam from a waterfall, leaving her shape outlined under the delicate film of linen.

She was very pale and motionless. One of her arms hung languidly over the side of the couch; the other she had raised to the frame of the opening where her hand seemed to clinch, perhaps in an effort to raise her body. In the immobility of her position and in her figure there was a frightful rigidity.

∞ VIII ∞

Subsequently Aurélia's behavior displayed inexplicable acts, so contradictory that they defeat the acumen of the most profound physiologist.

Convinced that the heart also has its logic, although different from that which reigns over the mind, the narrator of this event would wish to probe the reason for these singular movements engendered in Aurélia's soul.

Since, however, he has not been endowed with the lucidity required for the study of psychological phenomena, he will limit himself to what he knows, leaving to the sagacity of each the fathoming of the true cause of such contrary impulses.

Let us return, therefore, to the course of Aurélia's new existence until the evening of her wedding, when the exalted state that inspired her during the scene that had taken place with Seixas suddenly struck her, and she lay prostrate on the rug of the nuptial chamber.

She did not exactly faint, or if so, it was merely a brief swoon. But she spent the rest of the night there, lacking the strength or resolve to rise, in an intense lethargy that, while not completely extinguishing her mind, lulled it into heavy somnolence.

She was aware of her pain; she suffered bitterly, but at that moment she had not the acuity to discern the reason for her despair and appraise the situation she herself had created.

At dawn, sleep, though troubled, brought respite from her anguish. She slept for about an hour, having the floor for her bed, her head on the same bedframe intended as a step toward her happiness.

The morning glare filtering through the lace of the curtains awoke her. She rose hastily, impelled by a terrible idea that, like a flash of light, had crossed the confused shadow of her memories.

She ran to the door through which Seixas had left, and listened, deeply apprehensive. Several times she placed her hand on the key only to remove it in fright. Aimlessly, she walked quickly about the house and finally approached the window, automatically, with no purpose.

It was at this point that she saw Seixas furtively cross the garden and enter the house. Silence still reigned over this entire part of the building, so she could hear the light sound of her husband's steps in the adjoining apartment.

A bitter, scornful laughter clinched her lips.

"He is a coward!"

After what had taken place between them on the evening of their wedding, Aurélia concluded that Seixas had only two means of breaking the humiliating bondage to which she had subjected him. He could kill her, or he could kill himself.

She had prepared herself for either of these two solutions. It is true that sometimes her heart nourished an impossible hope. If the man she loved were to kneel at her feet and beg her to forgive him, would she be strong enough to resist and salvage the dignity of her love?

But she did not have to undergo this eventuality. At her first words, Seixas had withdrawn, to display thereafter an effrontery that she had never expected and that produced in her soul an unspeakable horror. The tie that bound her to this man had become a degradation, almost an infamy.

Meanwhile, by expelling him from her presence, she still hoped that the words proffered by her husband were but a bitter irony. She could not admit that she had loved such a dissolute and vile being. The cynicism that had earlier offended her must engender some reaction.

It was upon seeing Seixas in the morning that she fully understood what a miserable creature he was. Then her soul underwent a transformation in which all good and affectionate feelings foundered, leaving on the surface only the aggressive and vicious instincts that constitute the lees of the heart.

When Aurélia had devised the marriage that she eventually effected, she was not inspired by calculated vengeance. Her idea, one she cherished and that filled her with hope, was to manifest to Seixas the immensity of the passion that he had failed to understand; by sacrificing her freedom and all hope to join a man she neither loved, nor could ever love, she would lay bare before his eyes the bleak wasteland her soul had become after losing this love that comprised all her existence. This posthumous marriage of an extinct love was but a splendid funeral, before which Seixas should feel mean and ridiculous as, before the bier, the haughty become aware of human misery.

The feeling that drove Aurélia might be called pride, but not revenge. It was rather the exaltation of her love which she craved, not Seixas's humiliation, although this was essential to the desired effect. She did not hate the man who had deluded her; she rebelled against the disappointment and wished to overcome it, subjugate it, compelling the cold heart that did not reciprocate her affection to admire her in the splendor of her passion.

But at that moment, recalling the words Seixas had uttered some hours before, seeing him calm, ready to accept as natural the terrible situation, thinking about the lack of dignity with which the man submitted himself to continuous degradation, Aurélia had felt a true urge for revenge.

Seixas wished to insult her with his insolent audacity. Very well, then, she accepted the challenge. If this miserable creature was not utterly devoid of the last traces of self-respect and shame, she intended to vex him with her most virulent sarcasm. Unless his soul was dead, he should feel the brand of her red-hot iron.

It was in this state of mind that Aurélia dressed for breakfast; and she was still in this state of mind during the afternoon when she left with her husband to make her calls.

Nevertheless, when on the day following the wedding, she sat in the rocking chair and saw Seixas come into the dining room, her resolution wavered. The young man's noble and distinguished appearance, the natural elegance of his gesture, restored the prestige that such gifts never fail to exert in lofty spirits, and to which hers was already accustomed.

The thought of revenge did not leave her, but the bitterness and anger incited by yesterday's resentment were sheathed in the courteous form and delicate tone that seldom, and only in a moment of violent turmoil, forsake people of breeding.

In the alternatives for this wish for revenge, often counteracted by the generous impulses of her soul, the first month following the wedding slipped away.

If in surrendering to the inner irritation that exasperated her mind, she delighted in flogging her husband's dignity with her inexorable sarcasm, when she retired after one of these scenes, she did so to unburden the tears and the sobs that swelled in her breast. She then realized that the victim of her wrath was not the man she hated but her own heart that had worshiped this creature, unworthy of such saintly affection.

When weary of this constant orgasm of the soul, always obdurate from scorn, she imperceptibly reverted to her gentle nature, her relationship with her husband took on a loving expression. Then suddenly she would be invaded by a deadly coldness and would shudder, frightened by the idea of belonging to such a man.

Thus had Aurélia arrived at that moonlit evening when Seixas spoke of poetry and she listened, leaning on his arm in the rapture from which she had been painfully wrenched by a word from her husband.

Later, by herself, she thought about the incident and was filled with horror. For a moment, albeit a fleeting one, she even lamented Seixas failing to deceive her on that occasion by lulling, or rather dulling her self-respect. By the time that illusion vanished, it would have been too late and she would irrevocably belong to her husband.

This feeling, which she, having hardly uttered, rebuffed with all the strength of her soul, nevertheless, left within her a deep sorrow, along with the panic of such hallucinations. Hence the irritability that dominated her since then, and reached its peak on the afternoon of the visits.

Entering her dressing room, Aurélia was feverish—feverish from the passion that inflamed her. She opened every door and window and lunged, dressed as she was, onto the couch, remaining there motionless as Seixas saw her through the keyhole.

Frightened at such immobility, her husband was about to knock when a slave woman passed in front of the illuminated scene, and it suddenly vanished. The door of the dressing room, reflected in the mirror, closed.

The next day Aurélia stayed in her apartment all morning. When he returned from his office, Seixas found her pale and downcast.

At dinner it was Dona Firmina who kept the conversation going. The day before, the widow had spent the evening at a neighbor's, where there was a weekly gathering. Someone happened to mention Abreu, who was said to have sunk into poverty. At this point they recalled all the extravaganzas and prodigalities through which the young man had squandered, in slightly over a year, the substantial inheritance left by his father.

Dona Firmina, repeating what she had heard, deplored Abreu's fate—he had sacrificed such a beautiful future. Infusing her judgment with that stern morality usually cultivated for use on others and not for oneself, she accused the young man with excessive rigor.

"It is not his fault, Dona Firmina," observed Aurélia, returning from her abstraction.

"Whose is it then?" asked the widow.

"Of whoever made him wealthy, without rearing him for wealth. Gold emanates a kind of miasma that produces fever and causes lightheadedness and delirium. One must have a very strong spirit to resist the infection, or a kindly saint to ward off the poison; otherwise one invariably succumbs to it."

"Do you mean to say that wealth is an evil, Aurélia?"

"It is not an evil; it often becomes a blessing; but, whatever the case, it is dangerous. Those who train with weapons think that everything can be resolved by force. The same happens with money. Those who possess it in large amounts become convinced that everything can be bought."

They had finished dinner. Aurélia rose from the table and amused herself feeding the canaries bits of bread she crumbled in the palm of her hand.

Meanwhile Seixas had lighted his cigar and, lost in thought, strolled down the path winding between beds of daisies and grassy carpets, and disappeared in a grove of palm trees. The young man recalled scenes from the day before, compared them with the words just uttered by Aurélia, and searched for an explanation to the enigma.

He was interrupted by the girl's voice beside him.

"This stroll every afternoon must already bore you. Why not go horseback riding? You should enjoy yourself."

Aurélia spoke while playing with the flowers to avoid meeting Seixas's eyes.

"Your company can never bore me."

"Always, it becomes monotonous."

"Besides, it is my *duty*," replied Seixas, emphasizing the word.

Aurélia moved away; she took a few steps, looked at the red flowers on a vine called *ladies' earrings*, and secure in the resolve that disquieted her, turned to her husband.

"Our destinies are joined forever. Fate has denied me the happiness I had dreamed of. It was my fancy that no other woman would have you as long as I live. But I do not intend to condemn you to the torture of this existence we have been living for over a month. I will not hold you; you are free. Enjoy your time as you wish; you owe me no explanations."

Aurélia stood quietly, awaiting an answer.

"Do you wish to be left alone, madam?" Seixas asked. "Order and I will leave, now as on any other occasion."

"You did not understand me. There is a way of easing the weight of this chain that links us fatally and of sparing you the constant outbursts of my eccentric character. It is a divorce that I offer you."

"A divorce?" Seixas exclaimed briskly.

"You may proceed with it whenever you wish," Aurélia replied firmly, and left.

◑ IX ◐

Surprised and shaken by the girl's proposal, Seixas reflected for a moment.

As a result of his reflection, he moved closer to his wife, busy at this moment watching some goldfish in the pond effervesce at the surface of the water to devour pieces of a rose apple with which she tempted them.

"These fish amuse you now," Fernando said. "If tomorrow they bore you, will you have them thrown out and let them starve?"

The girl lifted bewildered eyes to her husband.

"Perhaps you never happened to think about this social problem," continued Fernando. "Does the master have the right to dismiss the captive whenever he so pleases?"

"I don't think anyone will doubt it," Aurélia answered.

"So, by your understanding, after having deprived a man of his freedom, after debasing him before his own conscience, after having transformed him into an instrument, it is legitimate, under the pretext of emancipation, to abandon this creature who had been kidnapped from society? I believe the contrary."

"But what does this have to do—?"

"Everything. You, madam, have made me your husband; I have no other mission in this world. Since you have imposed this destiny upon me and have sacrificed my future, you have no right to deny me what I have paid for so dearly. I have paid at the cost of my freedom."

"That freedom I return to you."

"And along with it, can you return what I lost by estranging it?"

"You are perhaps afraid of the scandal the divorce will produce. We need not publicize our decision; we can live totally apart from each other in the same city, or even in the same house. If need be, we have the excuse of trips because of illness or change of climate or to tour Europe."

"You will do whatever you wish. My obligation is to obey you, as a slave, so long as I do not fail you as the husband you have purchased."

Aurélia stared disdainfully at Seixas's countenance.

"Do you believe I can change my feelings toward you?"

"Have no fear. Were I not convinced that love between us is an impossibility, I would not be here now."

A strange smile brightened Aurélia's face as she trembled with a gesture of sublime hauteur.

"What then is the reason for you not to accept what I offer you?"

"What you offer me, madam, cost you one hundred thousand, and to accept alms of such value is to steal from the prodigal who throws it away."

"As you wish!" said Aurélia derisively. "Surely you imagine that your presence annoys me and therefore you enjoy the idea of imposing it to vex me. You are wrong. You may stay; it was not for my sake, but for your own that I offered you the separation. Do you reject it? Good; you cannot complain about whatever comes to pass."

In spite of Seixas's refusal, following that afternoon his relationship with Aurélia became more elusive. The girl made no effort, as during the first weeks, to spend a great amount of time in her husband's company. He, in turn, fearful of becoming inopportune, remained aloof as long as his wife did not indicate that she wished him near her.

There were days when they did not see each other. Seixas left very early for his office; Aurélia would have dinner with some friend. Only the following day, at four in the afternoon, would they meet again.

Fernando would avail himself of these afternoons spent alone at home, since Dona Firmina accompanied Aurélia, to visit his mother, who still lived in the same house on Hospício Street.

It was a matter of disapproval among Dona Camila's acquaintances that her son should abandon her thus to an obscure and indigent life instead of summoning her to his company or at least helping her subsist at a different level of decency and wealth.

Dona Camila did not complain. But in spite of her extreme love for that son, and of the selflessness of her endearment, she had found it strange that Fernando, after his marriage, did not think to give his sisters any gift at all.

Very seldom did Fernando appear at his mother's house, and then only in passing. Dona Camila overlooked this, although she lamented that her son's position and social obligations did not allow her to have him for longer periods of time.

At first, Mariquinhas prodded her mother for the two of them to go to Seixas's house in Laranjeiras and even to spend the day there. Her mother, unaccustomed to society, feared Aurélia's criticism. However, this reason would not deter her if Fernando insisted; but he, on the contrary, pretended not to understand and changed the subject at his sister's first hints.

This evasiveness on the part of her husband's family did not escape Aurélia. One afternoon when Seixas received in her presence a note from Nicota, she questioned him:

"After the evening of our wedding, your family has never come back to this house! Is it because of me?"

"No, it is my fault. I never mentioned it to them again."

"And why not?"

"They believe I am happy. I do not want to rob them of that sweet delusion."

"Those who come here and those we visit, are they not deluded?"

"They are indifferent. A mother's eye can read her son's soul like an open book: what they do not see, they guess."

"Do you want to wager?"

"About what?"

"I can deceive her as I have deceived everyone."

"Possibly; she is not your mother."

Nicota's note informed Fernando of the day set for her wedding, which was celebrated the following week, on a Saturday according to the usual custom.

Seixas hid this detail from his wife. On the afternoon the wedding was to take place, he went out with the excuse of paying a visit to a minister and attended the ceremony. He took his sister a piece of jewelry, but one of insignificant value for his wealth.

This stinginess, added to the fact that he went on foot, made those in attendance suspect that his unexpected opulence had affected Seixas's character to the point of transforming him from a spendthrift into a refined miser.

Another wedding took place at this time. It was that of Dr. Torquato Ribeiro to Adelaide Amaral.

Some days earlier, the bridegroom received, through Lemos, a message from Aurélia, requesting her receipt for the fifty *mil-réis*, as the time had come to repay it. Ribeiro went to Laranjeiras, wondering about the surprise the girl might have planned for him.

"Here is what I owe you; the three ciphers are Adelaide's gift."

Ribeiro opened the paper; it was a check made to the bearer for fifty thousand on the Bank of Brazil. He made a gesture of refusal, but the girl interrupted him:

"You have no right to reject it. It was the price of my happiness. My uncle guaranteed to Amaral that you had this money; otherwise he would not consent to undo his daughter's marriage to Fernando, and the latter would not be my husband."

"How are we ever going to repay you for this enormous kindness?" the young man asked, deeply touched.

"By being happy," answered the young lady.

"It would suffice me to be as happy as you are."

"As happy as I?"

"Yes. Aren't you happy?"

"Very. You cannot even imagine how much!"

Aurélia was Adelaide's matron of honor and Seixas was forced to attend that wedding, which unfolded, so to speak, before his eyes a past he had tried in vain to escape. There they were together, before the altar, two women he had betrayed in turn, and not driven by passion, but seduced by self-interest.

When, lost in contemplations, he was yielding to the melancholy of these reminiscences, Aurélia approached and whispered in his ear:

"Look cheerful. I want everyone, but especially this woman, to believe that I am happy, very happy. You owe me at least this ridiculous satisfaction in exchange for what you have stolen from me."

Taking Seixas's arm, and leaning against him with that voluptuous pride of the woman who surrenders to a great love, she walked toward the door of the church where her car awaited her.

At that moment, as during the evening at Amaral's house, none could help but envy the happiness of the beautiful couple whom God had endowed with all gifts: beauty, grace, youth, love, health, and riches.

They had all this, and were nothing but two wretched people!

No one could imagine what a torture this joyful and ostentatious celebration was for those two souls, burning in the drawing room lights and tormenting each other with the smiles that fell from their lips.

The following day, a Sunday, Aurélia decided to confine herself to her apartment and did not see her husband until Wednesday.

Neither Dona Firmina nor the servants questioned the fact, although they suspected some strain between the newlyweds.

Since on these occasions husband and wife closeted themselves in different locations, the house servants, ignorant of the interdiction to which the nuptial chamber had been condemned, assumed that they communicated through that interior connection.

Aurélia's elusiveness repeated itself several times thereafter. Seixas noticed that she avoided him and suspected that his presence was beginning to annoy her. He was not wrong. Since she no longer could find within herself the anger and sarcasm that in the beginning delighted her heart, her husband's proximity oppressed her.

Seixas did not antagonize her. He stayed home, at his wife's beck and call, but spared her the displeasure of seeing him.

This was part of the decision he had made, but it was not without great effort and bitter struggle that he found it within himself to remain by the side of this woman for whom, he sensed, he had truly become a scourge.

One powerful reason restrained him, we must suppose, so strong that it subdued at every instant the rebellion of his sense of honor, wounded by the scornful aversion directed at him.

That is when he began to frantically labor in search of a means to escape the terrible conflict. All the ideas his feverish mind suggested, he eagerly accepted, only to reject them immediately, discouraged.

Finally, he decided. Before going to his office he sought out Lemos, whom he had met only in passing since the wedding. The old man welcomed him in his jovial manner:

"What an honor, my friend! This humble house does not deserve you!"

"I must speak to you!" answered Seixas.

The old man blinked his eyes. He guessed that Seixas had not sought him out at that moment to make a courtesy call.

"I wish to consult with you," the young man went on, hesitating. "I have learned that bonds will come down considerably and that it would be advisable to sell them now and buy them back later, perhaps in two months."

"That is not bad, but there is a better thing these days," Lemos said.

"What?"

"Selling pounds sterling."

"I do not have them."

"That does not prevent you."

"I do not understand."

"Sell to deliver at the end of the month, at twelve. In the meantime they will certainly come down to ten, and in two weeks, without spending a penny, you make a few thousand, which never hurt anyone."

"Now I understand. Ten thousand pounds sterling would be—"

"Twenty thousand."

"And, if on the contrary, they go up?"

"You lose the difference."

"That's the risk."

"There is only one way of profiting without risk—not paying."

Seixas said good-bye, despite Lemos's overtures to take him to Commerce Square.

On this very day he met Abreu who, after having squandered his inheritance, had become a gambler and, according to rumor, lived by gaming. From their conversation, Aurélia's husband learned the address of a house where each evening roulette lovers congregated.

That evening Seixas left the house surreptitiously and, calling a tilbury, went to town. However, as he crossed the threshold of the door whereby one penetrated Cacus's Pit, he was overcome by such terror that he took to his heels, fleeing down the street and not stopping until he reached home.

⚬ **X** ⚬

On the ground floor, on the left side, the house at Laranjeiras had a veranda in the country style, decorated with live palms and clusters of orchids.

It served as a billiard room, and there Aurélia and her husband used to spend the afternoon when the weather was unappealing for a stroll in the garden.

It was there that Seixas found two large paintings, each on an easel. The canvas bore the outline of two portraits, Aurélia's and his own, that a famous painter, a disciple of Vítor Meireles and Pedro Américo, had sketched from a photograph, to give the final touches in the presence of the models.

At her husband's questioning look, Aurélia answered:

"It is an indispensable decoration for the drawing room."

"Do you consider it indispensable? It would seem to me, on the contrary, unsuitable to reproduce, even by this means, a presence that must annoy you so much."

"You cannot portray the soul. Fortunately!" observed Aurélia with the mysterious smile that, for some time now, had accompanied her words with their covert meaning.

Seixas passively carried out his role as model. The afternoon sessions had been reserved for him so as not to interfere with his work at the office.

Aurélia exited, leaving him more at ease.

On the following day, in the morning, when the painter returned to work on her portrait, before resuming her position, the girl made some comments about the cold and dry expression on Seixas's face.

"I painted what I saw. If you wish an imaginative portrait, that is something else," answered the artist.

"You are right. My husband has not been well. It might be better to interrupt the work for a few days. I will notify you when the time comes."

That afternoon Seixas found Aurélia completely different from what she had been of late. Her sweet expression, and especially the innocence and honesty of her manners, restored to his memory the image of the beautiful girl from Santa Teresa whom he had once loved.

He let himself be enticed by this illusion, although he was convinced that he would see it vanish suddenly and painfully as the others had. But his soul needed the respite and even more the solace of a comforting belief; he surrendered to the sweet chimera and tried to convince himself that he was reliving an idyll from his past.

Aurélia led the conversation toward subjects of the greatest appeal to a poetic and elegant spirit like Seixas's.

She spoke of music, verse, flowers, the arts. When her speech was not whetted by irony, she possessed such exuberant affection and tenderness that it emanated from her lips and spilled about her an atmosphere of love.

In the evening she played the piano and sang her husband's favorite passages.

She surely was not, in spite of Dona Firmina's praises, a virtuoso, or even an outstanding or adept pupil. But few possessed her artistic temperament. She played from inspiration, and her singing was her soul's emotions resounding spontaneously like the arpeggios of the breeze in the bosom of the forest.

The following days passed in the same gentle intimacy. During the afternoon, in the garden, they either admired the flowers together or read from the same book some romance less interesting than their own.

Seixas had the task of reading, while Aurélia sat beside him and listened. Sometimes, either because she became momentarily distracted or because she was impatiently anticipating the narrative, she would lean forward to glance at the page, onto which a ringlet of her brown hair came to play.

It was in the course of one of these scenes that the painter reappeared. Seixas manifested his contrariety, but Aurélia's kindness succeeded in dispelling it. He maintained during the session the same affable and gracious expression that had earlier brightened his noble mien and which had been his countenance in the past, when the overturning of his existence had not yet clothed him in melancholy severity.

The following morning, examining the painter's work, Aurélia, quivering with emotion, saw the man she had loved smile at her. There he was before her, looking out from the canvas, where the artist's brush had fixed him with marvelous felicity. It was one of those portraits in which the model, instead of imposing himself, inspires the artist; they cease to be copies and become creations.

Aurélia was still enraptured in her contemplation when the artist arrived and received her praises along with her sincere gratitude. The painter thought he had produced only a work of art. How could he suspect this woman's secret, the widow of that living husband?

"You must make a copy of this portrait to hang in the drawing room alongside mine. As for this one, I would like it to have the suit I remember seeing my husband wear when I met him. I want to surprise him. Do you understand?"

"Absolutely."

"I ask you, though, not to touch the face."

"You may rest assured."

Aurélia described to the painter the suit that should appear in her husband's portrait, then assumed her position to have her own done.

When he returned from his office, Seixas noticed that his wife no longer displayed the same disposition of spirit with which he had left her the day before. She did not revert to her former irritability, but little by little she withdrew and eventually isolated herself completely.

She spent her days locked in her dressing room. When she appeared, she was always lost in thought and had the look of those people accustomed to living in a fantasy world who, feeling disconcerted when they come down to reality, take refuge in their chimeras.

The house at Laranjeiras had turned into a true cloister, inhabited by two cenobites who did not see each other and did not communicate, except at dinnertime.

When they rose from the table, Aurélia would hide behind a thick bower, where, from afar, she followed with her eyes the figure of her husband, who strolled around the garden.

In the evening, each took a book. Seixas would read; Aurélia availed herself of these free moments to return to her thoughts and to the sweet reveries she abandoned when she left her dressing room.

Dona Firmina at first wondered about Aurélia's behavior; but she was a woman of good judgment, and very practical. She soon guessed the reason for those changes, and took the first opportunity to show how keen and perceptive she was:

"Don't you find Aurélia different from what she used to be, Mr. Seixas?"

Fernando, astounded by the question, turned his eyes toward his wife, whose pale features, illuminated at that moment by a reflection from the setting sun, had the diaphanous appearance of wax.

"Some temporary indisposition. She should get out of the city, spend some time away, in Tijuca or Petrópolis."

"I am not sick," answered Aurélia indifferently.

"Sick you are not, Aurélia; but it is something like it," replied the widow. "And strolls in the countryside are excellent for the melancholy and fainting spells you have been suffering from."

"You are mistaken; I am not suffering from anything."

"Oh, please do not dissimulate! Everyone can see that it is—"

"What?" insisted Aurélia completely unaware of the widow's intention.

"A baby!"

The young woman burst out laughing; but in such an exaggerated and harsh way that Dona Firmina became even more convinced. Fernando stood up with the excuse of watering the beds of Parma violets that lined the pedestals of the bronze statues.

Months went by. Suddenly, for no apparent reason, with the contrast and the unexpectedness that characterized this unique woman's decisions, there was a revolution in the Laranjeiras house, and in the existence of its dwellers. Aurélia left the seclusion, to which she had for so long condemned herself, to plunge into the other extreme. She displayed an eagerness for amusements as never before, not even when single. She began to frequent society again, but in a frenzy and without respite.

The theater and the balls alone did not satisfy her; on those evenings when she was not invited out or there was no performance, she would improvise a party which, in liveliness and gaiety, owed nothing to the most beautiful functions in the court. She had a gift for gathering Rio's belles to her house. She loved to surround herself with this court of beauties.

The days she devoted to visits to Ouvidor Street, or picnics in the Botanical Garden or at Tijuca. She had the idea to turn Botafogo Beach into a promenade in the likeness of Paris's *Bois de Boulogne*, Vienna's *Prater*, or London's Hyde Park. Some days, around four o'clock, she and her friends would ride in an open car along the extended curve of the picturesque bay, delighting their eyes with the enchanting landscape and breathing the cool sea breeze.

Passersby stared in amazement, and their expressions conveyed the malice of their assumptions. Aurélia cared not at all about these gossips, but her friends were annoyed, and she had to give up the lovely ride to see the migratory birds.

This longing for parties and diversions following her inexplicable apathy and withdrawal might arouse the suspicion that Aurélia sought in society not pleasure but perhaps forgetfulness. Could she be trying to confound her spirit, and thus wrest it from the musings and reveries that had absorbed her for so many days?

"You must be wondering about this fever for amusement?" she mentioned to her husband. "It is a fever, yes; but it is not dangerous. I want the world to consider me happy. The pride of being envied might console me in the humiliation of never having been loved. At least I will enjoy an appearance of bliss. After all, what is everything in this world but an illusion, not to say a lie? Therefore, I apologize if I disturb you by taking you from your customary pursuits to accompany me. You surely admit that I deserve this compensation."

"It is my obligation to accompany you, and you will always find me ready to fulfill it. Young, beautiful, and rich, you should enjoy the life that smiles upon you. The world has this virtue—what it does not absorb, it wastes. In times to come you will see your existence from a quite different perspective, and nothing will remain of the past but the memory of a child's nightmare."

"This is precisely what I seek. I would give anything to erase these beliefs or, rather, these unpleasant childhood illusions with which my soul was raised, and resign myself to life's reality. Oh! If only I could! . . ."

The ellipsis gave way on the girl's lips to a scornful smile.

"Then we would understand each other!"

Ransom

∞ **I** ∞

There was a ball in São Clemente.

Aurélia was present as usual, dazzling in her magnificence, both of spirit and luxury. Her dress was a masterpiece of elegance; her jewelry was worth a fortune, but no one noticed it. What people saw and admired was she, her beauty, a thing of splendor which filled up the room.

The ball, far from tiring her, on the contrary, invigorated her. Like tropical flowers, those daughters of the sun that display brilliant hues on the hottest part of the day, it was precisely in this sea of light and passions that Aurélia revealed the full opulence of her beauty.

To one side, Seixas contemplated her.

From midnight on, the other young women began to wilt; exhaustion faded their color or flushed their faces. Their bodies betrayed this excessive tiredness in the languor of their inflections or in the rigidity of their gestures.

Aurélia, on the contrary, as the evening progressed, radiated more enchantment and seemed to enter the plenitude of her charm. The artistic precision of her attire slowly disappeared in the excitement of the ball. Like the first outlines that emerge at last from the passionate chisel of the artist, fired by inspiration, her statue received its finishing touches from the crowd's admiration.

While around her the vortex swirled, she maintained her unalterable serenity. Her bosom heaved gently under the influx of sweet emotions; her smile ensconced itself blissfully on her slightly parted lips, through which her peaceful breath escaped. Her eyes, her entire body, emanated a celestial effusion that seemed to radiate from her. When this taking on of her beauty was complete, the ball was ending.

Aurélia made a gesture to her husband and, covering herself with the cashmere shawl he offered her, entwined her arm in his. Amid the adulation that trailed after her, she departed, leaning proudly against the chest of this most envied of men whom she dragged behind her like a trophy.

The car was at the door. She sat down patting the ample flounces of her skirt to make room for her husband.

"What a beautiful evening!" she exclaimed, resting her head on the cushions to immerse her eyes in the blue of the star-laden sky.

With this motion her shoulder touched Seixas's, and ringlets of chestnut brown hair, shaken by the movement of the car, caressed the young man's face, emitting an inebriating perfume. From time to time, the light from the gas came through the small door of the car, opposite the lamp, and outlined Aurélia's beautiful countenance and neck, which the shawl, slipping off, had uncovered.

From his position, looking over the girl's shoulder, he saw in the transparent shadow, when her low-necked dress rose with the movement of her breath, the harmonious lines of her magnificent bosom swelling in voluptuous contours.

"That star is so bright!" said the girl.

"Which one?" asked Seixas, leaning over to look.

"There, above the wall, can't you see?"

Seixas saw only her. He shook his head.

Aurélia absentmindedly clasped her husband's hand and pointed in the direction of the star.

"It is true!" answered Fernando, seeing one star or another.

Drawing back her hand, Aurélia rested it on her knee, no doubt unaware that she still had her husband's locked in hers.

"I do not know what it is about starlight!" whispered the girl. "It is something I have noticed since I was a child. Whenever I watch the stars this way and imbibe their rays I feel a kind of dizziness, which makes me sleepy. Perhaps the light they twinkle intoxicates us? It seems as if I had drunk a glass of champagne, but made from the juice of those golden clusters up there in the sky."

Aurélia's eyes directed these words, cloaked in a bewitching smile, at her husband.

"It must have been ambrosia, the drink of the gods," returned Fernando, responding to the witticism.

"But, joking aside! They have made me so sleepy! Could it be exhaustion?"

"It could be! You danced so much!"

"So you noticed?"

"What did you expect me to do?"

Aurélia waited a moment so as not to interrupt her husband; seeing that he remained silent, she arranged herself with the gracious movement of birds ruffling to go to sleep.

"I cannot go on! I am dizzy!"

She then sank into the cushions; little by little, her languid body sagged from the swaying of the car and her head finally rested on her husband's arm; her perfumed breath bathed Seixas's face as he felt the sweet impress of that seductive shape. It was as if he inhaled and imbibed her beauty.

Fernando did not know what to do. Sometimes he wished he could forget everything and remember only that he was this woman's husband and that he had her in his arms.

But when he dared, a mortal cold invaded his heart, and he remained immobile, in fear of himself.

However, no one knows what might have happened if the car had not come to an abrupt stop at the door of the house; startled, Aurélia realized what had happened and made room to allow Seixas to descend and offer her his hand.

"I have never felt so tired! I think I am sick," she said, alighting from the car.

"You should not have stayed out so late!" observed Fernando solicitously.

"Give me your arm!" whispered the girl with a wan gesture.

Seixas was beginning to be concerned, especially when he saw her hanging on his arm, dragging herself toward the stairs.

"Are you really indisposed?"

"I am sick, very sick!" she answered in an unsteady voice.

In her eyes, however, and in the corners of her mouth, there was a twinkle of mischievousness that belied her words.

Seixas returned the pleasantry.

"It is a very serious disease, is it not? It attacks you every night and leaves you unconscious for several hours. It is called sleepiness."

"I do not know; I have never had it," retorted the girl, lowering her lids and veiling her beautiful eyes.

When they arrived at the sitting room, where they usually parted company, Aurélia turned toward the dressing room. At the door, Fernando stopped.

"Carry me, for I cannot take one more step," said Aurélia, gently luring him.

Seixas took her to the couch, where she collapsed, struck by exhaustion or sleepiness. Since she did not immediately release her husband's arm, he leaned forward as a consequence of her movement and found himself bending over her.

Aurélia gathered in her dress making room at the edge of the couch and, with her hand, beckoned for her husband to sit down. Meanwhile, with her head flung over the velvet rest, her bare throat sketched against its blue background a masterpiece of sculpture chiseled from the purest Paros marble.

Seixas averted his gaze as if seeing an abyss before him. He felt its fascination, and recognized that he lacked the strength to escape the dizziness.

"Until tomorrow," he said, hesitating.

"See if I have a temperature!"

Aurélia reached for her husband's hand and brought it to her forehead. As he leaned over her with this movement, Seixas's arm brushed against the contour of a heaving breast. The girl shuddered as if struck by a deep tremor and, in a nervous spasm, gripped her husband's hand, still clasped in hers.

"Aurélia," muttered Fernando, who little by little had slid off the couch and was on his knees, searching his wife's eyes.

She lifted her head slightly so the light of her eyes would stream onto her husband's face, and smiled. What a smile! A maelstrom into which sank reason, dignity, virtue, every human arrogance.

Seixas was about to rush away, but Aurélia's eyes seared him; from those scintillating pupils escaped an intense fire that penetrated his soul like boiling lava. He turned his face toward the door, as if fearing that it might be open.

Aurélia had lowered her eyelids and let her head fall to the cushion in that delightful abandon with which the body surrenders after strenuous exercise. Fernando, in the same position, admired the beautiful woman lying there, throbbing before his eyes, and felt her against his chest, where the lace ruffles edging her dress seethed, swelling to the brisk rhythm of her breathing.

Still, he did not dare. Never during the days when he smuggled love had any woman, however wary of his desire, inspired the respect, or rather, the dread, that restrained him at that moment beside his wife.

The girl raised an arm in a gesture implying annoyance and dropped it on the back of the couch, from where it slipped in exhaustion onto Seixas's shoulder. Under the sweet pressure of this chain encircling him, he lowered his head and his lips lightly caressed the braids of hair that cascaded in ringlets over her shoulders and spilled onto Aurélia's face.

But she had turned her head, hiding her face in the velvet quilt in a sudden gesture, while withdrawing her hand to conceal her visage. This movement, perhaps only chastity's feeble resistance, was enough to check Seixas's impulse.

After a moment of perplexity, he was about to rise when Aurélia emerged hastily from the inertia and languor that had prostrated her and, sitting on the couch, had her husband again kneel at her feet. Then, resting her hand on his forehead, she bent his head and fixed upon his countenance a long, penetrating gaze that seemed to sink into the man's conscience and probe his secrets.

"You are not deceiving me? You love me then?" she asked tenderly.

"You still do not believe it?"

"Did you finally conquer the impossible?"

"It conquered me."

"That fortunate I am not!" exclaimed the girl, rising from the couch, and pacing about the room with faint steps and her head lowered.

Fernando, who followed her with amazed eyes, saw her approach a picture resting on a stand against the opposite wall.

The blue curtain of the canopy was drawn aside; in the gaslight that clearly illuminated this corner, the full-length portrait of an elegant gentleman stood out against the background paneling.

It was his portrait; but of the young man he had been two years before, with a touch of the extreme elegance he still maintained and with the ineffable smile that had vanished beneath the severe and melancholy expression of Aurélia's husband.

"The man I loved, and love, is this one," said Aurélia, pointing to the portrait. "You, sir, have his features, the same elegance, and the same aristocratic air. But what you lack is his soul, which I keep here in my breast and which I feel throb within me and possess me when he looks at me."

Aurélia gazed lovingly at the portrait. Ravished by the power of the feelings that swelled in her breast, she impressed on the image's cold and lifeless lips a fervent kiss, vibrant, impetuous; one of those exuberant kisses that are the true explosions of a soul torn by the fire of a buried passion, long repressed.

Seixas was dumbfounded. Feeling that he was being mocked by this woman, who subjugated him to his regret, he listened to her words, watched her movements but could not understand her. He summoned reason, and it fled, leaving him in a frenzy.

Aurélia had just turned toward him, lofty with ecstasy, tremulous with love, her eyes aflame, her lips tumescent, and her breasts leaping to the impulses of passion:

"Why does my heart, which quivers so before this image, remain cold at your side? Why does your gaze not penetrate it like the beam of that unmoving eye? Why does the touch of your hand not pass on to mine that flame that intoxicates me like nectar?"

Suddenly Aurélia stopped. A warm wave flushed her gentle face. Her passionate impetuosity cut short by a rush of modesty, she was distraught like a flower of the night at the first rays of dawn. She lifted the cashmere shawl that had slipped from her shoulders to her waist and, wrapping herself with the shiver of a chill, huddled at the end of the couch.

Seixas approached her, with his usual courtesy; in a voice already tranquil, and quite natural, he said:

"Good night."

Aurélia opened the cashmere enough to extend the slender fingers of her right hand and offered them to her husband.

"Already?" she asked, raising her eyes, half beseeching, half despotic.

Her husband shuddered at the subtle touch of her fingers gently pressing the palm of his hand:

"Are you ordering me to stay?" he said, his voice trembling.

Aurélia smiled.

"No. What for?"

What was meant by this phrase, imbued with the smile that, so to speak, provided its tone, no one can guess.

Seixas left, bearing in his soul the greatest humiliation this woman's scorn could inflict upon him.

๏ II ๏

One evening the conversation happened to turn to the subject of Brazilian literature.

A rare occasion. Among us everything can be fashionable in the salons, except our country's literature, which remains at the door or, at best, retires to the smoking room, there to serve as topic for two or three incorrigible men.

On this evening, an exception was made. Someone whose lips burned with the desire to dogmatically condemn a book he had recently read, although it had been published some time before, took advantage of this moment for the literary execution.

"Have you read *Diva*?"

The response was a silence filled with surprise. No one had heard of the book, nor did anyone think it was worth wasting time on such things.

"She is a fantastic character, impossible!" ruled the critic.

He went on to add a few things about the novel, criticizing the style as incorrect, abounding with gallicisms, and riddled with grammatical errors. The dénouement raised especially bitter censure.

Criticism, no matter how malignant, always produces the useful effect of whetting curiosity. The most rigorous censor, despite himself, pays homage to the author and recommends him.

In the morning Aurélia had someone buy her the novel, and she read it in one sitting, rocking in her wicker chair, by the opening of a window shaded by the jack-fruit trees, whose flowers emanated the perfume of magnolias.

In the evening the critic came by.

"I read *Diva*," she said, after having returned his greeting.

"Well? Is she not an impossible woman?"

"I do not know anyone like that. But, actually, only Augusto Sá, the man she loved, could have known her, the only one to whom she bared her soul."

"In any case she is an unrealistic character."

"And what is more unrealistic than truth itself?" refuted Aurélia, repeating a famous phrase. "I know a girl . . . If anyone wrote her story, they would agree with you: 'It is impossible! There never was such a woman.' Nonetheless, I knew her."

Little did Aurélia imagine that the author of *Diva* would later have the honor of indirectly receiving her confidences and also pen a novel about her life, to which she was alluding.

That evening, among the news of the day that sustained the conversation, was an item that profoundly disturbed Aurélia. It was rumored that Eduardo Abreu was dominated by the idea of suicide. One of his friends, returning with him on the ferry from Niterói, had prevented him from throwing himself into the sea; another one had caught him with a revolver in his pocket.

On the following day there was a performance at the opera house. Aurélia wrote a note to Adelaide Ribeiro offering her box and promising her company. The two ladies were not on intimate terms; they had merely exchanged the obligatory visit after their respective weddings.

Aurélia took advantage of the pretext of the new opera not to strengthen their formal relations but to have the opportunity to speak with Dr. Torquato Ribeiro.

At eight o'clock, when Aurélia entered her box on Seixas's arm, she found Adelaide and her husband already there.

The two ladies, aware that they would spend the evening face to face, instinctively, without premeditation but responding to an irresistible rivalry, had dressed with extreme care. Both were at the height of their beauty. But an odd contrast: Adelaide, the poor one, appeared in the most elaborate luxury, very stylish with all the fashionable refinements. Aurélia, the millionaire, affected extreme simplicity. She wore lace and pearls, and had only a single flower, her own grace.

As the curtain rose, the owner of the box, as usual, occupied the side toward the stage, reserving the place of honor for her guest. The husbands alternated, Ribeiro sitting next to Aurélia and Seixas by Adelaide.

Once the initial curiosity always aroused by the decorations and the cos-tumes of a production not previously seen had passed, Aurélia, turning to attend to the friend who was speaking to her, noticed Seixas's position and attitude.

He had leaned against the divider of the box and was watching the scene over Adelaide's shoulder; but it seemed to Aurélia that her husband's glance did not reach the stage and refracted, like a ray of light before the obstacle set in its path, at the smallest movement of the slender body of Ribeiro's wife's.

If Adelaide leaned forward to exchange some observation, she gracefully flared before Fernando her shoulders, jasperated by the gaslight shining fully upon them. If the girl languidly rested against the column, it was her lovely bosom, framed by a nymphlike, low-necked gown, that offered itself to Fernando's eyes.

Aurélia shook her mother-of-pearl fan with a quick and fluttering move-ment, causing the slats to rattle violently against each other. Two or three shattered between her taut fingers.

Sometimes she darted an imperial glance at her husband to warn him of the impropriety. Other times she examined Ribeiro's face to discern the ef-fect that this coquetry of his wife's produced in him. But Seixas was totally absorbed in the play, or in what lay en route to the play, and Ribeiro, with his binoculars, was surveying the boxes.

Adelaide, completely luxuriating in the satisfaction of eminence, did not even notice her friend's impatience, nor did she realize that the excessive outpour of her bodice, with the languishing sway of her body, exposed her bosom almost entirely to the eyes of the man behind her. Does the statue feel the glance that insinuates itself among the transparent veils? The fash-ionable woman has the skin of a statue when she dresses for the ball.

Finally Aurélia could no longer contain herself.

"Shall we change places, Fernando? The gaslight bothers my eyes."

"Sit here!" said Adelaide, offering her chair.

"No. It is better there; I will be in the dark."

During the intermission they left to walk about the salon. It was Aurélia who suggested this, wishing an occasion to say a few words in private to Torquato. Before they left, however, she insisted that Adelaide wear her mantle.

"You may catch a cold. It is damp."

"On the contrary; it is hot!"

"Do not take risks."

And she covered Adelaide's shoulders with her own mantle, which of-fered better protection.

Seixas offered his arm to Adelaide, as was the custom; Aurélia followed on Ribeiro's arm and, not letting them out of sight, began to talk to the gentleman.

"Yesterday I heard some disturbing news; Eduardo Abreu tried to commit suicide."

"I have already been told."

"And it seems that he has not abandoned the idea. I would like to rescue him from his folly; it is my duty, and I owe it to my mother's memory. Can I count on you, sir?"

"Allow me not to answer that question. Tell me what I must do."

"Thank you. I need only for you to bring him to my house and have him visit often. He was rich; he lost his fortune, and with it his friends, consideration, everything that made life sweet. No wonder he looks at the world as an enemy whom he must flee. If, however, amid this moral desert in which he finds himself, some idea, or wish, or consoling feeling were to emerge, this link might tie him again to life."

"But are you not afraid?" observed Ribeiro reluctantly.

"You think his passion may not be totally extinguished? That is precisely what I am counting on."

"And your husband?"

"He is my husband," the girl answered, lifting her head in serene pride.

Ribeiro understood the word and the gesture. Truly, could the man who had the supreme good fortune of being this woman's beloved husband suspect her?

"Imagine yourself in his place, you, sir, who know part of my life. After what I gave him, would you consider yourself entitled to that pitiful sacrifice of the life of a wretch?"

"Certainly not."

At that moment, Aurélia who had been distracted by the conversation, saw Adelaide, the mantle removed, suspended from, or rather, entwined on her husband's arm with a wantonness that she, his wife, would not dare display in public.

Aurélia, on an impulse she could not contain, despite the self-control to which she had accustomed herself, left Ribeiro's arm and dashed to the other couple, separating the two by interposing herself between them. She then recovered, noting the amazement portrayed on the faces of the others, and tried to dissemble, affecting laughter and entwining the arm of Ribeiro's wife in hers.

"Listen, I want to tell you a secret, Dona Adelaide!"

She walked away, taking her friend. The secret was some witty remark about a certain strumpet who was walking past, and then an allusion to the impudence of certain ladies who take pride in imitating those they most disdain.

"Give me my mantle!" said Aurélia gruffly to Seixas.

Before he could comply, she took from his hand the cashmere Adelaide had given him to hold, wrapped herself in it, and took her husband's arm.

"Shall we go?"

Taken aback, Seixas allowed himself to be led, believing that they were returning to the box. When they arrived at the stairs, Aurélia waited to bid Adelaide farewell.

"Are you leaving already?" asked the friend ever more surprised.

"I promised my godmother, Dona Margarida Ferreira, to see her this evening. I stopped by only to enjoy your company."

Aurélia thought about this on the way from the salon to their box; it was an excellent explanation for the ungainliness of removing her husband's arm from her friend, and the best excuse to put an end, once and for all, to the unpleasant incident.

Seixas followed his wife, without any comment. They climbed into the car; the coachman, having received no orders, headed toward Laranjeiras. Dona Margarida Ferreira lived in Andaraí.

"Are you not going to your godmother's?"

The answer was brief and cold:

"No, it is too late."

Aurélia blamed herself for that moment of weakness. How could she, having taken away from her rival the man she loved and having spurned this victory as unworthy of her noble soul, give that rival the pleasure of fearing her seductions?

Discontented and annoyed, she was considering revenge for this eclipse of her pride.

"What is jealousy?" she said suddenly, in a sharp tone, not looking at her husband.

Seixas understood that a row was on its way and prepared for it, summoning all the calculated resignation with which he cloaked himself.

"Does it call for a physiological definition, or is the question merely a topic of conversation?"

"Do you believe in the physiology of the heart? Do you not find it absurd, this would-be science proposing to explain and define the incomprehensible, something even the one who feels it cannot understand, and that is felt, often with no awareness of this moral phenomenon? There is only one physiologist, but He does not define, He judges. It is God, who formed His creature from the clay of the earth—as it is taught in the Scripture—and forgot to knead, on his left, a portion of the chaos from which He had taken him. As for jealousy, we all know more or less the meaning of this word. What I wanted to know was your opinion on this: is jealousy the product of love?"

"That is what people generally believe."

"And you, sir?"

"Since I have never felt it, I cannot have an opinion of my own."

"Well, I have one, and from experience. Jealousy is born not of love, but of pride. What hurts in this feeling, believe me, is not being deprived of the pleasure enjoyed by another, when we too might enjoy it and more. It is only the displeasure of seeing the rival possess a good that belongs to us or that we covet, to which we think we have exclusive rights, and of which we admit no sharing. Is there any jealousy more impassionate than that of the miser for his gold, the minister for his portfolio, the ambitious for glory? You can be jealous of a friend, as well as of a cherished trinket, or a favorite pet. When I was a child I felt it for my dolls."

Aurélia remained silent, awaiting a reply; the pause lengthened, so she continued:

"An example. A short while ago, at the theater, when I saw the way Adelaide Ribeiro held your arm, I was jealous of you. However, I do not love you, as you well know, and I cannot love you!"

"That is the decisive proof. And you, madam, do not believe in physiology? Do you need any better definition? Jealousy is the master's zeal for the object that belongs to him."

"Or the person!" added Aurélia viciously.

"For the object that belongs to him," insisted Seixas, "be it animate or inanimate."

"We have yet another proof in support of my opinion. You, sir, who have loved so much and so often, have never been jealous; you have just so confessed."

"And because jealousy is a symptom of pride, or in other words, of dignity, the consequence—"

"—Is logical; but I dismiss it. I would rather you recited one of your poems to me. For instance, 'The Whim.'"

∞ III ∞

Aurélia's parties, or receptions, as Alfredo Moreira called them, in the Parisian fashion, were the most brilliant given at the court in those days.

With no infernal gallops or extravagant dance steps that turn quadrilles and waltzes into veritable madmen's pinwheels or whirlpools of people touched by the tarantula, an urbane enthusiasm always prevailed that stimulated the pleasure and spread joy without wrinkling the young women or wedging the ladies between the gentlemen.

Aurélia had discovered an ingenious way of obtaining this result. When the young men, who would set the tone for the gathering, withdrew with feigned reluctance, and showed no haste to choose their partners and take them to the center of the room, the lady of the house would announce the *married couples' quadrille*.

This quadrille, as the name implies, was danced exclusively by the husbands with their wives. No one could escape; no exemptions were accepted, neither of age nor of sickness. Aurélia was inflexible, and none could resist her gentle tyranny. If she had these despotic and peevish whims, they were offset by her superior tact, as she captivated one and all with her delicate and graceful amiability.

The absurdity of ages and the obligation of gallantry between two better-halves, sometimes so mismatched, amused everybody, even the rheumatic old men. Inwardly, the matrons enjoyed this fantasy for it rejuvenated them, although they offered every excuse, as decency required.

What they most enjoyed, however, was piquing the young men, who, in addition to being excluded and losing the lovely partners chosen from among the married ladies, also suffered the ricochet of the single girls' sulkiness, annoyed because they could not dance and were forced into the role of spinster aunts, occupying the place of their mothers, who had taken theirs.

As a result, the young men, wary of such an outlandish quadrille, displayed an exemplary activity at the first bowing of the fiddle and maintained a constant state of animation in the room, without Aurélia having to bother begging *my dear gentlemen* the special favor of dancing.

Lísia Soares claimed that this invention was nothing but a pretext of Aurélia's to dance with her husband, with whom she was more and more in love, even to the point of lending herself to such ridicule.

Eduardo Abreu, who had not been seen in society for a long time, appeared at these parties. Aurélia welcomed him with affectionate distinction and always reserved for him one of the quadrilles that her numerous admirers so contested.

She had just danced with him, and was strolling about the room on his arm. Seeing them go by, Alfredo Moreira, with the redistilled spirit that a frivolous life imparts to the salon *roués*, said to his companion:

"A sentimental retrospective!"

"I don't understand the riddle," replied the other man.

"Don't you know that Abreu was madly in love with Aurélia and did the craziest things in order to marry her?"

"Now I see."

"She refused to marry him because she was in love with Seixas; but now that she is married to him, she might transfer her love to the young forsaken lily."

"It seems that way."

This excerpt of dialogue took place in the artificial passageway installed along the dining room on evenings when there was a gathering, with palm-trees, acacias, and magnolias planted in ceramic vases and wooden boxes.

Fernando, who had taken refuge for a moment in that corner, and sat smoking on a rustic sofa in the shade of a plantain bush, heard the vicious comments of the two *roués*. Searching with his eyes for the target of those gibes, he saw his wife speaking to a gentleman with tender and seductive insistence, which reminded him of the days of his first loves.

"She loves him," he murmured.

Afterward he saw nothing else. The couple had disappeared from the room, and he had sunk into his soul. He recovered his senses only when his wife's voice roused him with a start.

"I have been looking for you for quite a while!" said Aurélia, sitting beside him and observing him anxiously. "Are you troubled?"

"No, madam; a short time ago I had the pleasure of seeing you dance with Abreu."

Aurélia cast a quick and penetrating look at her husband.

"It is true; I danced with him. He is one of my usual partners," she answered flightily. "And you, sir, why didn't you dance, too?"

"Because you did not order me, madam."

"Is that the reason? Well, I will give you a partner. Would you offer me your arm?" replied Aurélia, smiling.

"It would be ridiculous to offer you that which is yours. You order, *senhora*, and are obeyed."

Aurélia took her husband's arm and walked slowly along the passageway.

"Why do you call me *senhóra*?" she asked, sounding the open *ó* in a rich voice.

"A speech defect!"

"But to the others you say *senhôra*, with a closed *ô*; I have noticed, even this evening."

"That, I believe, is the true pronunciation of the word; but we Brazilians, to distinguish a relationship of power and authority from the polite form, use the variant, which sounds stronger and has a certain metallic vibration. The subject says to the sovereign, as the slave to his mistress, *senhóra*. Perhaps, not thinking about it, I confuse them."

"Does that mean that you consider yourself my slave?" asked Aurélia, staring at Seixas.

"I believe I stated as much to you from the first day, or rather, from the evening that marks our common existence; and my presence here, my remaining in your house under any other condition would have meant adding to the initial humiliation an unspeakable indignity."

Aurélia replied, giving her voice a sad and deeply felt inflection.

"Is it not time we ceased these reprisals between us? They are nothing but word tricks. With such serious reasons to remain eternally separated, we have no need to go on constantly tweaking each other with these childish games. I set the bad example; I should be the first one to do an act of contrition. You, sir, you are my husband, and nothing but my husband."

"What I said is no banality, but a deep conviction, a serious matter, the most serious of my life; soon you will recognize it. I did not use the word slave in the domestic sense; that would be utterly ridiculous. But you, madam, should know that marriage began as the purchase of a woman by a man; and even in this century, in England, as a symbol of divorce, the husband would take the forsworn woman to the market place and sell her at auction. You are also aware that in the East there are slaves who dwell in sumptuous palaces, treated like queens."

"The sultanas?"

"So, this power, or this luxury, that man has claimed for himself, why can the woman of this century and this society not enjoy it, provided her hands abound with gold, which is after all the great legislator, like the supreme pontiff?"

Seixas's words were bitter and seared his lips.

"I am a husband! It is true, as Scheherezade was the sultan's wife."

"Minus the handkerchief!" retorted Aurélia scornfully.

But the irony could not quell the irresistible surge of shame that lowered her eye and covered her cheeks and neck with a vivid blush.

"Let us spare from our mutual sarcasm the august sanctity of conjugal love," she said emotionally. "God did not grant us that ineffable joy, the pure source of all that is noble and grand for the heart. We have been left—I at least—orphans and disinherited of this celestial blessing. But that is no reason to deny it our veneration."

Having just uttered these words, heartfelt and from her soul, she regretted her surrender to emotion, and pealing a silvery laugh, affected her habitual spirited tone:

"Would you care to know my opinion? What you call slavery is nothing but violence that the strong exert over the weak; and, in this respect, we are all more or less slaves—to law, opinion, social conventions, prejudice; some to their poverty, others to their wealth. As for true slaves, I know only one tyrant that creates them—love, and it was not for me that it captured you."

At that moment they were in the drawing room, before the chair occupied by Adelaide Ribeiro.

"Dona Adelaide, do me a favor. Keep this runaway for me, and hold him captive, at least during this dance."

"Is this a deposit?" asked Adelaide mischievously. "I accept, but take no responsibility."

"There is no risk."

While Ribeiro's wife fixed the puffs and the train of her elegant dress to take the arm of the partner the lady of the house had so kindly offered her, Aurélia, pressing against her husband's side, whispered these words in his ear, with feeling:

"I give you back your freedom. I had told you once; now I have done it."

"And I refused then as now," answered her husband in the same tone.

"Why?" questioned the young woman, a sprightly note of inquiry in her voice and in her look.

"Not because I wish to hinder your own. Rest assured."

"Certainly not!" said Aurélia with a disdainful frown.

"The reason is different."

"I would like to know it."

"I hope to God that one day you will know."

They had withdrawn a few steps in order not to be heard. Aurélia stared into her husband's eyes, agitated by the tone of his last words, and was preparing to demand an explanation when she heard the rustle of Adelaide's dress approaching.

She dropped her husband's arm and walked away.

The music signaled the quadrille. Alfredo Moreira came through the room, fluttering like a satyr in the forest searching for a flower. Fernando guessed that this flower was a partner and presented him with Adelaide Ribeiro, risking a breach of the code of the salon by breaking the rules of etiquette.

"Are you missing a partner, Moreira? Here is Dona Adelaide, who no doubt will enjoy the exchange, for, instead of one who has retired, it offers her a gentleman who is the prince of Rio's elegance."

Without waiting for an answer, he left the lady to the *roué* who swelled like a tulip, fingering the tips of his waxed mustache. Seixas counted on his position as master of the house, engaged in seeing to it that his guests danced, to justify the stratagem used to exempt himself from the quadrille.

Thus he frustrated Aurélia's whim, which had annoyed him. Why? He could not easily sort the reasons in the clash of the impressions of the moment. His wish to convince his wife of his indifference toward Adelaide; disgust at having lent himself to this deceit; the need to maintain the gravity of a situation that was becoming more complicated—all this crossed his mind.

The gathering went on in lively fashion. More guests had arrived and the party had turned into a ball, as often happened.

The flute sounded the sparkling prelude to a Strauss waltz.

The renowned waltzers stepped aside, doubtlessly to increase their attraction. The neophytes and the older people hesitated about taking the lead. One of the more daring drew a blank; he did not find a partner.

Suddenly a murmur ran through the room, *the waltz of the married couples*, followed quickly by Aurélia's crystalline laughter, the fresh, clear trill that sometimes escaped her lips, as if her pearly teeth raveled between these rubies, brushing against each other.

The ravishing woman crossed the room on the arm of the old General Baron T., who, in order not to deny his martial bearing, proved at that moment a heroism superior to that which he had displayed during the late war with Paraguay, where he had been a kind of Bayard, *sans peur*, but not *sans reproche*.

The illustrious warrior, who never averted his face from the cannon, were it Krupp, did admit, however, the possibility of bending at times to prevent the bullet from clipping the feather on his hat or the shrapnel from singeing his beard, radiant as a sunlit cloud. But to bow his arched and lofty chest, to totter on his firm leg, stiff and straight, when he had on his arm the most beautiful woman in the world, was cowardice, even worse, an indignity he could not commit.

Lísia Soares accused Aurélia of suggesting that so-called waltz of the married couples. She defended herself.

"It was the general's idea; he is dying to dance a waltz with the baroness. Memories of his youth!"

The famous warrior did not retreat; still, never had a cavalry charge against a square or trench, under crossfire from a battery of cannons, cost him so dearly as that waltz he danced determined to die like a hero.

∽ **IV** ∾

Aurélia was busily gathering various couples and directing them to the middle of the room; judges of every high rank and quality, decrepit counselors, stuffy viscounts, scowling marquises: all attempted to perform compliantly, better to lighten the penitence.

It was then that Lísia Soares approached on Fernando's arm. The mischievous girl had a sardonic smile on her lips; her glance pierced like a pin.

"Are you so busy with the others that you forget yourself?" she said.

"How so?" asked Aurélia, turning around.

"Do not dissemble. Justice begins at home; here is your husband. Set the example."

Aurélia understood that her friend, piqued because she could not waltz with Alfredo Moreira, sought vengeance.

From the first time she appeared in society, after the period of mourning her mother, Aurélia, who despite her bold and lively word, was chastely demure about her person, decided not to waltz to avoid risking a dance with one of these partners who bring to life the poetic comparison of the vine entwined with the mossy trunk.

She had declared, therefore, that she did not know how to waltz, and that she could never learn because the quick turns made her dizzy. There was some truth to this second part. When she had waltzed with her friends at school she had so enjoyed this brash dance that she would let herself be swept away and, ignoring the rhythm of the music, would whirl with astounding speed until dizziness forced her to sit down.

Convinced that she really did not know how to waltz, Lísia thought of retaliating by forcing her to cut a pathetic figure in the room, or else recant her eccentricity and put an end to that waltz of the married couples. What encouraged the girl most was the suspicion that Aurélia had done it maliciously, solely to prevent her from dancing with Moreira.

In this she was unjust. I do not know the reason behind Aurélia's act; but that she at that moment had forgotten Lísia's and Moreira's existence, of this I am certain.

"Do not be mean, Lísia!" said Aurélia in a querulous manner that did not succeed in concealing the subtle raillery in her look.

"No, dear: you do not excuse anyone, so come on."

"I do not know how to waltz."

"That's what makes it interesting. Neither did my father."

"She knows; she used to be my partner in school," observed a lady.

"You have to dance."

"The punishment must fit the crime," said a gouty old attorney returning from the waltz, exhausted as he had never been after the most complicated defense in court.

"A case of fair reprisal!" added an old diplomat who had made a career of eternal *availability*, no pun intended.

"The Crown yields to popular opinion!" proclaimed a minister for whom the Crown and popular opinion in Brazil were two sides of the same coin in which he received his salary.

The married ladies insisted to avenge themselves for the transfer that the lady of the house had perpetrated against them; the young women because of spite, the young men because they wanted to break Aurélia's spell and have her, from then on, as a sure waltz partner.

"There is no need for this revolution. I will submit," said Aurélia genteelly bowing her head.

Walking toward her husband who was standing before her and whom Lísia had not permitted to leave, she took his arm resolutely and allowed herself to be led to the middle of the room.

"Why do you hesitate? If you do not want to waltz, I will take the refusal upon myself," whispered Seixas.

"It is a matter of pride. Do you understand the power this question of honor holds for us women?" answered Aurélia, also in a low voice.

"At this moment, no; I do not understand."

"Look at Lísia savoring the humiliation of my not knowing how to waltz, and the fiasco that awaits me! Besides—"

Her voice took on a vibrant note.

"Besides, you, sir, might think I am afraid."

Aurélia placed her hand on her husband's shoulder and, infusing her figure with a graceful, undulating movement like the fluttering of a butterfly quivering in the bosom of a cactus, she stood before her partner and offered him her dainty waist.

It was the first time, and they had been married for more than six months; it was the first time that Seixas's arm clasped Aurélia's waist. It was clear then why both shuddered at the mutual contact, as this living tie bound them together.

The elegant couple swayed to the tempo of the ravishing music. And everyone admired them, except Lísia Soares who had expected to humiliate Aurélia, but now chafed in resentment at the sight of the sylphlike grace with which Aurélia waltzed, triumphantly.

That evening, Aurélia was wearing a gold-tone tulle dress, which enveloped her like a veil of light. With the twirls of the waltz, the ethereal waves of the skirt and the flowing sleeve on the arm she raised to rest against her partner, floated like diaphanous clouds imbued with sunshine, enfolding her and her gentleman like the brilliant glow that follows a sunset.

It seemed they both had taken wing, swept to the heavens by a radiant assumption.

Aurélia's head was defiantly inclined on her shoulder in a majestic gesture, with a provocative expression that would probably have appeared inelegant on another face, but, on hers, conveyed an irresistible seduction and a fatal and dazzling beauty.

No one had ever affixed to canvas, or carved in marble such a sublime image of temptation as that embodied in the fascinating hauteur of that magnificent woman.

At the first notes, this quick dialogue began, cut short by the pirouettes of the dance:

"I do not know how to waltz slowly."

"So let us quicken the pace."

"Will it not make you dizzy?"

"No, my head is strong."

"And your heart?"

"It is already calloused."

"Well, with me it is the opposite."

"Your heart?"

"It has never faltered."

The girl continued to utter intermittent phrases.

"It is the head that is weak." "But how unique!" "I am strange in everything." "Slowly makes me dizzy." "The house is turning around me." "Not fast, no." "When everything disappears—" "When I no longer see anything—" "Then, yes!" "Then I enjoy waltzing!" "And I can waltz forever!"

They passed near the orchestra. Seixas told the conductor:

"Speed up the rhythm."

The conductor's baton gave the signal.

"More!" said Aurélia.

The beats of the baton became more frequent.

"Still more!" ordered the young lady.

The baton whistled. The instruments thundered; the notes were no longer played in scales but in gushes. It was no longer a Strauss waltz; it was a musical whirlwind, a pampas gale like those coming from the inspired hands of Liszt.

The beautiful couple moved with abandon, leaving those unable to keep pace with that impetuous torrent to trot classically. The eyes that tried to follow them blurred; they swept past, clouded by the oscillating atmosphere that the velocity of their rotation established around them.

Aurélia lowered her lids; her long fringed lashes, brushing her satiny cheeks, shaded the intense fire of her eyes, escaping now in subtle sparks and striking Seixas's face with the refulgence of a star.

The waltz is the child of Germany's mists, of blonde valkyries from the North. Perhaps over those icy regions, with the gentle splendors of snow, the heavens spill a serenity and innocence enjoyed by the fortunate; perhaps, when attending a ball, the peoples of fertile Germania change their temperament from that with which they march to war, and beer runs in their veins instead of blood.

If this is so, the waltz may in those countries enjoy the honors of a ballroom dance. At a different latitude, it should be exiled to the public dance halls, where jaded men seek the strong sensations the drunkard asks of alcohol.

There is in this unrestrained dance something that recalls the mysteries consecrated to Venus by pagan Greece, or the bacchantes' delirium as they brandished the thyrsus. "It is," in the words of the great poet, "the impure and lascivious waltz, exfoliating women and flowers."

Never has language, which that king of words named Victor Hugo subjugates and manipulates like a frisky charger, served a more eloquent expression of thought. It is indeed the exfoliating of a woman, the peeling of her beauty and of her person, that the immodest waltz effects in the middle of the room, in full light, under the eyes of the avid and curious crowd.

Older ladies do not like the waltz, except for the pleasure of feeling ravished by the whirlwind. There is delight, a pure and innocent voluptuousness, in this intoxication by speed. In the quick turns, the woman feels wings grow on her and thinks she is flying: the silk cocoon bursts, the butterfly unfurls.

But therein, precisely, lies the danger. The innocent rapture of the dance delivers the breathless, inebriate woman to the temptations of her partner, though refined, still a man, whom she unwittingly provokes, with the chaste sway of her figure, and transfixes, with the warm emanations from her body.

What a waltz is, that handsome couple whirling in the room demonstrated; they were preserved, however, from malicious eyes by the chaste and holy glory of conjugal grace that God had vouchsafed them.

Fernando regretted having acceded to his wife's desire and he, one of the most dauntless waltzers of the court, began to fear becoming dizzy.

His gaze, delirious with the enchantments that crowned Aurélia's beauty at that moment, attempted to free itself and strayed about the room. But it soon returned, drawn by that powerful force, and became absorbed in the ecstasy of adoration.

When Aurélia's hand rested on his shoulder, its gentle and tender pressure transmitting the sweetness of her warmth, it was as if his entire body were there, at that point at which a magnetic flow held him in contact with the girl.

Then this strange sensation became still more intense. He was no longer aware of himself even to notice distinctly the pressure of the fingers on his shoulder. What was happening in him was truly an intussusception of the exquisite form of that woman, whom he saw before him, but felt inside him.

Aurélia does not allow, as do some others, her partner to draw her to his chest. Between their trunks is maintained the distance necessary to prevent their touching in the whirl of the dance, so much so that they leave an opening through which the gaslight shines.

Nonetheless, the vivid sensation that Fernando experiences at this moment is of a close, intimate contact with the girl's tremulous body, as if he held her enclasped in his arms; his soul, much the same as the mold that frames soft wax, received into itself the beauteous statue and felt its lovely touch.

If Aurélia's bosom heaved rapidly in the breathlessness of the waltz, though the ruffles of her neckline did not even brush his vest, he, closing his eyes and retreating within himself, could feel against his chest the firm roundness of the voluptuous breast.

If a lascivious reserve, peculiar to the feline species, impressed upon Aurélia's back an undulating suppleness that, expanding with the nervous shock, convulsed her slender figure, this electric vibration resounded throughout Seixas's body.

It was a true transfusion caused by the touch of the woman's hand on her husband's shoulder, and of his hand on her waist; but, above all, by their eyes immersing themselves into each other and the intermingling of their breath.

There is no flower of such delicate scent as the pure and fresh mouth of a young woman.

I know of other, livelier perfumes, some strong and exciting—none has the magic sweetness of the breath of roses, the fragrance of her soul, that Aurélia infused on the gentleman's lips.

Delightfully engulfed as he was, Seixas experienced a momentary recovery and foresaw the danger. He attempted then to stop and bring to an end this terrible test to which his wife had submitted him, surely for the purpose of subjecting him to her dominion, as she had done once before, that evening on the sofa, that cruel evening still alive in poignant memory.

Preparing to stop, he diminished the pace of their steps. Aurélia noticed the subtle movement, or perhaps she felt the repercussion of her husband's thought, even before he fulfilled it. Her lips murmured a beseeching word: "No!"

Her lids rose; her large eyes, full of light and love, flooded Seixas's face and then closed, taking with them all his will and conscience, like a wave that, after washing ashore, recedes, bearing in its core everything found on its way.

Seixas abdicated his reason and flung himself anew into the whirlwind.

All this happened in brief moments, the time it took the waltzing couple to describe two or three ellipses around the vast ballroom.

The four corners of the house were decorated with tall, artistically wrought flower stands of authentic bronze, an idea of Aurélia's, who ordered them from Europe.

They were rustic groupings where room had been made for the vases; but, instead of flowers, they held live plants and thus formed a grove in each corner of the room, combining to give it a bucolic appearance much appreciated these days, and rightly so.

There is nothing more charming than to bring the countryside to the city and even to the home, there to entwine the unparalleled pomp of nature with the splendors of luxury.

In the grip of the waltz, the beautiful couple, avid for space and feeling straitened in the room, had extended the ellipse to the farthest point, turning behind one of the flower stands, where at that moment there was no one.

There was an apex, quick as thought, in which the couple found itself concealed by the long palms of a musacea graciously arching into an umbel. At that moment a flash of lightning blinded them both.

Firm roses, each on its stem, sway in the evening breeze; delicately tilting their chalices, they curl at the brushing of their petals. Thus did Aurélia's and Fernando's heads meet, and their lips lightly touched as they subtly turned.

It was an evanescent instant. The elegant couple had vanished behind the foliage and was already emerging from the shadow, wafting in the dazzling glare of the room that they would once more traverse in a fleeting ellipse.

But Fernando felt an icy breath on his cheek. He looked: Aurélia had fainted in his arms. The gentle head did not droop toward her breast when she lost consciousness. As if bound by the magnetism of the eyes that had enraptured her, she leaned toward her partner's shoulder, with her face toward him.

Her pale lips moved softly, as if her soul, which had remained, were speaking to the other soul that had passed that way.

Seixas lifted his wife in his arms and carried her out of the room.

∞ **V** ∞

Amid the flurry caused by the incident, as doctors rushed to help, salts were brought and the friends ran around, some concerned, others curious, there was a barrage of comments:

"How reckless!"

"What furor! I saw it at once."

"And she is not used to waltzing."

"She wanted to act strong."

"That is not it, madam; it was her dress. Do you see how tight it is at the waist?"

"Come now! Romantic gestures!" said Lísia, clicking her tongue with disdain. To Adelaide she added:

"Do you believe she fainted?"

"Do you think she was pretending?"

"Flirting with her husband. She wanted him to pick her up in the middle of the room for everybody to see. She likes to show how Seixas adores and dotes on her! No wonder! A doll worth a million!—"

The girl went on about the subject. She had the all-too-common failing of talking like an organ grinder, believing that in this way she stunned others with an airy spirit, when, on the contrary, she watered down what nature had given her.

Meanwhile, Seixas had taken his wife to her dressing room and placed the beautiful swooned body on a couch. He was disturbed, but not anxious. As he carried the young woman he had felt the warmth of her skin and the beat of her heart. The accident was at worst a minor syncope.

Indeed, before they could flood her with ether or ammonia and unfasten her waist, Aurélia opened her eyes and waved away the people crowded around the couch.

"It is nothing, dizziness, and it is over."

The doctor who verified her pulse confirmed this, recommending only, in addition to rest, loosening the dress in order to breathe more easily.

"It is not necessary; just give me some room," answered Aurélia.

The ladies all withdrew and returned to the drawing room. Dona Firmina lingered a while with no intention of leaving the girl, but Aurélia asked her to assume her role as hostess.

"Fernando will stay. You go to the drawing room and have the dance resume. I am fine; there is nothing wrong with me. It is only if they feel ill at ease that they will bother me; I will imagine that I am sick!"

Dona Firmina laughed, bent down to kiss the girl on the forehead, and returned to the drawing room. As she approached the door, she saw some curious guests peeking inside, and drew the curtains, closing them with the latch.

Aurélia still lay on the couch, on her back, in the reclined position in which Seixas had placed her on the cushions. When Dona Firmina left, she again closed her eyes and immersed herself in the delightful dream from which she had been awakened.

Her hand groped unsurely along the edge of the couch and found Seixas, who was sitting by her side contemplating the lovely woman, even more beautiful in this languid deliquescence than in her dazzling radiance.

"Did I fall in the drawing room?" murmured Aurélia, without opening her eyes, blushing slightly.

"No," answered Seixas.

"Who caught me?"

"Would I entrust you to anyone else?" said Fernando.

The girl's fingers responded by squeezing her husband's hand.

"When I realized you had fainted, I took you in my arms and brought you here."

"Where?"

"Your dressing room. Don't you recognize it?"

"I cannot remember."

Seixas fell silent. Aurélia remained immobile, clutching her husband's hand, sometimes contracting it at a subtle vibration.

At this moment, someone knocked discreetly at the door. Seixas moved as if to rise and see who it was; but as the hand she held withdrew, Aurélia sprang up and, throwing both arms around her husband's neck, bent him under this irresistible yoke.

Seixas was forced to sit down once more, and Aurélia, also dropping to the couch, kept him enclasped in this sweet chain, while she darted an angry glance at the door and rose her bosom in recoil like a serpent ready to lunge.

What was going through the girl's mind at this moment, exalted as she was by the evening's commotion?

It seemed to Aurélia that she had found at last the embodiment of her ideal, the man she adored, and whose ghost had cruelly scorned her until that second, vanishing when she believed she had him before her eyes.

Now that she had found him and he was beside her, had taken possession of her life, it seemed to her that in the delirium of her hallucination they wanted to vie for him, wresting him from her arms and leaving her once more in the widowhood that was consuming her.

"No! I do not want it!" she exclaimed vehemently.

The knocking continued.

"They may open it, Aurélia, and see us!"

Her husband's words, or rather the fear that dictated them, aroused in Aurélia an even more impassioned siege of anger.

"What do I care what these people think? What do I care about this world that separated us! I despise it. But I will not allow it to steal my husband, no! You belong to me, Fernando; you are mine, only mine, I bought you, oh yes! I bought you at a very dear price—"

Fernando had risen as if impelled by the violent release of a spring, so lost in thought that he did not hear the end of the sentence:

"For it was at the price of my tears and of my life's illusions," concluded the girl, who, with Seixas's movement, had also risen, suspended by the chain with which she encircled his neck.

Seixas had quelled the impetus that drove him and managed to smother it in scorn, an outlet for such great tempests of the soul. He sat down once more and whispered in his wife's ear, as she drowned him in her gaze:

"Your handkerchief?"

"My handkerchief?" repeated the girl mechanically.

And picking up her lace handkerchief that lay on the sofa, she looked at him as if searching for an explanation to her husband's strange question.

Suddenly she began to tremble with such force that she leapt to her feet, sublime in her wrath and indignation.

Not a ringlet of hair curling with unaltered perfection around the nape of her neck had come undone, not one ruffle of her gossamer dress had been crushed; yet anyone who beheld Aurélia at that moment would believe the disarray of the lovely gown, such was the exasperation that transpired from all of her being.

The serene dawn of her beauty, gilded just a moment before by the niveous rays of the light filtered through the opaque crystal, had suddenly transmuted into an evening ablaze by the sinister flashes of a storm. The star had turned to lightning; the angel had shed its celestial wings and donned luciferous fulgency. Aurélia burst out laughing:

"You are right!—It is the only possible love between us!"

The young woman's hand, which crumpled the handkerchief convulsively, lifted to fling it at Seixas, with the scornful words she had just proffered. But it was merely pretense; about halfway through the gesture her hand recoiled forcefully.

"If it were possible for me to descend from my virtue, and even from my pride, there is one man for whom I would never stoop! Of all my indignities, the worst would be the profanation of the only love of my life!"

The hiss of the girl's voice as she uttered these phrases mingled with the shredding of the lace handkerchief that she had just torn to pieces. Then, bringing the strips close to the gas burning in a lamp holder beside the dresser mirror, she conveyed them to the flame and left them to be consumed on the marble.

Some will accuse Seixas of having spoken, at the time his wife confessed to him her love and offered him spontaneous forgiveness, that word that entailed a cruel affront.

He himself, who a moment before could not find an expression eloquent enough for his revolt, now stood there repentant, staring with sympathetic eyes at his wife, who opened a window and leaned against the balcony to envelop herself in the breeze and the darkness of the night.

And not only did he repent. For the first time he doubted that thing he called his honor.

The very night Aurélia had inflicted upon him the atrocious humiliation of that monstrous partnership between sarcasm and shame, Seixas deemed himself hopeless for such a woman. He could never again love her, and even less accept her love.

Until the moment of that outrageous revelation, his behavior might be reprehensible before a stern moral code, but it was nothing more than a marriage of convenience, something banal and frequent, not only tolerated, but even honored by society.

Since, however, this marriage of convenience had been converted into an actual commercial pact, he considered it despicable to involve his soul and sink it into this sordid transaction.

His body, yes, was sold; he could not extricate himself from the disgraceful obligation, for he had received his pay. But his soul, never! Even if he looked upon this woman as an unscrupulous speculator, he felt that honor had not abandoned him; and if earlier it was beginning to fade, this accident had restored its vigor.

This was the idea that Seixas, under the impact of his suspicions regarding Abreu, had proffered to Aurélia in a vague fashion during the dialogue exchanged with her at the beginning of the evening.

However, it was time for the waltz and, enslaved by his wife's beauty and by her prodigious charm, he forgot all protestations of dignity; he experienced only the worship of his idol, from which his apostasy was unable to wrench him away.

The fainting had quelled in him his lover's exaltation. Sitting at the head of the couch, where Aurélia still lay with closed eyes, squeezing his hand with the intermittent pulsations of her fingers, he could not evade a thought that beckoned him.

That sudden swoon, under the circumstances in which it had occurred, and so promptly dissipated—could it have been simulated? Could the girl have been playing a scene in this matrimonial comedy that amused her?

Seixas, despite the revolution that had taken place within him in the past six months, had not completely expended his habits of a man of society, for whom life is a series of conventions and ceremonies, dictated by custom.

The salon routine knows not the impetuous and unruly movements of passion. There all is done according to rules and regulations. A girl who, from the age of seven, is in the habit of offering her lips to the caress of friends of the family, receives her first kiss with graceful, but calm modesty.

And the man who had drunk of so many playful mouths, as if they were the pink crystal chalices from which he sipped muscatel—could this man, who had held in his arms so many cool and smiling sweethearts, understand that the wingtip of a kiss, because that is all it was, might cause someone to faint?

In her relationship with her husband, especially at times of excitement, Aurélia displayed gestures and attitudes of great dramatic expression. These natural movements were merely signs of the passions and feelings in her soul; they seemed artistic because they were clothed in supreme elegance.

Seixas, while admiring them as a poet, suspected they were theatrical, and hence his assumption that, with all this surrendering, Aurélia was preparing for him a new humiliation, similar to, if not worse than, that of the night of the ball, in that same dressing room.

It was in this state of mind that the phrase *I bought you at a very dear price*, which Aurélia's lips trilled with sprightly intonation, pierced him like the point of a stiletto. He heard nothing further; there grew in his conscience an immense desert filled only with the idea of that debasing transaction.

The thought that had dominated him before the waltz, and which a fleeting rapture had lulled, reappeared.

He took refuge in sarcasm, which since the wedding had served to divert the upswelling of his anger. With no intention of doing harm, only as bitter irony, he uttered the word he now regretted.

Meanwhile Aurélia, at the window, cast her gaze over the blue of the atmosphere against which was silhouetted the outline of the mountains. A nebula winked its uncertain glimmer.

The young woman gazed at it for a moment and imagined seeing the track of her soul ascending toward it to the heavens.

"The evening air may do you harm, especially as distraught as you are," said Fernando diffidently.

Thinking that the girl did not hear him, he drew closer and repeated his observation.

"You are wrong! I am calm, perfectly calm!" said the girl, and as proof of her statement she left the balcony and stood by the glow of the gaslight.

Her face and her entire demeanor displayed the imperturbable serenity that she assumed when she wished to contain and subdue the impulses of her passion.

Fernando took one step forward and was perhaps about to apologize, when the door opened. Since no one had answered, the person who had knocked earlier persisted, but this time decided to lift the latch. It was Dona Firmina, who came to inquire after the girl.

"Wonderful! Up and about?"

"And ready to dance!" answered Aurélia, laughing.

She went to the dressing table to correct the slight discomposure of her gown, curled a lock of hair, adjusted the ruffles of her skirt, and took her husband's arm to enter the drawing room.

"Do not be reckless, Aurélia!" said Dona Firmina.

"Have no fear! Now I am protected."

The widow did not understand. Aurélia, walking away, quickly shot this admonition at her husband, whose looks still showed traces of the upheaval he had suffered.

"Let us be miserable, but not ridiculous. Anything, except offer my life as a spectacle to this contemptible world."

All these incidents were brief and occurred so quickly that a quarter of an hour after she had fainted, Aurélia entered the salon on her husband's arm, as fresh and exuberant as at the start of the ball, and even more dazzling in her beauty.

Her guests, upon seeing her, came to greet her but could not congratulate her because the orchestra was again pouring forth a turbulent Strauss waltz, and Aurélia was whirling about the room with her husband.

"It is madness!"

This was the voice heard from all sides. Seixas had tried to dissuade her, but she had silenced him with one remark:

"It is the reparation, sir, that you owe me."

They waltzed for as long as they had the first time, and not the slightest commotion flustered those two hearts, which shortly before had been joined in the selfsame pulsation but now beat in rhythmic isolation stirred only by the motion, like the hands of a clock. Between them lay an icy ocean.

When the waltz was over, Aurélia smilingly received the congratulations of her friends and guests; Seixas, censures and admonishment for having consented to a second dance with his wife.

"It could have been fatal for her!"

"I had to cure myself of my dizziness," interjected Aurélia, laughing. "It was his duty."

"And now, are you cured?" asked the general.

"Oh! Forever!"

The ball went on, growing more and more lively.

∽ VI ∾

The last guest had left. Seixas was returning from accompanying Dona Margarida Ferreira to her car. Aurélia, who awaited him, bade him good night and was about to retire. Fernando intercepted her:

"I would like to explain something to you!"

"It is pointless."

"It was not my intention to offend you."

"Of course; such a kind gentleman could never harm a lady."

"I overheard something unpleasant that deeply disturbed me and made me act unnaturally. I was not calm; in any case, I was only referring to my position, and did not mean any allusion—"

"It is yesterday's story you are telling me," exclaimed Aurélia pointing to the face of the clock which indicated two A.M. We will discuss it tomorrow. Let us go to sleep."

With a smiling curtsy to her husband, she left him in the room and retired to her apartment, where the slave girl was waiting to undress her.

"You may go; I do not need you."

Aurélia retained from her days of poverty the custom of handling her personal needs; because she did not like to deliver her body to the care of others, nor allow any eyes but her own to invade her natural modesty, she would, whenever possible, dispense with the slave girl, who no longer found such behavior strange.

Once she locked the door from inside, the girl in an instant carried out her metamorphosis. The gown worn at the ball lay on the carpet in front of the mirror like the wings of a butterfly expired in the bosom of a flower; from it, out of that collapsed silk, emerged the chaste girl enveloped in her pure white cambric robe.

Seated on the couch where she had been a few hours earlier with Seixas, she became pensive. Finally she rose to draw aside the curtain over the portrait and light the nearby lamp.

She contemplated the portrait and addressed it, as if there stood before her the man whose image she saw.

"You love me!" she exclaimed jubilantly. "Even though you deny it, I know you; I see it in you, and feel it in myself! A well-bred man as you are only offends a woman when he loves her passionately! You offended me because my love was stronger than you, because it annihilated your nature and turned you from the gentleman that you are into a fierce tyrant. Do not apologize, no! It was not you; it was jealousy, a coarse and brutal sentiment. I know it well!— You love me!— We may still be happy!— Oh! then we shall doubly live, to make good these days we did not live at all!"

The gentle lady leaned against the frame of the painting, and once again became pensive.

"And why can't we be happy from this moment on? He is there, thinking about me; perhaps waiting for me! All I have to do is open that door. He will beg my forgiveness, I will take him in my arms, and we will be together for evermore!"

A wonderful smile illuminated the lovely woman. She descended from the platform and crossed the bedroom with trembling but eager steps, her cheeks burning.

She approached the door, drew the blue portière, and put her ear to the door; she smiled. Softly she whispered her husband's name and recalled the passionate notes with which the diva Stolz sang the aria of *La Favorite*: "*Oh! mio Fernando!*"

Finally, she looked for the key. It was not in the lock. She herself had removed it and kept it in the drawer of her pink *araribá* desk.

Impatiently she went back to retrieve it. When her hand touched the steel, the coldness of the metal made her shiver. She cast the key aside and shut the drawer.

"No! It is too soon! He must love me enough to win me, not merely enough to allow himself to be won. I can, I no longer doubt it, I can, at the moment that suits me, bring him here to my feet, imploring, inebriated with love, subject to my call. I can force him to sacrifice everything for me, his dignity, his pride, the final scruples of his conscience. But the next day both of us would wake from that terrible nightmare, I to despise him, he to hate me. Then, truly, never again would we forgive each other; neither I him, for my desecrated love, nor he me, for his abased character. Then, truly, would the eternal separation begin."

After a short interval, she again spoke to the portrait:

"When he convinces me of his love and plucks from my heart the last root of this loathsome doubt that lacerates it; when I find you within it, my ideal, the master of my love; when you and he become one, and I cannot distinguish the two of you either in my affection or in my memories—on that day, I shall belong to him—No, I already belong to him, now and always, since I fell in love with him!— On that day, he will take possession of my soul, and make it his!"

Withdrawing, the young woman still bore the thought of her love, which rose to the heavens with the first words of her evening prayer:

"May You grant, dear God, that it be brief!" she said, crossing her hands, as she knelt on the footstool and gazed at a crucifix of silver and ebony.

When she finished praying, Aurélia extinguished the gas, leaving only a lantern on the dresser with its faint glimmer to illuminate the face on the portrait.

From her bed, where she had just nestled like a dove between fine Irish sheets, her head on the pillow, she saw through the open door, there in the dressing room, the cherished image; and, with her eyes fixed on it, she fell asleep, drifting as always from one dream to the next or, rather, continuing the one and only dream that was her whole life.

The clash of these two souls, bound by some fate to be dashed one against the other, always caused estrangement and coldness for some time. Remission was more perceptible and enduring after the night of the ball, for the crisis had also been more violent.

During these intervals, Aurélia observed her husband and witnessed the transformation taking place in his character, once weak, mundane, and inconstant, now restored to his generous nature by a wholesome influence .

She imagined, or rather saw, that thoughts of her filled and completely dominated her husband's life. At every moment, in the most inconsequential circumstance, this absolute possession that had taken hold of his soul became manifest. There was in Fernando something like a resonance of her.

She knew that her husband's attention, though solicited by matters of utmost importance or people of high position, was never far from her. In society, as at home, she discerned through its disguises the gaze that sought her, often in the reflection in the mirror or through an opening in the curtain; and when not the eye, the ear was bound to her voice.

The flowers that Seixas watered were hydrangeas, a favorite of hers, Aurélia. When he approached the aviary, the lady's darling canaries merited every caress. In the garden, as in the house, the favorite spots were those she had chosen.

Aurélia did not like Byron, though she admired him. The poet she loved was Shakespeare, in whom she found not the mere singer, but the sublime sculptor of passion.

She often thought she could be the heroine of that great epic of a woman, written by the immortal poet. On the day of her wedding, her delirious imagination even dreamed of a death similar to Desdemona's.

Seixas had renounced the poet of his earlier fancies, and grown fond of the English playwright, whom he once thought monstrous and ridiculous. He read the same books as she; their thoughts met on the pages that the other had already perused, and mingled. They mutually applauded or censured.

Few women had as devoted a husband as Aurélia, so bound to her life. Seixas was absent only during his work hours; the rest of the day he spent in her company, in domestic intimacy, or paying visits and attending gatherings.

From the first days, determined to be passively obedient, her husband had imposed upon himself the task of presenting a detailed account of the hours spent out of the house, of the events of his journeys, of whom he had met, and even of the work at his office.

What had been only an irony on the part of the husband became a habit; and she, who in the beginning was annoyed with the feigned subservience, was unable, later, to relinquish this confidence, which restored to her the small fraction of Seixas's existence spent away from her.

But it was not only the possession of her by love that had been wrought in Seixas; it was also the assimilation of character.

As with all souls that are regenerated, Seixas's exercised over him a severe discipline. It embodied strictures that in other circumstances would seem ridiculous. An excuse, a harmless justification would assume the proportions of a lie. Constant and general amiability was hypocritical; indifferent people had no rights beyond politeness, and could not encroach upon the privileges of friendship.

Sometimes, Aurélia, standing apart, had heard him, while talking about others, condemn the life of enticements and gallantry in which he had consumed the early years of his youth. At any opportunity he revealed his present stern and austere way of regarding society, and of solving the practical matters of existence.

Like soft wax, the man of heart and honor had been molded by the touch of Aurélia's hands. If the artist who chisels the marble swells with enthusiasm watching his conception emerge from under the burin, one can imagine the girl's joy, feeling her soul shaping the statue of her ideal, the incarnation of her love.

Thus, despite the estrangement that resulted from the ball, the drama of this passion was moving toward a happy dénouement when an incident arose that complicated matters and disturbed its course, precipitating the conclusion.

The impression of the violent scene had faded, and gradually a tranquil intimacy began to return.

Fernando had left for his office. Upon arriving in the city he encountered a business man, an old acquaintance.

"What a pleasure to meet you. I have some good news for you. That concession has finally come about."

"Which concession?" asked Seixas, surprised.

"Well, now! Have you forgotten? You no longer care about such trifles? Our concession for the copper mines . . ."

"Oh! Now I recall!" interrupted the young man, a bit disturbed.

"Well, Fróis managed to sell it in London. They paid a pittance for it—fifty thousand. In any case, it is better than nothing, because, my dear fellow, I never expected to see copper from those mines even in a pot. The news came on the last steamer; I intended to look you up day after day but did not have the time. Fortunately I ran into you. I apologize."

"Do not mention it, Mr. Barbosa."

"After deducting some expenses that were incurred, each of us is entitled to slightly more than fifteen thousand. When you care to receive your share, just send the voucher I wrote you."

"The voucher?"

"I bet you sold it?"

"No; I must have it at home."

"So, when I receive it . . . Good day."

Barbosa bade farewell, and Seixas went on his way, but abstracted and confused. The news given by the business man suggested various and contradictory thoughts.

That concession was an epilogue to his former existence, which had ended with his marriage. Investment fever had begun to develop, and a sharper had come up with the idea of exploiting some copper mines in São Paulo; in order to obtain the concession he had decided to invite to join the speculations a businessman who would provide the funds and a government employee who would open the administrative channels.

Seixas happened to have ties to Fróis, and became the chosen employee. Through his intercession, the petition rose to the minister like a balloon full of the gas of pompous information. It was soon expedited. The cabinet official caught him smoking a cigar with his minister and providing him with the most extensive clarification, not about the proposed enterprise, but about a beautiful woman, of whom His Excellency was enamored.

Once the concession had been granted, Fróis attempted to negotiate, hopeful of obtaining at least three hundred thousand. But these hopes withered, and the three associates began to believe that their copper mines on paper were worth less than the old pots for which street peddlers always pay a few pennies.

Seixas gave it no further thought, and since then had remained ignorant of Fróis's efforts and of his calculations of probability until receiving, at that moment, news of the sale of the concession, which suddenly and unexpectedly brought him a profit of fifteen thousand.

The first and most vivid reaction that the news produced in Seixas was one of happiness at earning that amount, which for him was of incalculable price. Still, he was assailed by a certain feeling of displeasure because of the origin of the money. If, in the past, the intervention of a public official in such ventures seemed licit to him, he no longer viewed these things with the same tolerance.

Nevertheless, whatever his scruples, he needed this money and deemed himself entitled to spend it in such a far-reaching undertaking as the one he intended for it, with the proviso of later returning the same amount through indirect means to satisfy these scruples of conscience.

Having made his decision, he was overtaken by fear concerning the voucher written by the business man as the one capitalizing the enterprise. He did not recall seeing the paper for a long time, perhaps three years. Where could it be? When he burned his papers on the eve of his wedding, would this useless item have been spared?

Seixas must have attributed great importance to this matter, for, back at work in his office, he interrupted his strict diligence. He took a tilbury and rushed home, expecting to return in an hour.

∞ VII ∞

It must have been eleven o'clock when the tilbury arrived at Laranjeiras. Seixas, although with no thought of hiding, preferred, to avoid arousing curiosity, for no one at home to notice his return. He had the tilbury stop some distance away and, without a sound, climbed the private staircase that led to his apartment.

The door to the study was locked from inside, and he had forgotten that morning to take the key. He was thus obliged to go around through the sitting room. At that time, Aurélia and Dona Firmina were usually in another part of the house; he would pass unseen.

He found it strange that the door to the sitting room was closed, though not latched; he supposed that, as it was not fastened to the baseboard by the bolt, the wind must have blown it shut.

He slowly pushed it open and entered, only to stop short at the threshold, pale and stunned.

On the sofa along the wall, to his left, he saw Aurélia sitting and talking in a spirited and intense fashion to Eduardo Abreu, who occupied the chair beside her, his head lowered.

Lifting his eyes without daring to look at the girl, the young man saw the bewildered figure of Seixas standing in the doorway, staring at him; on an irresistible impulse, he rose to his feet.

It was then that Aurélia caught sight of her husband, whose unexpected presence and altered countenance disturbed her, albeit quickly and almost imperceptibly. With her usual self-assurance, she promptly recovered.

"You may come in, Fernando!" she said, smiling.

"I do not want to disturb you," answered Seixas, finding difficulty in releasing his voice from his dry lips.

"It is urgent business," she replied, "but it can well stand a few minutes' delay. Sit down, Mr. Abreu!"

Seixas took some automatic steps into the room.

"You did not go to your office today?" asked Aurélia to conceal her husband's and her guest's confusion.

"I came to look for a paper I left behind. By your leave."

Seixas took advantage of the first opportunity to flee that place, where he feared he might create a ridiculous or terrible scene. Giving a desultory bow, he left hurriedly for his apartment.

If until then he had needed money, now, more so than ever. He went directly to his desk, opened the drawer where he kept his old papers, spread them on the carpet along with other objects, and finding at last the voucher he was seeking, left hastily by his private staircase.

He stopped at the door to let Abreu, who was descending, pass; when he saw him in the distance, he climbed into the tilbury and returned to the city.

Aurélia, as soon as her husband had left, extended her hand to Abreu, saying:

"You have no right to refuse, and I hope you will not deprive me of this pleasure. Good-bye, and may you be happy."

Moved, the young man shook the delicate hand offered him so sincerely, and murmuring expressions of appreciation, took his leave.

He had no sooner disappeared down the stairs than Aurélia went toward her husband's study. She knocked at the door and called his name; receiving no reply, she went in. The first thing she saw was the open desk drawer and the pile of papers strewn about the floor.

She confirmed that Seixas was not at home and assumed that he had left by his private staircase, locking the door and taking the key.

Glancing at the scattered papers and resisting the urge to apprise herself of these relics of a past that did not belong to her, she turned toward the door to leave. It was then that she discovered amongst the bundles of letters, a piece of embroidery.

She picked it up to examine it, out of simple artistic curiosity. It was a ribbon to mark book pages. Embroidered in gold thread was, on one side the word *love*; on the other, in a semicircle, the name *Rodrigues de Seixas*; in its center was a monogram: an *F* intertwined with an *A*.

This gift from Adelaide Amaral, and the allusion to the future union implied by the married name, were not news to Aurélia. She knew of things perhaps even more poignant to her love, but time had obliterated them from memory. They comprised the scar that this cruel memento had reopened and ulcerated.

All that painful past from which she had just begun to disengage herself rose before her like a relentless specter. In the hour she stood there motionless, she again suffered all the distress and anguish she had endured for two years. That scarlet ribbon seared her eyes and fingers like a flaming blade, and she could not muster the strength to take her eyes and her hand from the gold and crimson letters that intertwined the name of her husband with the name of another woman.

At last her indignation erupted. Silk squeaked between the small twitching hands that tried in vain to rip it apart. Failing in her intent, she lifted the ribbon to her mouth and in an arrogant fit of anger cut with her teeth the threads forming the letters and reduced her rival's gift to tatters.

She then flung away the fragments in disgust, but into a spot that would not escape her husband's eyes, and locked herself in her dressing room.

Seixas arrived at his customary time. Ordinarily he entered through the sitting room, where he always found his wife, already dressed for the evening, waiting for him. They would exchange a few words, and afterward he would go to his room to prepare for dinner.

On that day he went up by his private staircase. He was already his own master but preferred to avoid an encounter, naturally because he was in need of those moments.

In fact, as soon as he reached his study, without bothering to gather the papers that lay on the floor, or noticing the fragments of the ribbon that were on his desk, he opened his combination drawer and removed a little notebook from which he copied some figures. Using these, he began a series of calculations and operations that absorbed him till the moment the servant came to call him for dinner.

Aurélia could not disguise her irritation. She pelted her husband with jibes and epigrams. The sarcastic vein did not spare even the inoffensive Dona Firmina; but the principal target was Adelaide, upon whom allusions rained.

Seixas appeared indifferent to the provocations. He allowed the jeers to pass without retort; but his disdainful and haughty countenance confronted the woman's annoyance with a cold and mute resistance that added to her irritation.

Aurélia's vexed pride whetted the edge of her weapons, in order to defeat that threatening attitude that offended her; but she did not succeed. The constant battles had finally annealed Fernando's character and refined his temperament.

As she rose from the table, she cast her husband a challenging glance, and left to wait for him in the garden, in that secluded place where they had the habit of meeting in the evening to talk more freely.

Fernando found her seated on a rustic bench, in the proud and imperious position of a queen waiting to hear the pleas of her subjects prostrate at her feet. Her right arm rested on the leafy crown of a jessamine, whose flowers she crushed between her fingers.

Seixas sat down, facing her:

"I do not have, and have never had, madam, any aspirations for your love. It would be utter madness, and finding myself in the calm and cold use of my full reason, I see the barrier that separates us. Nor do I have the right to ask for accounts of your feelings, or even of your actions, so long as they do not offend that which a man values above all possessions. In abdicating to you my freedom and with it my person, one thing, nevertheless, I did not transfer to you, and could not have done so: my honor."

"And what good to me is that rubbish, *your honor*? Can you tell me?" asked Aurélia, the most poignant mockery in her gaze.

"Remember, madam, that you made me your husband, and that I still remain such. Though I might sell you that title and the obligations corresponding to it, the origin is unimportant; it exists, and attests to the right recognized, or better, granted me by you, yourself: the right bestowed upon every husband, if not to his wife's loyalty, at least to the respect of conjugal faithfulness and to family decorum."

"Oh! You would like to maintain appearances? And that is enough for you?"

"For the time being!"

Aurélia glanced at him, hoping to catch her husband's thought from the expression on his face:

"Would you be kind enough to tell me what this scandal is that you are complaining about?"

"You no longer remember? Do you consider natural the liberties you have allowed this man, Eduardo Abreu, to take? It must be a month ago, at an evening party, you spoke to him in a way that lent material for Moreira's jokes. On that occasion I did not punish that fool's insolence to avoid a scene."

"Was that the evening of the waltz?"

"Not satisfied with this, you carry the impropriety to the point of receiving that same young man, in your husband's absence, alone, and entertaining private conversation, as I found you!"

"Have you finished?"

"I think that is sufficient."

"Well, it is my turn to answer. As you admitted, I owe you no account of my actions; only the man I loved would have the right to ask it of me. I would, however, like to imagine that you were that man, an absurd hypothesis I bring up only to show you that even then, your oversensitivity seems strange."

"Oh! Do I resemble an Othello!" said Fernando taunting her.

"No, Othello was right about all his outrages and brutalities; he loved, passionately. But you are here, sir, only as an advocate of decency."

Crushed by this sarcasm against which he could not react, Fernando felt an urge to confess to the woman all the madness of the love he felt, and then, when she exulted in her triumph and his humiliation, prostrate her at his feet.

∞ VIII ∞

Aurélia's eyes remained fixed on the white, velvety petals of a Cape jasmine:

"Modesty is the purest veil of a lady. Fortunate the woman who lives in the shadow of maternal zeal only to leave it for the gentle shelter of sanctified love. Her virtue possesses, like this flower, an immaculate complexion and a lively perfume. That blessing was not for me; I found myself alone in the world with no protection, no guidance, no counsel, obliged to make my way in life through an unknown world. Very early I was exposed to suspicions, insolences, and base passions; I became accustomed to struggling with this society, which terrifies me, to cloaking myself in my pride, as I had neither a mother's devotion nor a husband to protect me."

The woman's touching and melancholy expression as she uttered these words moved Seixas, who had already forgotten his resentment.

"When I was an innocent girl who never left her mother's company, and had never been alone in a man's presence except for the only one I loved, and have loved in this world, that man left me for another woman, or for something else, and linked his name to that of a woman who was engaged to someone else. Afterward, finding myself alone in the world, chaperoned by an elderly relative, a mother for the sake of appearances and an obliging friend, who made me feel even more alone, assuming the role of a shield, this impudent man married me without the least repulsion."

The girl fixed her gaze on her husband:

"Confess that the gentleman's scruples and his panic about a scandal arrive too late and at the wrong time."

"These scruples were born of the present situation."

"You are wrong again. This position is a responsibility, not a right. You spoke, sir, of your honor. I believe that honor is an impetus from the heart. What remains of honor to one who has alienated himself from his heart? If you have any honor, which I believe, it belongs to me; I can use and abuse it as I please."

"So, you consider yourself freed from any reserve?"

"To you and to the world I consider myself freed from everything; I owe them nothing. What they give me is only tribute to wealth, and wealth pays for everything with luxury and dissipation. I am my own mistress and intend to enjoy my independence with no other restrictions than my fancy. It is the only good left me from the shipwreck that is my life, and this at least I will defend against the world."

"I thank you for disabusing me in time, madam. I believed that by sacrificing my freedom I was not renouncing my honor before the world and would not be subjected to being judged as unworthy. You see it differently; I applaud this collision. It comes in time to break an intolerable situation that has already lasted too long for the dignity of us both."

"Especially of one who, having alienated his person in a free and premeditated marriage, keeps gifts from a former fiancée."

Seixas, surprised, questioned his wife with his eyes.

"I never thought I had acquired your love, nor did I count on the faithfulness you vowed; but the least I expected from you, sir, was the honesty of a business man, who, having sold the merchandise, does not foist another brand upon the buyer."

Seixas could not understand this allusion, whose meaning he grasped only later when, upon entering his study, he saw the shattered remains of

Adelaide's gift. He wanted to ask for an explanation, but saw a servant approaching them.

"Mr. Eduardo Abreu is here and wishes to speak to you, madam."

"Fine!" said Aurélia, dismissing with a gesture the servant who left.

Seixas could hardly contain himself until this moment:

"You cannot see that man!"

"Such was my intention. I saw him this morning for the last time, but in view of your suspicion I changed my mind," replied Aurélia coldly.

"Then you should know that today, after he left your house, I came face to face with him on the street and openly refused to greet him, turning my back on him."

"Even more reason for me to see him. We must convince him that you were merely distracted so he will not think that you have honored him with a suspicion that slanders me."

Aurélia took her husband's arm and headed toward the sitting room, where they found Eduardo Abreu.

The two gentlemen exchanged a dry and formal greeting; afterward Seixas went to lean against the window beside Dona Firmina, leaving his wife at her ease with her guest.

"I am sorry to insist; loyalty to duty justifies it. Today I had the occasion to rebuff a certain vicious insinuation by a frivolous individual and shortly thereafter, running into Mr. Seixas, I noticed a considerable difference in the way he treated me."

"He must have been worried."

"I was troubled by the thought of being the unwitting cause or even the pretext of some suspicion. I therefore came to free you from the promise you made of the secret about your benefits, and to confess to your husband, I myself, all that I owe you so that he may admire even more the nobility of your soul."

"That confession you shall not make; it would seriously offend my dignity. My husband has no need of your testimony to maintain me in high esteem, impervious to the assault of evil tongues. The day I needed to justify myself, I would be divorced, because trust, the first tie of love and the true glory of marriage, would have been extinguished. Therefore, rest assured, your secret has cast no shadow over my happiness."

The young woman said these words with such emotion that she convinced Abreu, and his fears vanished.

For his part, Seixas had reflected. On the verge of a definitive resolution that ought to effect a profound change in his destiny, this ridiculous outburst struck him as a weakness, resembling frets of petty jealousy, which he believed he did not feel. Making an effort therefore, he approached Abreu with the cordiality with which he usually treated him, and thus confirmed the explanation given by Aurélia about the incident that morning.

That evening there was a party.

The gathering, though not very crowded, was lively. Fernando was happy; never had he doted so ostensively on his wife as this evening. He did not leave her side; the most delicate flowers, the most gallant courtesies uttered in that select society were those from him to Aurélia.

Aurélia, on the other hand, appeared concerned.

Her husband's pleasantness after the scene in the garden troubled her, to her regret. Try as she might, she could not rid her mind of the words proffered by Seixas that afternoon about a rupture that would solve the supposed conflict.

What did he intend to do? On this problem she exhausted her mind during the night.

The next day, Seixas had breakfast at eight as usual and left for his office. At that time, Aurélia was still in bed; but her bedroom, which was on the second floor, had windows over the garden; from the corner window one could see perfectly the part of the dining room where the table stood.

The young woman had one devotion each morning; when she heard Seixas's steps on the stairs she leapt from her bed and, wrapped in her damask blanket in order to waste no time donning her robe, ran to the window. There, hiding behind the curtains, she stood for some time looking at her husband, as if to wish him good-morning. If she was very tired from the day before, if sleep tugged at her, she would return to her still-warm nest, and doze in renewed slumber.

This morning, however, although she had retired late and felt the need to rest, she lingered gazing at Seixas's countenance with a feeling of sadness that she could not dispel. A vague foreboding warned her not to let her husband leave under the impression of the merciless sarcasm she had hurled at him the day before.

But the pride of her love triumphed, still hurt by the bitter memories that the sight of Adelaide's gift had awakened in her soul.

Seixas left and, to disguise her impatience, soon after breakfast she got into the car with Dona Firmina and left to spend her time on Ouvidor Street, at the fashion shops and at her friends'. She searched among the Parisian novelties, among the temptations of luxury, for some enticement that might captivate her thoughts and turn them from her anxieties.

She managed to remain aloof until four o'clock when she arrived home.

Seixas was not in, which was extraordinary. There was no precedent for his arriving past this hour. Aurélia dissembled to avoid revealing her restlessness to Dona Firmina and to the servants. She retired to her apartment to change, but leaned against the window frame, her eyes on the road.

At five o'clock the woman slave came to call her:

"Are you not having dinner, madam? It's on the table."

"Who asked to serve it?"

"It is five o'clock."

"And the master?"

"He asked José to let you know that he might not be back today till very late."

"When did the master speak to José?"

"This morning, in the city."

"And he did not mention the reason why he would be late?"

"I do not know; I will call him."

Interrogating José was no help, so Aurélia remained just as restless. But to prevent Dona Firmina from noticing, she attributed her husband's absence to a conference he must be having with the minister about important tasks at the office.

As they were about to sit down at the table, the door opened and Seixas entered.

The surprise allowed Aurélia time to dominate the first impulse of her happiness, which quickly faded at the sight of Seixas's countenance. In the rigid and serious expression on his face he bore the imprint of an inflexible resolve.

Nonetheless, he did not depart from his natural politeness. He courteously apologized to his wife for his delay:

"I had to conclude some urgent business, of which I shall inform you."

"And did you conclude it?"

"Fortunately."

"I asked in order to know if I should wait for you tomorrow."

"No, I think there will be no more waiting for me," replied Seixas with a fleeting smile.

Aurélia saw the smile, and sensed the special tone of his voice.

When dinner was finished and they were strolling along the winding paths cut through the grass, Seixas told his wife:

"I want to speak to you in private."

"Let us sit down, then," said Aurélia, pointing to the spot where they usually spent the evenings.

"No, not here in the garden. I would rather it be a more secluded place, where no one will interrupt us."

"In my dressing room?"

"That will be fine."

"Or in your study?"

"In your dressing room; it is better."

"Now?" asked Aurélia, feigning indifference.

"No; in the evening will do. If it suits you, after tea, before you retire."

"As you wish!" said Aurélia, opening the leaves of the violets, looking for a flower.

Seixas took the young woman's watering can, stored with other gardening tools in a rustic nest cut into the wall, and amused himself by watering the beds of daisies and the pots of hydrangeas.

Once, returning from the fountain where he had gone for water, as he walked by Aurélia, the young woman asked him casually, as if they had not interrupted the dialogue:

"Is it about the matter you mentioned?"

"Precisely."

Seixas stood before Aurélia, assuming she would ask him another question, while the young woman hoped for an explanation that she did not want to request directly.

Seeing that her husband remained silent, she returned to the violets, and he went about his task.

☙ IX ❧

It was ten o'clock in the evening.

Aurélia, who had left the sitting room earlier, after exchanging with her husband a meaningful look, was at that moment in her dressing room, sitting before the elegant pink *araribá* desk which was embossed with fire-gilded bronze.

At this time, the young woman had on a green satin robe tied at the waist by a cord of gold threads. It was the same she had worn on the night of her wedding, and she had not touched it since then. By some kind of superstition she remembered to put it on again, at this time when, if she could believe her premonitions, her destiny and her life were to be finally settled.

The girl had leaned her forehead on her right hand; her bare arm, resting on the table, emerged from the ruffles of cambric trimming the sleeves of her robe. She remained absorbed in deep meditation until the chime of the pendulum clock sounding the hour roused her.

She then rose and took a key from the drawer; she crossed the nuptial chamber, which was dark, illuminated only by the reflection from the dressing room, and boldly opened the door that, eleven months before, she had locked in a frenzy of indignation and horror.

Pushing the door loudly in order to be heard in the other room, and tying back the portière to leave the passage free, she quickly returned, after uttering these words:

"Whenever you like!"

As Fernando penetrated the nuptial chamber, full of shadows and silences, he forgot for a moment the poignant memory that it should rekindle and which seemed to have been extinguished with the darkness. What he sensed was the air redolent with perfume, enveloping him like the atmosphere of a heaven in which he was the fallen angel.

Aurélia awaited her husband, once again seated at her desk. She had pushed back the arm of the lamp so that the gaslight, intercepted by a jasper reflector in the shape of Aurora's chariot, left her immersed in a diaphanous twilight that lent to her beauty tender and mellow tones.

Seixas sat on the chair indicated by Aurélia, in front of her, and after concentrating for an instant, searching for a way to begin, he yielded to the inspiration of the moment.

"This is the second time I have seen you in that robe. The first was about eleven months ago, not exactly in this place, but near here, in that room."

"Would you like us to talk in the same place?" asked the young woman guilelessly.

"No, madam. This place is more appropriate for the matter we will be discussing. I recalled that circumstance only because of the coincidence of your image before my eyes, just as I saw you that evening, so that I seem to be continuing an interrupted interview. Do you remember?"

"Perfectly."

"I assumed I had done something quite ordinary that the world had accepted under the name of marriage of convenience. You have disabused me, madam; you defined my position with great clarity, demonstrated that I had effected a commercial transaction, and displayed your title of sale, which of course you still have."

"It is my greatest treasure," said the girl in a tone in which one could not distinguish between irony and emotion.

Seixas thanked her with a slight nod and proceeded:

"Had I at that moment possessed the twenty thousand that I received from your guardian as an advance on the dowry, the problem would have solved itself. The misunderstanding would have been undone: I would have returned your money and redeemed my pledge, and we would have separated like two contractors in good faith who, acknowledging their mistake, release each other from a mutual obligation."

Seixas stopped as if awaiting a contradiction, which was not forthcoming. Aurélia, resting against the armchair with her eyes half closed, listened, fingering a mother-of-pearl dagger used as a letter opener.

"But I no longer had the twenty thousand on that occasion, nor any-where to obtain it. Under those circumstances I was left with two alterna-tives: betray the obligation and become a swindler, or respect the dictates of the contract and honor my word. Despite the impression you rightly have of me, do me the justice of believing that the first of these alternatives, I consid-ered only to reject it. The man who sells himself may depreciate himself, but he rules over what belongs to him. He who, having been sold, extricates himself from his owner, steals from the other. From this infamy I have saved myself, by accepting the consummated fact that I could no longer abjure and submitting faithfully, with the greatest scruple, to the will I had recog-nized as law, and from which I had estranged myself. I call upon your con-science; however severe its feelings about me, I am certain that you will not deny me one virtue: loyalty to my word."

"No, sir; you have honored it like a gentleman."

"This is what I wished to hear from your mouth before informing you of the reason for this conference. The amount I lacked eleven months ago, on the night of your wedding, has finally come into my possession. I have it on me; I am carrying it in this wallet and with it have come to negotiate my ransom."

These words burst from Seixas's lips with an ardor he could scarcely con-trol. As if they had lifted a heavy weight from his chest, he breathed rapidly, impatiently gripping the wallet he had taken from his pocket.

Were he not so concerned with his own turmoil, he would certainly have noticed the deep blow suffered by Aurélia, whose body, leaning against the chair, shook like the blade of a steel spring.

Startled and shaken, she had raised to her mouth the mother-of-pearl blade and clenched her beautiful teeth on it.

As he was about to open his wallet, Seixas interrupted his gesture.

"Before I conclude the negotiation, I must reveal to you the origin of this money, to dispel any suspicion that I might have obtained it through your credit and as your husband. No, madam, I have acquired it exclusively on my own; and for the greater peace of my conscience it antedates our wed-ding. Approximately six thousand represents the product of my salary and the jewelry and trinkets I sold soon after my captivity, already with my re-demption in mind. I still had a long wait and perhaps would have lacked the resignation to bring it to term, had God not abbreviated this torture by work-ing a miracle in my favor. I was a partner in a concession granted four years ago, which I no longer remembered. The day before yesterday, at the same time that you, madam, subjected me to the harshest of all tests, heaven sent me an unexpected rescue to break at last this shameful bondage. I received word that the concession had been sold, and it brought me a profit of over fifteen thousand. Here is the proof."

Aurélia received from Seixas several papers and glanced over them. They comprised a declaration by Barbosa, relative to the concession, and bills of sale from the jewelry and other objects.

"Now our account," continued Seixas, unfolding a sheet of paper. "You, madam, paid me one hundred thousand; eighty by a check drawn against the Bank of Brazil, which I return untouched, and twenty in cash, received 330 days ago. At 6% interest this amount has earned you $1,084.71. I therefore owe you $21,084.71, besides the check. Am I right?"

Aurélia examined the current account; she took the pen and deftly calculated the interest.

"It is accurate."

Then Seixas opened the wallet and removed with the check twenty-one bundles of bills of one thousand each, plus the change, which he placed on the table:

"Please be kind enough to count it."

As phlegmatic as a business man, the young woman opened the bundles one by one and slowly counted the bills. When she completed this operation, she turned to Seixas and asked him, as if she were speaking to the agent charged with receiving the dividends from her stocks:

"It is correct. Do you want a receipt?"

"There is no need for that. Returning the bill of sale will be sufficient."

"That is true. I did not remember."

Aurélia hesitated a moment. She seemed to be trying to recall where she had put the paper; but the true reason was quite different. She was deliberating, afraid of revealing her agitation if she stood up.

"Do me a favor and open that small drawer, the second one. Inside, there must be a bundle of paper tied with a blue ribbon—precisely! . . . Do you recognize the ribbon? It was the first thing I received from your hand, with a bunch of violets. Oh! Forgive me; we are negotiating. Here is your note."

The young woman had taken a paper from the bundle and gave it to Seixas, who put it in his wallet.

"At last the link that bound us has been broken. I have regained my freedom, and the possession of my self. I am no longer your husband. Do you comprehend the solemnity of this moment, madam?"

"It is the moment of our separation," confirmed Aurélia.

"We may yet meet in this world, but as two strangers."

"Never again, I believe," said Aurélia in a tone of profound conviction.

"In any case, since this is the last time I shall address you, I would now like to explain something that I was not permitted to do eleven months ago, on our wedding night. I would have at that time seemed a wretch looking for pity and you, madam, who trod on my integrity, would not have believed a word of what I told you."

"The explanation is superfluous."

"Listen to me; it is my desire that some distant day, when you reflect on this event, you restore part of your regard for me; nothing else. The society in which I was raised molded me into a man after its kind; luxuries gilded my vices, and I could not see behind their fascination the materialism toward which they dragged me. I became accustomed to considering wealth the prime life force of existence, and example taught me that marriage was as legitimate a means of acquiring it as inheritance or any honest speculation. Nevertheless, madam, even then you would have found me beyond temptation if, soon after your guardian sought me out, there had not arisen a situation that terrified me. Not only was I threatened with poverty and, what grieved me most, a poverty heavy with debt, but I also found myself as the cause, albeit involuntarily, of the unhappiness of my sister, whose savings I had consumed and who was about to forfeit a marriage opportunity for want of a trousseau. At the same time, my mother had been deprived of the meager assets my father left her, which I had recklessly squandered, thinking I could replace them later!—All of this crushed me. I am not defending myself; I should have resisted and struggled; nothing justifies abdicating one's dignity. Today I would know how to confront adversity and be a man; at that time I was nothing but a salon actor; I succumbed. But you, madam, have regenerated me and the instrument was this money. I am grateful to you."

Aurélia listened, motionless. Seixas concluded:

"That is what I wanted to tell you before we separated forever."

"Also I desire that you harbor no unjust suspicion of me. As your wife, I would not defend myself; given, however, that we are no longer anything to each other, I am entitled to demand the respect due a lady."

Aurélia briefly recounted what Eduardo Abreu had done when Dona Emília passed away, and her determination to save him from suicide.

"That, therefore, is the reason I called this young man to my house. His secret did not belong to me; and you and I, sir, did not share the bond that makes of two souls one."

Aurélia gathered up the check and bundles of money that lay on the table.

"This money is blessed. You say, sir, that it has regenerated you, and you have just repaid it so that in turn it will assist in the fulfillment of a charitable deed and serve another regeneration."

She opened a desk drawer and placed the valuables in it. Then she rang the bell and the slave woman appeared.

"Allow me," said Aurélia, turning to whisper an order to the slave.

She lighted the gas in the lamp holders of the nuptial chamber and left, while Aurélia spoke to her husband, pointing to the illuminated room:

"I do not want you to lose your way."

"There is no danger of that now."

"Now?" repeated the girl, with a look that disturbed Seixas.

There was a pause.

"Perhaps, to avoid public curiosity, you would like a pretext, madam?"

"For what?"

"A voyage to Europe would be best. The ship should be leaving within the next two weeks. Reasons of health will explain everything, the separation and the urgency. Later, when people find out, it will cause no surprise."

Though Aurélia betrayed some emotion, her voice was firm when she answered:

"If something must be done, it is better to do it quickly and not deceitfully."

Fernando promptly rose:

"In that case, I bid you farewell."

On her part, Aurélia also rose, out of courtesy to her husband.

"Good-bye, madam. Believe me—"

"No ceremonies!" interrupted the young woman. "What could we say to each other that we both have not already thought?"

"You are right."

Seixas retreated a step to the middle of the room and made a deep bow, which Aurélia reciprocated. He then slowly crossed the now illuminated nuptial chamber. As he was lifting the portière, he heard his wife's voice:

"Just a moment!" said Aurélia.

"Did you call me, madam?"

"The past no longer exists. It was not we who lived these eleven months, but those two who have just separated, forever. I am not your wife anymore; you, sir, are no longer my husband. We are two strangers. Is that not true?"

Seixas confirmed this with a nod.

"So, then, I kneel now at your feet, Fernando, and implore you to accept my love, this love that never ceased to be yours, even when I most cruelly offended you."

The young woman had grasped Seixas's hands and led him impetuously to the same place where nearly a year earlier she had inflicted a cruel affront on the young man kneeling at her feet.

"The woman who humiliated you, you see her prostrated in the same place where she insulted you, in the wrath of her passion. You see her imploring your forgiveness and happy because she adores you as the master of her soul."

Seixas lifted in his arms the lovely woman who had knelt at his feet; their lips were already uniting in a fervent kiss, when a doleful thought crossed his mind. With a somber gesture, he pulled back from Aurélia's beautiful face, illuminated by a dawn of love, and stared at her, his eyes filled with deep sadness.

"No, Aurélia! Your wealth has separated us forever."

The young lady disengaged herself from her husband's arms, ran to the dressing room, and returned with a sealed document that she handed to Seixas.

"What is this, Aurélia?"

"My will."

She broke the seal and gave the paper to Seixas to read. It was indeed a will, in which she confessed the immense love that she had for her husband and named him her sole heir.

"I wrote it immediately after our wedding; I thought I would die that night," said Aurélia with an exalted gesture.

Seixas gazed at her with tearful eyes.

"Does this wealth terrify you? Well then, make me live, my Fernando. It is the means you have to reject it. If that is not enough, I will dissipate it."

* * *

The curtains were drawn and the evening zephyrs, caressing the bosom of the flowers, sang the mysterious hymn of sanctified conjugal love.

This book is
set in Hiroshige, a typeface
created by Cynthia Hollandsworth.

Printed and bound
by Edwards Brothers in Ann Arbor, Michigan,
on 55 lb. Glatfelter Natural.

Designed and composed
for the University of Texas Press
by Rafael Fajardo.